Sentiment
Other
Stories

Vincent O'Sullivan

Solis Press

ALSO BY VINCENT O'SULLIVAN AND AVAILABLE FROM SOLIS PRESS:

The Good Girl
A Book of Bargains
Sentiment

Originally published in 1914 by Duckworth & Co., London and
contains words that may offend. This edition completely reset with
minor spelling changes and published in 2016 by Solis Press

Publisher's note: The version of "Sentiment" in this collection is very
similar to that published in the 1917 book *Sentiment* (which is also
available from Solis Press). In the 1917 edition there minor additions,
many of which refer to the First World War, and the significant
difference of the inclusion of a new final chapter.

ISBN: 978-1-910146-17-0

Published by Solis Press, PO Box 482,
Tunbridge Wells TN2 9QT, Kent, England

Web: www.solispress.com | *Twitter*: @SolisPress

Contents

Sentiment

"O Thou," etc.   The Poets

Chapter I

WILLIAM TORE ALONG THE platform of the suburban station
with a newspaper streaming in his hand, while angry or
encouraging shouts were hurled at him from several points by officials;
bounded upon the step of the slowly moving train; and was pitched
forward into the carriage by a brace of porters who stood ready. The
door was slammed; William picked himself off the knees and toes of
the other passengers, and gathered his hat from the floor at the far end
of the carriage where it had rebounded from the nose of a lady in the
corner. Then he sat down, opened his newspaper, and glancing round
on faces flushed with pain and indignation: "That was a close shave,"
he observed genially.

His companions could not trust themselves to reply, and habit had
inured William not to expect one unless it came in the form of sarcasm
or vituperation. He had never yet met the passenger who smiled amiably on his descent, and was thereupon prepared to engage in a spark-
ling conversation. Indeed, he was now so experienced that he could
derive the social order of his companions from their mode of receiving
him. The genteel, he found, eyed him with silent fury, moving as they
did in circles where a look is considered enough; but as you went down
the ladder you encountered irony and objurgation. "Bloated areo-
plane!" vociferated by a stout man, obviously a butcher, was the only
fragment which had ever attracted more than the transient attention of
William or lingered in his memory.

The scene, in fact, was repeated too often for him to class it any
longer among his vivid excitements. This hare-brained rush and plunge
took place about four times a week, and had degenerated in the estimation of William from a sporting event to a form of exercise. With this
in mind, he even so arranged matters as to arrive at the station when
the train was starting. He needed to relax the muscles before settling
himself to his desk in the offices of Messrs. Ibed Brothers and Co., the

well-known importers of perfumes and chemicals in Frog Lane, E.C. of whose business he formed a not at all indispensable part.

He had entered this office when he was twenty; and although it was now some three years that he had been occupying a clerical stool more or less insecurely, still his post remained insignificant and his salary he thought derisory. If his mother, a lady who supported existence at Tunbridge Wells chiefly on a military pension bestowed upon her as the widow of Lieutenant-Colonel Spring, D.S.O., had not sent him occasional contributions, he would have found life in London, which he regarded with the same eye as the redoubtable Corinthian Tom, a grey and hopeless affair. To sit at home at night he felt was paltry and even unmanly; the more obvious enjoyments of the town-dweller enticed him to the West End. There, by spending freely his own money, his mother's, and money of more ambiguous origin in the gilded haunts of pleasure, he acquired enough of the gilt to cover any stains left by the office.

For the clerks to receive private correspondence addressed to the care of the firm was an act discouraged at Ibed Brothers, the firm having deduced from its experience that such missives went to furthering amatory and other intrigues which it was desirable to keep from the eye of the home circle. When, therefore, William, approaching his desk that Saturday morning, saw propped up an envelope addressed in an irregular but unmistakably female hand, he had a movement of impatience.

"That woman is a blighter! What does she want to write here for?"

The contents, however, were innocent enough. Stamped on top of the paper in small silver letters was the address of the writer: The Firs, Palebrook, Hampshire—and the letter meandered over the spacious page.

June 11th.

"DEAR WILLIAM,—I really can't think of your number, so write to the office, though your uncle says he thinks it's against the rules, but if it is you must see Mr. Ibed and explain it is a letter from your aunt and he is sure to be nice about it."

William paused, and reflected a moment gloomily on the character of women. "Now who with any sense would expect me to go into Ibed and say I had a letter from my aunt?" And he resumed his reading, with his opinion of the writer's knowledge of life, which had been small enough before, considerably lessened.

> "We want you to come down here just as soon as ever you get this and stay a month. Your vacation must be commencing, I should think, so you can easily manage it. It is long since you were here, not since you were quite a small boy, but you will not find us changed. I have written to your mother and told her you were going to spend your holidays with us. Sabina Moll will be here part of the time. You remember Mr. Moll, don't you? We tried to get you into his office at Manchester before we arranged so well with Mr. Ibed. Give him my kindest regards. Your uncle sends his love, and I am your aff. aunt,
>
> "LAURA S. M. BURGER.
>
> "Mind you come *to-morrow* (*Saturday*) for a month. I have *special* reasons."

Letters from his aunt were by no means frequent enough to have laid the spirit of criticism. "Except for a Christmas card, price twopence, this is the first I've heard of her in near two years. I wonder what's up? 'Give him my kindest regards.' Oh, yes. Ibed doesn't care a rotten nut about her or about my uncle either. It wasn't them got me into the office; it was mother. They introduced mother to Ibed and she did the rest."

His thoughts lingered with a tenderness by no means usual upon the gay, still handsome widow at Tunbridge Wells, who took life so airily, whom nothing could mortify or depress. "Mother can do anything she likes," he reflected with a dash of bitterness. "With her looks and manner and way of jollying people along she could have married a millionaire before this. Why the devil hasn't she? That would have given me some chance, instead of being stuck in this dog-kennel which Aunt Laura is so proud to have found for me. I'll give Ibed her kindest regards, won't I? She must think I'm a kind of private secretary."

But all the same he was attracted by the invitation. He remembered Aunt Laura's house at Palebrook and its comforts. The Burgers were very well off. A vacation spent with them would be a different business from and altogether more desirable than a slim top room in his mother's boarding-house, dodging bored and aimless about the Pantiles, and smoking too much. Oh, yes, he would certainly put in a month with the Burgers.

But could he? Aunt Laura insisted upon his immediate appearance: the invitation seemed to depend on that. If he couldn't go now, perhaps he could not go at all. But the holidays at Ibed Brothers had not yet begun, and William's holiday lay far down the list near the last of August. He looked round upon his fellow-workers, meditatively gnawing a pen-handle.

"I'll go in and strike Ibed for an early vac.," he decided. "These fellows will be furious if I get it, but I don't care a horse-marine."

One of the partners, Mr. Behrens Ibed, had a fancy for dealing with the clerks personally. Was one to be rebuked or praised, his salary raised, or his name taken from the books, it was before Mr. Ibed, in person, that the patient plumed himself or wilted. And William, about an hour and a half later, found himself standing before a stout, good-humoured-looking, glossy little man, redolent, as it were, of his own perfumes. The black moustache spun out in points, the shining black hair which curled about the ears, the sallow complexion, were all but accessories to a pair of large lustrous brown eyes, laughing and jovial, though at certain moments they would suddenly turn hard and cold as an iceberg. But the prevailing expression was humour, even kindly humour; and in truth, whether Mr. Ibed was making a clerk happy by increasing his salary, or depriving a man of his livelihood, he liked to do it on a jest—though his jests often enough appealed to his listener much as judicial quips which set the court in a roar appeal to the prisoner in the dock.

"Well, Mr. Spring, what's gone wrong this morning?" He turned on William a face wreathed in smiles.

"I got a letter from my aunt——" William began awkwardly.

Mr. Ibed laughed sonorously. "Come, come, I'd no idea it was as bad as that. A letter from your aunt? Mr. Spring, this begins to look serious, sir. What does the lady accuse you of?"

With reservations, and a hashing of phrases, William shuffled through the facts and indicated his wishes.

"Hum! That's not so easy as you seem to think." Mr. Ibed looked hard at William, and something in the long-limbed, cool-faced young Saxon seemed to please him. "How's your mother?" he asked suddenly with decided interest.

"Oh, she's fairly well, I think," answered William gruffly. In secret he was flattered; but he always became gruff when he spoke of his family for fear that anybody should think he was carried away by inordinate affection.

"Fine woman, your mother," resumed the merchant with emphasis. "Right good sort, one of the best. You can tell her I said so. Well, look here, Mr. Spring—we stand to lose thousands by the loss of your services, but you can go."

William thanked him in the tone of one suffering from some indefinite sense of wrong, and slouched to the door.

"Oh, that's all right!" jocose Mr. Ibed fired a parting shot. "You can't enjoy yourself much if you think of those thousands your absence is going to cost us."

William approached Mr. Hamilton, the head clerk, a dour, iron-grey Scotsman. He tried to be airy, as though he were communicating a matter of infinitely little moment.

"Hullo, Mr. Hamilton, how's Scotland? By the way, I'm going for my holiday this afternoon. I've just seen the boss."

"Yill go one day and not be asked back, I'm thenkin'," said Hamilton, drawing down the corners of his mouth contemptuously into his beard. He seemed unmoved, but he eyed William with an unwonted glint of curiosity. A man who could have the date of his holiday advanced at Ibed Brothers must have some influence with the firm.

But the other clerks were by no means so self-contained. In fact, to most of these men, whose thoughts, however much they might hate the firm, necessarily centred on it as the chief interest of their existence, any variation of the rules had the effect of a revolution, and was a topic to be discussed for days. And the question of vacation, those few golden weeks of respite from the monotonous grind, was, together with the question of salary, the sorest question of all. William's companions were men of all ages, and most of the older ones suggested in some vague way that life had been too hard for them. You imagined, as you looked at them, the thousand lapses of dignity which an existence perforce genteel, that had to be kept up on inadequate means, had forced them into. But at this moment the eyes of all alike were lit by a similar flame of resentment and apprehension. Between the two main questions there was but a step, and one voiced the general fear.

"Have you got a rise?"

It was not that they had a corporate prejudice against William, or anything of that kind. Allowing for the peculiar conditions of the life of a clerk in a big firm, which tend to concentrate the thoughts of each individual on his private fortunes and to check any generous expansion towards his fellow-workers, it may be said that the young man was rather popular. True, he managed to irritate several of them on different sides by different traits. On many, his selfishness, disguised by no subtlety, but blatant and brutal as a schoolboy's, acted like the unexpected hoot of a motor horn at a street corner. Then, the domineering and harsh manner which had not yet been worn down since his sojourn at Wellington College, a manner which often annoys men who have not been themselves at one of the big schools and consequently do not know what depth of uncertainty and shyness it covers, made against him here. There was no "give and take" about William at the office; he made no more effort to conciliate and win friends than the average sixth-form boy who is good at games. Besides, he was unmarried, and to many of these men, who came to their desks day after day weighted by domestic cares, he seemed to flaunt an insolent freedom for which they bore him a dull grudge, no less deep because it had no logical basis. And in truth, a man harassed with the baby's croup, or the incidents and expenses of his wife's lying-in, might be forgiven if he resented the sight of William's fresh-coloured, handsome face, self-satisfied and rather pompous, as he started on Saturday afternoon for cricket, tennis, or the river, without a serious trouble in the world. To make it worse, the young man was wont to relate his pleasures with a callousness and want of tact which proceeded partly no doubt from hide-bound indifference to the feelings of others, and partly from the obtuseness betokened by his good-looking headpiece.

For all that, he was well enough liked on the whole, and any ordinary performance of his would have roused no special indignation. But in the present matter he had clearly been hoisted over the heads of others—he, too, of all the clerks in the office the most incompetent. He was a creature of privilege, unjustly and arbitrarily conferred. For his sake, the scheme of holidays would have to be dislocated and new allocations made. Not an eye in the room but regarded him venomously. He, on his part, conscious that he was a target for obloquy, shoved things about on his desk with an elaborate assumption of unconcern.

"No," he answered the question. "I didn't get a rise, if you are anxious to know." Then, thinking this remark conciliatory to the point of cowardice, he added: "Of course I could have got it if I had liked. I'd only to ask."

This was brought out with such an accent of concealed power that for a moment his hearers were dumbfounded. Perhaps it might be as well not to rile such a manifest favourite of the Ibeds. And it really looked as if William was dominating the situation, when old Hamilton came in from another room. After a moment, he approached the young man's desk.

"Well, my laddie-buck," he said, addressing the favourite most disrespectfully, "it'll be great pliskies you'll be havin' the night. And where do ye intend spendin' your holidays?"

The devil tempted William to swagger. "I'm going to stay at my aunt's place in Hampshire," he said incautiously.

The ears of the other clerks, stretched to preternatural keenness, caught the note of brag which sounded in this statement, and from that moment William was bombarded with his aunt. Was it his aunt who gave him his pretty ties and socks? Did his aunt take him out to walk on Sundays? Did his aunt tuck him up in bed at night?—such were the inanities with which William was pelted. Descriptions of his aunt were built up with great skill, and every clerk lent his wit. One older, one at all events more philosophical, would have ignored them for their very vapidness; but William flushed and wriggled, his stony demeanour at last broken down. Silent and furious, he left the office as soon as he could, pursued with kind regards to his aunt, love to his aunt, kisses to his aunt. At the street door, the office-boy presented him with a letter and then fled. He opened it and found it was a proposal of marriage to his aunt.

"Lot of bounders!" he thought, as he flopped sulkily down on his seat in the train which bore him to his suburb. "They simply can't understand anything outside their own rotten kind of life."

This reflection restored in a measure his equanimity. It was not that he objected particularly to the gibes at his aunt for what they were worth; but it made him furious that anything connected with him, whether it were an aunt or a boot-jack, should be laughed at. He was in fact so unusually demoralized that he brought out his aunt's name at his lodgings with some embarrassment, and scanned his landlady's face suspiciously for the shadow of a smile. But the landlady received the address with so much satisfactory respect and even awe, that William had regained full possession of his self-esteem and his usual stock of assurance by the time he got on board the 3.15 from Waterloo.

As he sat, flanked by *Leggy Bits*, *The Crimes of the World*, and other amusing publications, a thought flashed through his mind. "I ought to have gone round to see Penelope, I suppose. Forgot all about her. She's so infernally nervy. She'll make an awful row and love doing it." He yawned and stretched out his long legs. "Never mind; I'll write."

Now to this lady he was secretly engaged to be married.

Chapter II

PALEBROOK STATION LAY RATHER outside of the town, and this had to be traversed before you reached "The Firs," which also lay a little outside the town at the far end. William, lounging back in the brougham which had been sent to meet him, stared vacantly out of the window. Some might perhaps have regarded with interest the singular winding little town, seated so picturesquely above the sea, a haven grey and salted from centuries of driving blasts and sea-mew, and now filled with the rumour of Saturday evening traffic; but William found difficulty in getting up an interest in anything where his own fortunes were not in some measure involved. He was thinking now of what kind of a month his aunt and uncle could manage to give him.

"I suppose the old lot are here in this hole just the same as when I was down ages ago. There'll be tennis, and croquet, and a few evening parties, when the natives are unselfish enough to sit up and give them. And cards. O Lord, how I loathe cards! I don't remember any decent girls when I was here last, but I was young then, I expect. Anyhow, it's better than Tunbridge Wells. I wish I was a millionaire."

This idle wish, probably the wish oftenest and most generally expressed throughout the civilized nations every twenty-four hours, ushered to his thoughts the name of Sabina Moll, for her father was rich. He fell to wondering what she would be like. Old Moll, the father, whom he had seen while he was still at school, he remembered as an infamous bore with a Lancashire accent, who asked puzzle questions in arithmetic and tipped badly. If Sabina was like her father, and Aunt Laura expected him to be nice to her, she would find herself jolly well mistaken, that's all! Even good-nature has its limit, and for William one aspect of that limit was the representation of old Moll as a female.

The carriage passed through a low iron gate painted red, and rolled over a short gravelled drive to the house. It was a fair-sized modern dwelling, standing amid trees, and surrounded by well-kept lawns and flower-beds. Had there been anything to complain of about the house, this might well have been overlooked on account of its pleasant seat. Perched on the crest of a hill, at its foot the salt marsh stretched level like a table, and above this the wild fowl swept in great companies. Where the line broke against the sky, you perceived from the windows the gleam of the torn breakers on the harbour-bar, while through the most lonely night you might always have the cheerful spectacle of the lights of ships riding at anchor. So, I say, might one have reasoned to whom the sights offered to the eyes were more important than comforts to lull the body; but, as it happened, it was unnecessary to discuss the alternative at "The Firs." Certainly, William, for one, would not have worn such an amiable smile as he entered the house if the aspect of it had not assured him of rewards other than good views from the windows.

His uncle stood in the hall and welcomed him with unfeigned heartiness; and his aunt pushed complaisance so far as to come out too, and seized him by both hands with manifest enjoyment. For a second, William feared that she was going to kiss him.

"They're uncommonly civil," he mused when he got to his room. "I wonder why they're so awfully glad to see me?"

His bedroom was a pattern of prettiness and comfort—of that English comfort which foreigners envy and strive after in vain. Even to William's unobservant eye, it was plain that Aunt Laura had taken special trouble to make things pleasant for him. Things done for him he generally took as if he expected they ought to be done; but in the flowers so deftly arranged, in the magazines lying about, and other trifles, he perceived an element of personal supervision which indicated that he was not only a nephew but a guest, and what was more, a guest they were anxious to please. He took up a book from the table by his bedside—the only book in the room—attracted by the heavy gilt binding, and put it down quickly in disgust. It was a gift to Aunt Laura, and *Indian Love Poems* was the title. "What rot!" he commented. "If the Indians knew as much about love as I do they wouldn't write poetry about it. Why couldn't Aunt Laura stick some decent books around in case I got a reading fit?"

So, after all, he had discovered some kind of a grievance which saved him from any ridiculous lapse into gratitude. There was now no need to be expansive or to simulate the generous emotions; he was still free to face his relations from the advantageous standpoint of a person who has not been treated quite well. But as he worked through the long and perfectly cooked dinner, enhanced by full-bodied wines, and served, in a dining-room furnished in what seemed to him perfect taste, by two befrilled and noiseless maids, he found it hard to keep his injury in mind. Aunt and uncle, he found, were coming out strong, and he looked at them with a smile which was almost friendly. "If they keep this pace up for a month," he was thinking, "I shan't finish among the 'also ran.'"

"I've been looking at some of those papers you brought down," said his uncle. "We never get a glimpse of that kind of thing here. Quite spicy. Rather—rather—*French*, eh?"

"Tray French," answered William, whom the good cheer had gained to a reluctant kind of joviality.

"Throgmorton!" exclaimed Aunt Laura. When she used this name it was a sign that she was, or pretended to be, shocked, and her husband gave the chuckle of a sad dog in his plate. "I think," she went on smoothly in her rich melodious voice, "that one gets everything one wants in the sixpenny illustrated papers, don't you?" She turned to William. "And how was your mother looking when you saw her?"

"Ripping. Mother always looks well."

"Ah, there's a woman for you!" put in Mr. Burger. "None of your nonsense about *her*. What I call—I say, what *I* call a good specimen. Always laughing and in good humour. Wish we saw her here oftener, but she finds us too slow, I fancy. Now, I'm a kind of man who likes gaiety myself."

He was the husband of the sister—the much younger sister—of William's father, the deceased Lieutenant-Colonel, a detached position whence he could survey Mrs. Spring in untroubled lights, and admire what he called "the cut of her jib" without reserve. He did indeed like gaiety, as he said, and for years had yielded to this propensity in multifarious forms. Even still he had an occasional frisk, but he had long since laid aside the powdered gallantries of his youth. Fits of the gout, occurring with tedious periodicity, had warned him that tranquil courses were what he must for the most part follow in future if he would have peace. He recognized this mandate and acted upon it, though he would not acknowledge he did so to himself or anybody else. It is not so easy to cease to be a gay dog, and the reputation is clung to even after the substance is gone. Red-faced, pursy and active, nearer sixty than fifty, he expended his great fund of energy in tearing all over the country in a motor; in shooting partridges; or again, the gulls might see him, drenched with spray, beating up the Solent in a small yacht. It is certain that he never gave a serious thought to anyone or anything but himself and his own concerns. Good luck had attended him through life—though you may well doubt this if you remember the terrible name "Throgmorton" which his wife had just now tossed at him. But as a matter of fact, his first name was Herbert, the auxiliary Throgmorton having been thrown in by his father as an act of grace, because (as Mr. Burger loved to relate) on the very day of his son's birth he had made a most lucky financial venture, engineered by a firm operating in Throgmorton Street, E.C. Lulled in comfort, he had no children to ruffle his equanimity, or distract attention from himself, and his slightest wish was anticipated by admirable servants. What more would you have? His conversation, which was listened to with respect by those who ate his excellent dinners, was as a rule the enunciation of weather-beaten commonplaces specialized to the individual. Most of us, so like one another, thinking ready-made thoughts, galvanizing stale emotions, sharing with my brother the cut of my coat and a parcel of opinions, with my sister her dressmaker and a bundle of phrases, as like, really, as one copy of the same newspaper is to another, into whatever odd shapes you may fold it; so few among us one, solitary, able to stand alone—well, most of us feel that a special god looks out of a special star concerned particularly with our own distinct being. Do many people really think that the world will go on *precisely* the same on the day after their death? And if you take a man who is the head or centrepiece, whether of a family in a cottage, or a court in a palace, feared, if not respected, consulted in all exigencies, it will go hard but he will think his opinions as important to the world at large as he is himself to his own circle. He feels a need to assert himself, to shew his neighbours that there are other reasons, not merely fortuitous ones, which have placed him just where he is. Any of Mr. Burger's neighbours was as likely to take the same views and say the same things that he did; but at the moment they fell from his lips, in a voice which suggested the springing of a trap, he stamped them heavily as personal property. His favourite domestic amusement, from which twenty years of usage had not taken off the gloss, was to bring out wicked little things which shocked his wife and made her exclaim, "Throgmorton!" This happened pretty often.

It is possible, however, that she was not so much shocked as she appeared. If she had not been quite so buxom, or taller, she would have been very handsome, and as it was, her good looks were unquestionable—that kind of good looks which depends on an unharassed life. She had the good sense to let the grey seam her thick black hair, without resorting to the various "refreshers" in vogue; and this hair, in contrast with the still youthful-looking, serene face, the sultry brown eyes, and full sensuous mouth, gave her a very distinctive appearance, especially of an evening, when the values were enhanced by well-shaped arms and shoulders. She had, moreover, that extremely rare gift in women—a beautifully modulated speaking voice. As with so many other Englishwomen, what an impartial observer—especially a foreign observer—would deduce from her appearance was in such flagrant contradiction with her expressed views of conduct and her abject subjection to the narrowest social code, that some might have rashly put her down as a hypocrite, and wondered when and in what company she took the mask off. But there was no mask: she lived in accordance with her professions, and apparently without effort. And after all, viewing the narrowness of the plank she walked on, some of her evolutions were astonishingly free. Doubtless she considered that if the plank was narrow, it was strong enough to bear a lot of jumping about. Indeed, just here lay the secret of her charm for most men and some women: that she was constantly promising some piquant violation of her code, while you felt all the time that she would never violate it. She took herself seriously; was, of course, a regular church-goer, and a Primrose dame; ploughed through reports of Christian Endeavour and Charity Organization Societies; and was president of the local society for the reformation of female tramps. She had a reputation for benevolence, and she was in fact perfectly willing to do people a good turn when it did not put her to any considerable inconvenience; and this, as the world goes, is about as much as one can expect.

"Is Mr. Behrens Ibed in a good mood these days?" she asked William.

The very thought of Ibed Brothers was enough to freeze whatever spirits and good-humour William had shown up to this, and to spoil his dinner. He was on the point of answering tartly that he knew nothing about Ibed and hardly ever saw him; but he thought better of it. After all, there was nothing to be gained by making himself cheap before his uncle and aunt.

"I had a long talk with him this morning," he said carelessly. "The old boy is much as usual."

"Oh fie, William, you mustn't call Mr. Ibed old!" Aunt Laura smiled, shewing her even teeth. "He is a great favourite of mine. I like him so much. He was with us at Monte Carlo last winter, and we saw a great deal of him."

"*You* did, you mean," put in Mr. Burger. "I'm the kind of man who don't get on with your big City swells. To tell you the truth, my boy, I find them limited—what I call limited, eh?"

"Ibed's is Limited," said William solemnly, but nobody laughed. Mr. Burger was frowning prodigiously at his plate, thinking perhaps of injuries he had supported from some of those "damn City fellows," and Aunt Laura was drawing pensively with her thumb-nail on the cloth.

"Yes, I like him," she pursued in her sweet voice, which made it a delight to listen to her, no matter what trash she was talking. "He's so full of fun and good-humour. He jokes about everything; you would think he hadn't a care in the world. And I'm sure, William"—she smiled again—"he doesn't seem old—well, not too old," she corrected on a low note, which was like an admirable performance ended.

But William turned on her a look of gloomy disapproval which would have checked a flow of spirits in the least sensitive. He thought her silly. For him she was only Aunt Laura, ranged with his mother and King Edward the Seventh among the souvenirs of his boyhood, the things he had always known. The only time it had occurred to him that there might be anything exceptional about her was one day, in his first years at school, when she had come to see him, and Carr, the great half-back, had pronounced favourably on her looks and asked who she was. But the effect of this was transitory, and he had long since got back to considering his aunt dispassionately, with a lean to depreciation. Besides, he didn't believe in unbending much with relations; it might encourage them to take liberties.

"Well," he said, with a short dry laugh, "I call him old because he is really. He's around forty."

"Ha, ha, ha!" Uncle Herbert was immensely amused. "Wait till you get to my age, my boy, and you won't think forty old. I'm the kind of man who thinks that for a healthy man forty is the brink of life. I say, the brink of life. It's my opinion that a man is only as old as he feels, and I'm jiggered if I feel sixty, eh?"

William grunted in a way which might mean assent, and also might not.

"William seems much older than you, Herbert," said Aunt Laura softly.

Pardonably, she found her guest dull. She usually received a good deal of sentimental attention from young men, and she had not seen this young man for so long that he was almost a stranger to her—quite enough of a stranger, certainly, for her to criticize the man apart from the nephew. The evening in the drawing-room seemed to her long, and she wished somebody would come in. She sat with her feet on the fender, talking in detached sentences to the young man, trying to interest him, to find out his interests; Uncle Herbert dozed; and William made no attempt to add to the entertainment.

"I think I shall go to bed," she said, at half-past ten. She never got angry when she was living uncomfortable moments, but to prolong them beyond the strictly necessary tick of the clock seemed to her as idiotic as to take in the shape of punishment and pain what could, by a little dexterous manipulation, be turned into a pleasure. "I want you to light my candle for me, William," she resumed. "Come on upstairs."

On the first floor she turned into a little sitting-room where a rose-coloured lamp shed a dim light, and settled herself in one of the deep chairs.

"Bring up that chair near me," she directed William. "I want to talk to you seriously."

She smiled disarmingly to take the edge off the word, but William sat down solemn, with his brow furrowed. He was rather alarmed: what was he going to be bothered about now?

"You know Sabina Moll is coming?"

So that was all! "Yes; you said so in your letter."

"To-morrow afternoon. Now, listen to me, William. I want you to be very, very nice to her."

"Oh, I'll be all right." He made an effort. "What does she do specially?"

"Well"—Aunt Laura hesitated, vaguely smiling. "She is very fond of walking."

"Walking!" William did not warm up. "Doesn't she play any games or anything?"

"I think she played a little tennis when she was here last summer, and they say she is quite good at croquet."

There was a pause. Aunt Laura moved a little forward and put her soft hand, shining with rings, on William's huge knuckles.

"What a great big fellow you are for a nephew!"

Here, there was room for a compliment, but William did not place it. With her usual good-nature Aunt Laura overlooked the omission, and developed her little scheme for his benefit.

"Listen, William. You are quite old enough to be married. Wouldn't it be nice if you got to care for Sabina?"

William twisted around in his chair and snatched his hand away. "But I can't marry her!" he blurted out.

Aunt Laura drew back, alarmed. "You haven't made a fool of your-self in London?"

William had already seen his mistake. "Oh Lord, no," he said easily.

She drew a breath of relief. "My dear William, you don't know her yet. She is really very nice."

"I suppose so." William was pondering with his eyes fixed on the wall. "Is Sabina Moll anything like her father?"

"Like her father?" Aunt Laura laughed musically. "You absurd boy! Poor Sabina! No, I don't think she is very like her father."

"Well, that scores in her favour," said William. "I don't want to say anything against any friend of yours, Aunt Laura, but old Mr. Moll——"

"Ssh!" Aunt Laura again put her hand out, this time on his sleeve. "You mustn't, you wicked wretch. He's awfully rich. Simply rolling. Of course most of his fortune will go to his sons, but do you know that Sabina is going to have at least four thousand a year?"

Whatever other faults might be laid to William's charge, nobody could impute to him a disregard for his own interests. Brought up among the shifts of narrow means, and under conditions which often threw him among the luxuries of the well-to-do, he had come to look on poverty as the sole evil under the sun, and almost as a crime. Frankly and cordially, he despised people who had no money. He would have despised himself if he had ever thought that he was always going to be poor. He had but the vaguest notions how his condition was to be remedied, but he felt certain it would be—mainly, I suppose, because he considered it ought to be. The injustice of his lot was too flagrant not to obtain redress. He looked at his aunt with more respect and friendliness than he had shown since he had entered the house. There was one thing to be said for Aunt Laura: she knew how to keep in with rich people.

"Your mother would be so much pleased if anything came of it," she continued. "It would make such a difference. There would be no more clerking at Ibed's, for instance."

She had at last uttered the telling note with that mellifluous tongue of hers. After his ignominious departure from the office that morning, William's strongest desire was never to see Ibed's again. Coming down in the train, thinking over his battered dignity, he had almost determined to "chuck it." Exaggerating, as most of us do, the importance of the position he occupied in the lives of other people, he could only picture the clerks constantly thinking about him, impatiently awaiting his return for new enterprises of wit, devising in their leisure hours ridiculous situations for him and his aunt. For one who had so long taken his stand as the young superior god of the office, to drop to the mere butt was too galling: how could he ever stand it? What worse fall than that of the man who finds the chair in which he sits self-satisfied, confident of admiration, suddenly plucked from under him? No, Ibed's would never see him again if he could help it. Where would he find another post? How was he to live meanwhile? And there came singing into his ears, in his aunt's beautiful voice, the name of Sabina Moll and her four thousand a year.

He sat silent so long that Aunt Laura imagined him weighing foolish, unimportant questions of Sabina's looks and capacity for outdoor exercise. In reality, he was entangled in much more abstruse perplexities, weaving plots, estimating chances so dark that, easy as she was, if she had known them she must have cried out in horror. After a little, he glanced up at her with a smile.

"I believe Sabina and I will hit it off, Aunt Laura."

Recognizing all the concessions underlying these words, she diplomatically left the matter there, and rose. "I ought to be in bed. I shall lose all my beauty if you keep me up like this. Be off at once, you abominable youth!" Then, over her shoulder as he was going: "I expect you're glad there's no more Ibed's for some time?"

"Oh, I don't know," William drawled. "Good night, Aunt Laura."

As she put out the rose-coloured lamp she had two thoughts. The first was one which has occurred to all great founders, organizers and projectors in all ages of the world, impatient of the inadequate tools they have to work with. And the second was, that there were at least four men whom she liked much better than William, into whose hands she would have steered Sabina Moll and her fortune with much more pleasure. But then they were not her nephews.

Chapter III

"I ALWAYS MAINTAIN," SAID MR. BURGER, throwing aside the newspaper, "let other people talk as they like, that a good brisk walk after breakfast is an excellent thing—I say, a most excellent thing. What do you think of a stroll down to the town?"

He looked at William. Aunt Laura seldom appeared in the mornings. A house which ran so easily and comfortably must have been carefully supervised, but it was characteristic of that amiable woman that the supervision was not noticeable. And it was characteristic of the two men—the uncle clad in light grey, William in a blue serge coat, white flannel trousers, and patent-leather pumps, both bare-headed, both smoking pipes—that they should grumble at her as they sauntered along.

"What I say your aunt ought to do is to get out in the morning and go for a long walk. I'm always telling her that. She's getting so stout. She never walks anywhere. Stays in bed half the morning, and motors or drives when she goes out. Now, what I say is, that sort of thing ain't wholesome—I say, not wholesome. How do you think she's looking?" he asked, falling into that melancholy error of the middle-aged; for healthy youth seldom observes people from the point of view of their health or welfare, and selfish youth never.

"She seems all right," replied William carelessly.

"She never puts one foot before the other," insisted the uncle.

"Jolly slack life," says William.

Thus pleasantly conversing, they entered the town. As they passed through the streets, Mr. Burger nodded amicably right and left, and meanwhile explained to William some of the town's idiosyncrasies.

"The Fords live there—nice people, not very well off, branch of the Fords of Starke Abbey. I dare say they'll ask us in some evening soon. This red brick house is old Parry's, the banker. He lives there with his three daughters, old maids as ugly as the devil, always cutting up flannel. But rich, my boy—ten per centers."

"That's a very fine house over there," said William, pointing.

"H'm," mumbled Uncle Herbert dubiously. "Yes, I suppose it's fine enough. Ought to be, if money can do it. We don't go there. It belongs to Corder—you've heard of Corder who has the boot and shoe stores at Portsmouth, Southampton, all over the place? I meet him sometimes at the station and round about, but your aunt draws the line at the family."

"Well, after all," decided William, "boots and shoes, you know—retail too—Aunt Laura can't be expected to swallow that."

He soon learned that society at Palebrook was quite as exclusive as he could wish. Rigid lines divided people between whom there was really no difference, except perhaps a better acquaintance with the rules of etiquette. The cream was a composition of the families of a few retired Service men, of people living on their incomes, like the Burgers, of the coastguard lieutenant, the parson, the banker, and their belongings. To these were to be added a few elderly men, living in lodgings or small houses on the outskirts of the town, who were always hanging about, had always endless vacant hours on their hands, and were classified by the tradespeople as "retired gentlemen." The Corders and other families in businesses that were inelegant, although just as intelligent and well-mannered as the others, were barred out, and, what is more, did not seem to resent the insufferable insolence and condescension with which they were treated, but rather took it submissively, hoping in patience for some far-off lucky day when they would be accepted by the *élite*. It was even currently reported that the young Corders were ashamed of their father's business which kept them in opulence. You could hardly find a better proof of the truth of Pascal's maxim, that the value one attaches to the opinion of a town depends upon the length of time one stays in it; for to the mere passer, the casual observer, to be received in Palebrook society seemed about the most undesirable thing in the world. Meanwhile, the sons of the *élite*, coming down from the Universities, from Sandhurst, and the public schools, in vacation time, did all they could to intensify the class consciousness by excluding the sons of all those below the salt from whatever sports or entertainments

were forward. The public tennis courts, for instance, of the two parties lay together, divided by a rather low wall, and there they segregated themselves from each other in a remarkable manner. Nothing
was more comic than to watch them on a summer afternoon, when a
ball, occasionally dropping into a wrong court, was tossed back, and
received with a lofty "Oh thanks!" on the one side, and a "Thank *you!*"
respectfully uttered with an undertone of grievance on the other.

Below these jarring factions were the small shopkeepers—
Dissenters, for the most part, and fierce Radicals. Then, over the whole
town loomed the shadow of the Marquess of Wednesbury, whose seat
was about a mile away. Although this nobleman and his family never
showed the slightest interest in the place, although they made a point
of not knowing a soul in it except the solicitor who had to do with the
estate, although few in the town could say for certain when his lordship
was at Palebrook Court, his name for all that had an enormous effect
upon the community—on that part of it, at all events, with which we
are mainly concerned. It was said he used to boast that if he wanted to
raise money for any affair, he had only to let it be known in Palebrook
that the scheme had his patronage and the subscriptions poured in.
"Palebrook may yell against the House of Lords at election times," he
said again, "but those are only the scum of the people and Dissenters.
You take my word for it, Palebrook is one of the strongholds of old
English snobbery. Very proper thinking people down there. When I
represented the division I had a majority in the town every time, simply
because the well-to-do people put the lid on the shopkeepers by saying they'd get all their stuff from the Stores if the place voted wrong."
Possibly his attitude towards the town was the outcome of a deep pol-
icy. There was no valid reason for asking one Palebrook family to his
house more than another, and if he asked one, he would be obliged
(unless he wished to rouse a turmoil of jealousy) to ask the lot. Besides,
by secluding himself as he did at present, he made something of the
same impression on Palebrook as Queen Victoria by the same means is
said to have made on the nation at large.

At the turn of the street, Mr. Burger nudged his nephew. "Here!
we'll speak to this person, William. He's a regular character." And in a
moment William was introduced to the Reverend Arthur Smalt, who
gave him a chill hand, and looked at him oddly, with little green cruel
eyes, set in a head made up of close-growing white hair, a wrinkled,

obstinate-looking forehead, a short red nose, a weak, querulous mouth, and a stubborn chin. Clean-shaven, all these traits were unrelieved; and the expression of his face was a blend of obstinacy, ill-temper, dyspepsia and disappointment.

"That's what I call an odd fish," said Mr. Burger with a chuckle when the vicar had passed on. "He's the terror of the bishops. He's been in three dioceses. He's been in the Church, and out of it, and now he's back again. He's always disputing and writing to the *Times*, and whenever he changes his opinion he writes a book about it. We're Broad Church here at present, but he began High. He lives alone up there in that mouldy old vicarage with a brace of dogs that he scourges unmercifully, and his two terrors are that somebody will borrow money from him, or that some acquaintance of his will turn up that he'll be obliged to give a bed to. Best joke was that he ran away to London last year because he heard some friend of his, who was rather badly off, was coming to Palebrook. The friend came, and stayed at the inn all the time. Very decent fellow, too. I went fishing with him one day."

"But why do you keep such a blighter?" William asked.

"Keep him? We don't keep him. He's some kind of connexion of the Wednesburys, and the Marquess gave him the living. But they're afraid of their lives of him. They won't let him within a mile of the house. The only time he was there, he kept correcting the servants, and said their cooking was poisonous. Shouldn't be surprised if he was right about that." Uncle Herbert pulled out his watch. "Come, let's go back. I'm a great man for lunch—lunch is what I call an important meal."

On their way, they passed by a charming Queen Anne house which stood at some distance from the road, amid well-kept lawns and gardens. Just as they went by the gate, there came forth a dark, lean man of a pale visage, who hung his clothes on somewhat slovenly.

"Hullo, Stephen!" sang out Mr. Burger; "mind you come in to-night! We expect Sabina Moll this afternoon—your friend of last year."

The other stopped, and William disliked him at once; for although he had never seen Sabina Moll, his thoughts were upon her, and it galled him that any woman in whom he deigned to interest himself should be interested in others. Besides, there was something particularly antipathetic to him in this man with the clean-shaven, professional face, dark, clear-cut, and hard, whose unruffled, concentrated manner and bleak smile as he glanced at the youth implied some vague assumption of superiority and advantage. Instinctively, William felt that the brief, keen look from the stranger's black eyes was an attempt to sum him up, and that the judgment was not on the whole a favourable one. He had been so used from childhood to being petted, to have people make way for him and consult his moods, that any lack of the usual deference made him feel small, and whenever he was made to feel small he became morose.

"Who is that bounder?" he asked his uncle as they walked on.

"Bounder! My dear boy, how do you expect to succeed in life? Why, that's Stephen Ruggles, our great man. Hand and glove with the Wednesburys, and all that. Quite a personage, I assure you. They've been lawyers in Palebrook for ages. That fine house he came out of— that's his house. They say his ancestor built it in the time of Queen Anne, whenever that was. You're later from school than I am."

William strode ahead, sucking at his pipe, which was out. "Is he married?" he asked, after a bit.

"No, he is not. He'll be a good catch for somebody."

"It's about time she caught him if she's going to," said William; and added with a disagreeable laugh: "He's old enough."

"Yes," said Uncle Herbert, ruminating. "I suppose he must be somewhere between thirty and forty."

Chapter IV

WILLIAM ATE A HEAVY lunch, and then drowsed away the afternoon under the trees on the lawn, a jar of tobacco on the grass by his side, and a heap of illustrated papers and magazines, with a new novel on top to keep them from fluttering. About five o'clock a motorcar, driven by Mr. Burger, came through the gate, and on the back seat of this were a lady, and a nurse in uniform.

"Whew!" William whistled and his eyes darkened. "She's an invalid. If that's not about the limit! I won't marry a medicine bottle—simply won't, that's all about it. Aunt Laura might have warned me, I think. I'm going on strike."

But the car stopped, and the lady jumped out without any signs of feebleness. William from his distance watched Aunt Laura kiss her on the threshold, and then draw her into the house.

"She's small," William criticized. "She doesn't come up to Aunt Laura's shoulder, and she's not a tall woman. I rather like short girls; they're a change." He rose and stretched himself. "I suppose I had better show up. They'll all be wondering where I am and waiting for me to appear. I wonder why they didn't send the motor for me yesterday instead of that feeble cab thing?"

Laughter sounded from the drawing-room, and voices in brisk conversation. William, who had half imagined that they would be sitting in awkward impatience, anxiously expecting his arrival, felt rather disappointed. "They seem to be enjoying themselves," he thought resentfully. Then he coughed loud to attract attention and went in. Two other ladies from the neighbourhood were there, but Uncle Herbert was the only man. "Ah, here's William," said Aunt Laura, hardly turning her head, and she went on with her conversation. William stood about, and to show himself at ease attempted to start a talk with his uncle; but the uncle was listening amused to what the ladies were saying and gave him hardly any attention. It was very trying.

Sabina sat lost in a big chair with her feet scarcely touching the floor, and from the depths of the chair she talked calmly in a flat, rather hesitating voice. She wore a big white hat, and underneath it appeared a face which did not strike William as particularly pretty. She seemed older than he had thought she would be, and, remembering the nurse, he wondered if it were the effect of disease. But after a few minutes he was set right on that point.

"I don't mind so much having measles," Sabina was saying. "It's not at all a painful malady, do you think? At least not the way I had it. But I always fancy everybody is inclined to laugh. They think it's such a childish thing to have measles when one is grown up."

She smiled, and it was a rather mirthless smile. From the way one corner of the mouth went up it might even be called bitter; yet it was not unpleasant to see, because it managed to convey that whatever dissatisfaction the smile indicated was applied to herself more than to others. Her face was moulded on the same small plan as her body, and although it had not a single good feature, it yet managed to be what is called "pleasing." But this impression was due more to her still, unassertive manner than to any distinct quality revealed; for there was no sensibility in her face and little good-nature, perhaps because she had never found occasions in her life which called for the steady exercise of these virtues. Still, she had as a rule those very amiable and conciliating looks and manners which many young women now cultivate as a lesson to the women of a former generation whose method has been the offhand and the downright, and even the overpowering high-hand, in social intercourse. The impression you took from her person and manner was of a woman who had moved along from the cradle protected by a bodyguard of guineas, and consequently had never come in touch with any real thing in life, of which she was, for all practical purposes, as ignorant as when she was a baby. She looked anything between twenty and twenty-five: at night she looked scarcely the first, in the daytime fully the last, and in trying lights, or at moments when her nerves and digestion were wrong, considerably older.

William, feeling extremely snubbed, sat unnoticed till the two callers rose to go away. He strolled through the window out on the lawn chafing, and when he came back found Sabina by herself looking at a magazine.

She raised her eyes quickly and then fixed them on her book again. "Do you know this part of Hampshire?" she asked after a little, without looking up.

"Oh yes, fairly well. That is, I've been down here a couple of times before. I don't care about Hampshire. I've biked through Yorkshire," he added.

This did not seem to interest Sabina, who made some inarticulate sound and turned over a page of her magazine. William was wondering whether he wouldn't let her go to blazes, when, after a long enough pause, she spoke again.

"I've just had the measles," she said, "and your aunt thought this air would suit me."

He looked at her solemnly, thinking there was some chance she might still have it about her clothes. "Beastly selfishness!" he reflected. "If I catch measles it will spoil my holiday." Then a reassuring thought followed, and he spoke.

"I had measles when I was at school. It got me off a term. I don't believe you can get it twice."

"No?" queried Sabina; and there was silence again.

William shifted his legs and said he supposed she liked the country.

"Oh, anything is a change from Manchester. I hate Manchester!" She got up and stood for a little with a curious swaying motion of her little body and arms, such as a schoolgirl often has when she recites her lesson. In Sabina it was not graceful. She moved some things on a table near her, kicked the toe of one shoe with the heel of the other, and then went out of the room rather awkwardly and left William fuming. Her repellent manner, which a person with any powers of observation would have at once put down to intense shyness, seemed to him the insolence of the wealthy woman. "Of course, she knows I'm in Ibed's and she thinks I'm not good enough to talk to. She puts me in with her old father's beastly little clerks. I never met such a disagreeable woman. Nobody would stand her if she wasn't rich. But I'll show her a thing or two."

Young as he was, and although he knew more or less intimately several girls round about his own age, yet he was far from being in unison with some of our modern lights where women were concerned. The woman he always took his bearings by was the woman of thirty-five or forty years ago: that for him was a permanent type. Present-day aspects of the feminine spirit he either ignored, or regarded as sickening divergences from the proper type. That woman's development had been hampered was an abstract proposition in which he took no interest; if he had thought about it at all, he would have agreed that she was long ago fully developed on all the points where development could profitably take place. That any woman was in any way that mattered the equal of man was to him unthinkable, and his opinion of women who assumed masculine airs was the meanest, while the men who approved such travesties were either silly juveniles or senile.

Accordingly, at dinner that evening he attempted to show Sabina many things, and first of all that he was a rather important person. There is no stronger conviction among the professional classes than that they have a right to treat with some contempt the possessors of fortunes made in trade; and this feeling, when they are themselves reduced to Government pensions and narrow incomes, aids them enormously in maintaining their self-esteem when they are brought in contact with new-got wealth. William set out to shew Sabina Moll, indirectly of course, that people like the Moll family might consider themselves honoured and lucky beyond their wildest hopes by an alliance with the son of a deceased Lieutenant-Colonel.

"There's a friend of mine in town," he said, addressing his uncle with studied carelessness—"Clement Stagg, son of Stagg, the captain of H.M.S. *Irrecoverable*, who nearly got engaged to Flavour's daughter last year—I mean, the Flavour of Flavour and Blades, the Oxford Street tradesmen. They're millionaires, but Clem's mater and sisters simply wouldn't hear of the match."

At dinner-time, beyond a perfunctory performance of his duties as host, reduced to their simplest forms when the party was an intimate one, Uncle Herbert seldom paid much attention to what was going forward. Now he simply answered: "Indeed? God bless my soul!" as one who dreams, staring meanwhile anxiously at a dish presented to him. But Aunt Laura looked at William with troubled eyes, and thought that all her plans must crumble if the foolish boy could not be stopped. She considered her nephew with the feelings of a playwright who watches a drunken actor disorganize his play. What in the world would he knock over next?

He was now offering himself as the hardened man of the world, familiar with the devious ways of London life; he talked of theatres, and music-halls, and related anecdotes of "celebrities" which he had heard from one of the clerks who had had a maiden aunt on the stage, or recollected from the gossiping columns of the newspapers.

"I have seldom been at the theatre," said Sabina in a prim voice which seemed meant to convey that she was tired of the subject. "I suppose there are theatres in Manchester, but I have not been in them. I much prefer concerts, don't you?" she asked Aunt Laura. And she went on to explain that she liked attending travellers' lectures. "There was an awfully interesting man who gave a lecture on Japan one afternoon last February. Effie Patten, my Newnham College friend, was greatly captivated. She wanted us to go off there together, but father, as usual, wouldn't allow it."

"What a pity! It would have been so nice for you," said Aunt Laura soothingly. But William broke in:

"Did you mean to go alone?"

Sabina opened her eyes a little. "Yes; just my friend and I."

He was put to it to stifle a guffaw. His dislike of her was blending into contempt and pity. And he began to talk of his own travels, which had, however, been limited to England, the northern coast of France, and Lausanne. He held forth grandly on hotels, as he was used to do with the clerks at Ibed's; but his aunt, who guessed on what terms his mother had stayed at such places, looked hot and ashamed, and even Mr. Burger, when he was at leisure to listen, began to fidget.

"I know nothing about English hotels," said Sabina.

She spoke as if she were denying a knowledge of public-bars, and William, taking this as another example of her narrowness, enjoyed a moment of triumph. But the obvious embarrassment of the table gained upon him. For his aunt's uneasiness he cared nothing; she was only a woman, and, so far as he could see, a silly one. William liked the company of young women—in fact, he was rather a philanderer—but this sentiment kept house with a good, sound, Tory, Old Testament contempt for women as acting and thinking creatures, and he was possessed by the misguided notion that a man can argue a woman in or out of anything. But his uncle too appeared uneasy, and that was more serious. It was enough to check the flow of William's talk, which had been running so fluently. His spirits fell; a horrible suspicion dawned on him that he was not being admired and envied so much as he thought; and under the shock he saw a new meaning in Sabina's last remark. This he was now inclined to twist into the boast of a purse-proud woman, who is not subject to the accidents of common travellers, but has a private house to receive her wherever she stops. And for one moment he had an intolerable vision of Sabina, whom he so much wished to regard with contemptuous familiarity, moving among the haunts of the enormously wealthy, on social heights he could never hope to attain.

The vision was too poignant to last, and he told himself angrily it was nonsense; but it had shaken him for all that, and he carried the effects of it into the drawing-room, even as one carries dim effects of a nightmare out into a sunshine morning amid the labours of the day. Various people had come in: old Parry with his daughters, active, elderly, solemn women without physical attractions; the coastguard lieutenant, a disputatious, shouldering sort of man, who had a conviction that he was socially and in most other ways superior to the people he came in contact with at Palebrook, accompanied by his wife, a pretty Irishwoman, whose existence was passed in suckling babies and backing up her husband's assertions. Stephen Ruggles and five or six others made up the residue.

A stout girl played the "Carnival of Venice" on the piano with what was called "brilliant execution." Her sister combined with her then in a *duo* for piano and violin. Sabina was asked to play or sing. She swung over to the piano shyly and ungracefully, and Ruggles managed to throw two more cushions on the piano-stool without being observed, which saved her the embarrassment of asking for them. In her gratitude she gave him a look which established an understanding between them at once. Seated thus at the piano under the shaded lights, she looked attractive, with her flushed face, her hair made the most of, and red flowers in her dark hair. Her hands and arms too, on which she wore a good deal of jewellery, although they were heavily shaped, revealing no sign of fine stock in the Moll pedigree, were white and firm. Under her very thick eyebrows, which grew into a perverse tuft near the nose and indicated a considerable amount of animal passion and temper in the little body, her soft brown eyes glanced up timidly at Ruggles, who stood by her, watching the music over her shoulder. And as princesses of royal blood are called handsome on easier terms than other people—there being always the reservation understood: "handsome for a Royalty"—so Sabina Moll in a shrine of pounds sterling seemed wonderfully pretty, though had you met her in an omnibus or behind the counter of a shop she might have struck you as insignificant. She played, and then she sang, and the way she did both revealed the fact that her father had spent some money to have her taught, and nothing more. She was not even on a level with the usual drawing-room and village-concert amateur. It was better not to hear such playing and singing.

William moved about with his eyes on her, almost glowering at her. It was not that he had the least symptom of any feeling which could be capitulated under the term amorous for Sabina Moll; there were girls here far prettier than she was and with whom he felt he could get along much better; but he had been so used hitherto to being cajoled and sought after by young women that he could not sit easy under her indifference. His aunt, to anchor him, set him to playing Bridge. He had no excuse to refuse; but ere long he trumped his own trick when he was playing both hands, and shortly after revoked, which caused his partner, Miss Parry, a punctilious player, to call him to order in severe terms. Thereupon good-natured Aunt Laura, who was for putting everybody at ease, came up offering to play his hand, and desired him to go and talk to Sabina.

William lounged up to her and began a conversation on songs. He mentioned the ones he liked and the singers he had heard sing them. The names were unfamiliar to Sabina, and William shewed his surprise a little too emphatically.

"I'm afraid I've not had your advantages," Sabina dropped icily, with the little dry laugh which usually followed when she said something disagreeable.

William, however, was better armoured against such shafts than she guessed, and he accepted the remark literally. It was only too plain that she hadn't had his advantages! But he judged it well to change the conversation. He thought her stupid; but if she wanted serious and stodgy topics he was her man.

"Are you interested in politics?" he asked portentously.

"Very much," replied Sabina; but she proceeded to talk of contemporary questions in a way which was less than vague. Still, William was not much beforehand, and they might have got on very well with this subject, being both too ignorant of its details to fight over it, when Sabina faced him suddenly.

"No doubt you support the suffrage for women?"

William was flabbergasted. If she had asked him whether he was in favour of letting loose the lunatics in Bedlam he would not have been so much astounded. His experience had never brought him in contact with any women who regarded this question seriously, and it had been presented to him from the music-hall and musical-comedy stage, where the Suffragette was looked on as a catch for a laugh as certain as the henpecked husband, the foreigner, the long-haired or bald-headed man, and the policeman. He knew that such people as Suffragettes must exist in reality elsewhere than on the stage or parading the streets, but it had never occurred to him to picture them in civilized conditions, any more than the dancing restaurant-keepers, gay dressmakers, or other phantoms of the theatre.

He looked hard at her, suspiciously, to see if she was not trying to make a fool of him; but when he was satisfied that she was really serious he gave a contemptuous laugh.

"Do you mean the Votes for Women lot? I should jolly well think I don't support them. Why, everybody knows that they're absolutely mad. You've only got to look at them." And his mind presented a lank creature with short pale hair, dressed in broad checks, and with a pair of spectacles spanning a red nose. "You don't really believe in them yourself, do you?"

Sabina looked deeply hurt. "Of course I do," she answered crossly. She began to flounder through some arguments, trying to reconstruct the logical chain of proofs which she had so often heard her Newnham College friend, Effie Patten, adduce, but it was only too evident that she was not very well up in the polemics of the subject.

Ruggles drew near and supported her. He had overheard the dispute, and he professed to be a convinced advocate for women's enfranchisement. He pointed out the number of women who paid taxes, who managed households, who were the real breadwinners, and he quoted figures. He advanced some other stock arguments. He saw that neither of his hearers knew anything about the matter, and as he wished to please Sabina, who, he guessed, had thrown herself in with the party simply because some friend or friends of hers had done so, what he said became a sort of *argumentum ad invidiam.*

He looked better in evening dress than he had in the morning. He was straight and well-knit; his thick smooth black hair threw into relief the face, thin and pallid, which was not, however, the pallor of ill-health. What was perhaps the strangest thing about him was that when he smiled, which he did often, the smile was limited to the beautifully shaped mouth, while the eyes remained serious. His face, taken altogether, had that look of artificiality which is often seen on the faces of actors, and politicians, and barristers, men who counterfeit emotions, who live in the sight of the public and depend on the public applause.

William thought that Ruggles had come up purposely to insult him in the presence of Sabina. He did not believe there was a man in England who sincerely backed the female suffrage. And as he thus regarded the whole dispute as personal, he tried to take a fall out of Ruggles, hauling down bits of argument, scraps of information from dusty shelves of memory where they had somehow stuck. He recalled a news-placard he had seen of one of the evening papers.

"Look what Lloyd George said in the House!"

Ruggles smiled with irritating blandness. "Yes; what *did* Lloyd George say?"

William was floored. He had no more idea than the man in the moon—or Sabina. But she was looking up at Ruggles with undisguised admiration, and William went in for him again, talking very loud.

"I don't care; I tell you I've seen them. Possibly you haven't. I've seen them at Westminster, trying to pull down the House of Commons and being hauled off by the bobbies." His innate contempt for women added bitterness to his tongue. "You don't propose to hand over the government of the country to that kind of a lot, do you? No sensible man does, at least. What good would they be in time of war?"

"I should have thought," said Ruggles suavely, "that that's just what they have shown themselves fit for, from what you've been telling us."

Old Parry, the banker, coming up at the moment, burst into a loud laugh, and Sabina turned away. The banker had an anecdote to relate, and he was a circumstantial teller of a story. It was impossible to continue the dispute, and William retired in sullen disgust. "I had the best of it," he thought; "but they all lick that fellow's boots here. He's about clever enough to impress Palebrook. There isn't a man to be found in London, or anywhere else in England, I don't believe, who supports those fools of Suffragettes. It isn't manly, that's all about it."

With such thoughts he solaced himself during the rest of an evening which for the others seemed to go pleasantly, and for him in spasms of chagrin and wounded vanity and what he called a sensation of being hopelessly bored. Meanwhile Aunt Laura, who had missed nothing of all this, sighed as she thought that youth is often the greatest disadvantage of the young.

Chapter V

BUT BIOGRAPHERS AND HISTORIANS assure us that it is at moments when defeat seems certain that the genius of your hero and statesman shines out brightest. Aunt Laura, lying in bed, gave her thoughts to the situation as it actually was, and came down next morning determined to set a new face on it. She put herself in the way of William about half-past eleven, just as the young man was strolling down to Palebrook.

"Are you going out, William?"

"Yes. I thought I might run across the Ford girls. Uncle says—"

"Don't go for a minute. Come and sit out of doors with me while Sabina is getting ready. We are lunching with the Bartlets about five miles from here."

She dropped into a deep chair and stared at the sky, and in her charming mauve and lace frock and big straw hat she looked fresh and smiling as if she had not a care in the world.

"What a divine morning!" She breathed it in. "And how are you getting on with Sabina?"

William had woken with half a headache, convinced that he would never get on with Sabina, and that he did not care. "I don't think we have much in common," he said. "She seems rather narrow. I've determined to leave her to herself as much as possible."

His aunt looked at him reproachfully. "How can you be so foolish! Really, William, I thought you were a man, and you act like a very child."

William, as a rule, used his youth as a bludgeon; but although he rejoiced in his youth in the fullest sense, he did not care about being called a child. Aunt Laura saw a sullen look creeping over his face.

"You must know you do yourself," she added softly. "I believe you are doing it on purpose."

"Doing what?" asked William, astonished.

"Why, making Sabina cross."

William simply jumped at this unjust charge ladled out so coolly. "Making her cross? It's the other way about, I think."

"Rubbish!" She glanced him over serenely. "How could a little thing like that make a huge fellow like you cross?"

"I think that's rather steep," grumbled William. "It has nothing to do with size. I can't strike it up with her, that's all. We're not made for each other. Besides, there's Ruggles, I suppose you've noticed? He's the whole thing, it seems to me."

"No, he's not—at least, not yet. But I admit there's some danger. I don't believe Stephen is a bit in love with her, or Sabina with him; but she may be in love with him any day, and he may be in love with four thousand a year——" Aunt Laura fell a-musing.

"What a pig!" cried William. "I thought he was rich."

"Oh, rich!" She gazed at the whispering leaves. "I suppose none of us object to increase our incomes. You'll have to change your tactics, my young prince."

"I don't see what more I can do," he put in.

"You'll have to change your tactics. The world doesn't come readymade even to the most important of us. I had a long talk with Sabina last night in her bedroom, and I've thought the matter out. I'm going to tell you what you ought to do. I find that Sabina has become very serious: there's a friend of hers, some girl in Manchester, whom she tries to live up to. All she cares about at present are heavy things like politics and concerts and poetry——"

"Poetry?" repeated William in a dull voice.

"Poetry. So, you see, your conversation so far has been hardly of a kind to interest her. You must give up talking about race-courses and actresses and drinking-bars——"

"I never talked about drinking-bars." William flushed indignantly.

"Didn't you? Anyhow, what you must try to talk about in future are serious subjects. I expect you don't care much for such things, but you've got a good enough head, and you can manage quite easily, because she has only just begun too: she was quite ordinary last year, quite like the rest of us. Now I've picked out some books that my brother-in-law, the headmaster, left here years ago, and they've been lying about the attics ever since; but I've had them dusted and put in your room. They seem to be poetry and history and that kind of thing. You see, you can study them, and then you can tell her what you've studied. It's quite simple."

William did not think so. "Do you mean I'm to spend my holidays swotting over poetry and history?" he inquired, looking at her gloomily.

"There's Sabina! I must fly. Perhaps," she said airily, "you prefer to be a clerk at Ibed's all your life. Your mother can leave you nothing. Good-bye, William; see that they give you all you want." And she moved over the sward, a picture of grace, swinging her parasol negligently.

She had routed William. Her mention of Ibed's had the effect of checking any tendency to rebellion. Between the chance of four thousand a year and an ignominious return to Ibed's, who could debate? He got up and stretched himself. "I suppose I'm in for it." And he decided to go upstairs and examine the books.

There were about a dozen. Swinburne's *Poems and Ballads*, *John Inglesant*, Pater's *Imaginary Portraits*, FitzGerald's *Omar Khayyám*, Charles Kingsley's *Poems*, were among them. William opened one after the other in despair. How was he ever going to get any grip on such stuff? But fully conscious of all that depended on the business, he set himself doggedly to plough through some pages, and possessing, as Aunt Laura had said, a good enough head, he managed to subdue a certain amount of unruly matter to his intelligence.

After lunch he was at it again with commendable assiduity, leaving his uncle, with whom he had lunched, in consternation.

"But you said you'd come sailing, William?"

"Yes, but I want to read."

In that house, to put off anything for the sake of reading was unheard of. There was only one way to account for it, and Uncle Herbert looked at him anxiously.

"I think you said you have had the measles, didn't you?"

William nodded as he lit his pipe, adding that he felt all right.

"But God bless my soul, to stay in the house on a fine afternoon like this! It's quite possible you've picked up that affair from Sabina. It's very catching. Perhaps Whitmore had better have a look at you. I call him a thoroughly sound practitioner. I'll speak to your aunt about it to-night. You don't feel like walking down to him now, eh?"

Finally, he was left to his studies. About half-past four, glancing out of the window, he saw that Sabina had returned and was drifting through the garden alone.

He went out and strolled abstractedly in her direction, reading in his book—the *Imaginary Portraits*. As he drew near, he seemed to perceive her and started violently. He really did it very well.

"I was so taken up with my book," he explained.

"Is it a detective story?" Sabina asked slightingly. "I thought you had gone on the water with Mr. Burger."

"Yes, I was to have gone, but this is my day for study. I stayed in and read." A glow of no ill-founded pride came into his face as he said this, thinking of the abominable stuff he had wrestled with all the afternoon. Few men could do the same.

Sabina looked at him uncertainly. "Was your book so very interesting?"

"I don't know that people in general would find it interesting," William answered loftily. "It interested me. Or rather they did. I do not," he remarked pointedly, "confine myself to one book."

For the first time since they had met, Sabina had a slight sense of inferiority. That he had stayed in to whistle, to dance, to stand on his head—anything of that kind she would have heard from William with such equanimity as we have for the not altogether unexpected. But that he had stayed in to read, and to read out-of-the-way, serious books! She looked at him with a certain timidity which was something quite different from her habitual shyness.

"What is the name of your book?"

He showed her the title-page, with his heart in his mouth. Suppose she had read it—had mastered the stodgy pages!

"*Imaginary Portraits*," she murmured respectfully. "Walter Pater. Is he a great author?"

William breathed again. He felt kindly to the unknown Pater: she had never heard of Pater, so Pater had saved him. "I should rather think so. One of the best."

"Pater," she mused. "What a very odd name. I have never heard Effie Patten talk of him. I should be sure to remember if I had," and her little face looked strained and anxious.

"Rather deep for women," said William mysteriously. "Rather off it, I can tell you. It even takes me all my time to follow him. So you see——"

"Could you give me any notion of the subject of the book?" Sabina hesitated.

"Ah, there you are!" cried William. "And likewise, there you are again! The name Pater," he continued, steering away from dangerous ground, "this author took because it means Father. I know that as a fact. Pater means Father in Latin, just as Mater means Mother."

He astonished himself. He wished his aunt could hear him: he wished all Palebrook could hear him. He was getting to like his part. And there could be no doubt in the world about the intense respect which now shone in Sabina's eyes.

"I had no idea your nephew was so learned," he had the satisfaction of hearing her say during the evening. "We've been talking of such profound subjects. He knows Latin and heaps of things."

"Dear me, didn't you know that?" Aunt Laura raised her eyebrows lazily. "I believe he is a poet too, Sabina."

"What on earth possessed you to say I was a poet?" William inquired angrily when he caught her alone. "Haven't I enough to do to keep up the philosopher dodge? You don't want me to have brain fever, do you?"

"Oh, I'm so sorry!" His accomplice laughed idly. "I ought to have said 'philosopher' instead of 'poet.' Now we must stick to it."

Chapter VI

THOUGH WILLIAM MIGHT NOT be a professed philosopher, though he had not, in truth, a spoonful of scholastic philosophy anywhere about him, he yet found himself engaged on a subject of meditation which has occupied no small number of them, to wit: The cruelty and irresponsibility of women. Here was that woman, his aunt, machining with a light hand the most daring schemes, engaging him gaily to the most onerous burthens, and then absconding out of all danger, leaving him to half kill himself to satisfy her engagements.

It was poetry now. The sun was shining in a sky of tender blue through which little fleecy clouds went spinning; it was a matchless day for sailing, for tennis, for just loafing. But it was poetry now, alas! And with rage in his heart, William attacked for about the fiftieth time the "Laus Veneris," applying his stubborn memory to retain words devoid of sense. It is said that certain pupils have been known to learn propositions of Euclid by heart to such a point that when it comes to demonstrating, if the letters of the figure be changed, they are at once unhorsed; and William was pursuing an analogous mental process. Luckily, his memory was a good one, and had been to a certain extent exercised by cricket scores and at Ibed's.

It was twelve o'clock. His aunt came in, cool and fresh-looking as ever. "What a lovely day! Everybody is out." She sat herself on the arm of a chair and scrutinized her flushed and dishevelled nephew. "Well, how are you getting on?"

It was too much. "It's all right for you," he burst out. "You wouldn't care about it yourself. What would you think of being up against that"—and he thumped the *Poems and Ballads*—"since breakfast?"

"Dear me!" cooed his aunt. "I'm sure I sympathize with you. You look as if you had been working hard. Would you like some beef-tea?"

"Yes, I would." He took five or six leaves of the book between his thumb and forefinger and held the book towards her. "That!" he said significantly. He seemed to be moved by a slight frenzy.

Aunt Laura was impressed. "Good Heavens! don't overstrain yourself whatever you do. I'll have the beef-tea sent up at once. I had no idea," she continued, "that poetry was as hard as that. I thought it was—oh, you know—comic opera and that sort of thing."

"The comic has been left out of this opera," said William bitterly. He drummed moodily on the book. "You wouldn't like to hear me recite, I suppose?" he asked in a tone of injury.

"Oh, of all things!" she clasped her hands fervently. "Do recite something, William."

"I may as well do it before you," he went on rather ungraciously, "because I'll have to do it some time, and I'll be better for practice. I've taken this piece from another of those books." He pointed to a small volume.

And he began:

> "*Three fishers went sailing away to the West,*
> *Away to the West as the sun went down;*
> *Each thought on the woman who loved him the best,*
> *And the children stood watching them out of the town.*"

He worked through the poem, shouting, making what he considered appropriate gestures as he went. Memories of music-hall reciters aided him: he paused at the end of every stanza and deepened his voice. Aunt Laura, with her head on one side, her lips parted, watched him, full of admiration.

"Really, William, you're simply splendid. You're too thrilling for words. You know there's a song something like that. I'm sure I've heard it somewhere."

She said this lightly, not thinking it made any difference. Her notion of the way poetry is produced was vague. If she had been forced to give an opinion, she would have said that she supposed it was got out of other books. It never occurred to her that a poem was the special property of any one poet. This will only shock intellectual circles and culture-clubs; there are really any number of people up and down the world like her. She was the kind of person who attributes the play to the actors, and who can never tell the name of the author of a novel she has been reading. The similarity between what William had just recited and a song she hardly remembered struck her as an amusing coincidence—nothing more, and that was why she mentioned it.

But William saw much farther than that: he was a conscious plagiary. "Then I'll have to chuck it," he said desperately. "There's a morning's work gone to pot. I picked it out because it was seasidey and appropriate. Now it's no use."

"I'm really grieved, William," moaned his aunt, wishing she had kept quiet. "And you've turned out so intellectual and clever too, dear. Does it make so much difference?"

"Oh, it's not your fault, I suppose," William grumbled like a generous martyr. "But I can't very well trot out stale stuff, can I? Sabina would spot it at once." He turned to his table again wearily. "Well, more work. Look here, Aunt Laura, I'd like that beef-tea, please, as soon as it's convenient. This sort of thing makes you hungry. I'll bet any odds you like that I've got some stuff here"—and he slapped his hand down on *Poems and Ballads*—"that you've never heard anyone sing out of an asylum."

Compensation awaited him at lunch in the shape of Sabina's reverent manner. She listened whenever the philosopher and poet spoke as if she were at a solemn service in church. He was wise enough not to speak often. He was on his aunt's left hand, and whenever she thought he was breaking away from his personage she kicked him on the leg. Uncle Herbert, too, had been evidently schooled, and looked on a little mystified, trying to think how the uncle of a great man should act.

Afterwards, out on the lawn, William was lounging and smoking, pretending to read, when Sabina came and sat near him, or rather over against him with a piece of embroidery work in her hand. She did not speak: no doubt she feared to disturb his high meditations and was waiting to be spoken to. Through half-closed lids he contemplated her. Even to the most fatuous there was nothing in her attitude to betoken love; but there was an interest and respect which denoted that she must regard the young man sprawling there as an intellectual giant. Aunt Laura had evidently given it to her strong. Enlightened by the hint from his aunt, he was quite shrewd enough to see that this admiration of intellectual effort and the arts was not native in Sabina; it was not even a personal impulse, but the suggestion of a friend—Effie Patten of Newnham College—whom she adored. Neither had it lasted for long: she could hardly be very well up in her subjects. He thought that under these circumstances he would be particularly dull if he could not impress her. She did not love him yet, of course, but it would go hard, since she was in such excellent dispositions, if he could not make her love him. As for his love for her—well, that would take care of itself. With Sabina's four thousand pounds a year jingling in his pocket, he could go and take Ibed by the nose at the head of his clerks.

Other thoughts, less comfortable, assailed him. He brushed them away. "That would somehow work out all right." The bees droned by; the flowers swooned languorously in the warm afternoon; butterflies, splendidly gaudy, dandered over the grass; the old sun-dial, ivy-clad, cast a long shadow; in the tree near by a thrush was singing, and Sabina in her chair became a pink blur. ...

"Mr. Spring—I hope I don't interrupt your thoughts—but I wonder would you mind writing in my album?"

It was Sabina speaking timidly as she held out the pretty book.

"I have a number of rather well-known people. Members of Parliament whom father has helped, and all that. I always make him take my book when he is presiding at a big meeting. I have several Cabinet Ministers. I have also a number of people we met on the steamer when we went out to New York. See, here is the great woman novelist, and over here is one of the great leaders of the Woman Suffrage movement—But I forgot; you are not on our side in that." She hesitated, blushing a little. "I have no poet, and so I thought——"

It was touching. In an age when the poet has been relegated among English-speaking people to the position of the palmist and the "beauty specialist" in the popular esteem, this thrill of veneration, swelling up in a heart nurtured in commercialdom, for the singing-man, the creator of unpractical ideals, the pursuer of unprofitable loveliness, was something to the credit of our general humanity. For bear in mind that her sentiment was in no way implicated with any attraction to the person of the youth before her; what she gave was a pure tribute, rendered to a man born with a gift which segregated him from the herd of mortals. William himself saw this well enough, but he felt no shame; on the contrary, he considered that what admiration she had to spare he had fairly earned.

"I'll take the book into the house and find a pen and ink," he said, with a rising sense of importance. This was to be a man indeed! But he wished it had been for something which enrolled his sympathies more than poetry.

Sabina, however, had come all prepared. "Perhaps this might do?" and she held out a little gold fountain-pen.

"Capitally." He wrote his name in neat letters: "William Parkman Montagu Spring."

She was looking over his shoulder.

"How many names you have!"

"Family names," said William. Then, with his irresistible tendency to bounce, he added consequentially: "My mother was one of the Montagus."

It occurred to Sabina, who had nothing to learn about social values, that they were a rather extended and variegated clan, stretching from the peerage to the moneylender and second-hand clothes dealer; but she did not make any attempt to locate William's kindred. Who he was interested her not at all; she was only concerned with what he was.

"Perhaps you will read some of your poems one day?" she ventured after a moment.

He had expected this. "One day—oh, yes. I'm getting up some things. They'll be ready shortly."

⁂

They had to be ready sooner than he anticipated. The very next morning his aunt came into his room.

"The Parrys have asked us all for to-night. It will be a large party. They hope you will recite some of your poems."

He turned pale. "They hope I'll recite——"

"Yes. I'm afraid you are going to mind, William, but Miss Parry sent that message by Sabina."

"Well, if you haven't got me into a hole! My God, if you haven't got me into a hole!" He lost control of himself altogether. "Look here, do you mean to say I'll have to get up and spout before a room full of people?"

"I'm afraid so," she said, toying with a flower in her belt.

"Well, I won't, my friend. You can risk your little bob on that with perfect safety. I say, with—perfect—safety. I'll go back to London first."

"Ibed's!" murmured Aunt Laura, looking out of the window.

This word, as usual, acted as a cold douche. "How on earth did they know I was a poet?" he asked sullenly at length.

"Sabina, of course. You don't expect she would keep a thing like that quiet? Why, she's proud of it."

"Is she? And do you mean to say that the whole shop knows I'm a poet?"

"I'm afraid so," said Aunt Laura again.

"Well, it's a shame," he cried, breaking down. "I say, it's a shame. My whole holiday is spoiled. Nobody will ask me to anything while I've got that reputation. Who wants a poet moping around? People will think I'm no good at games, and lost in my thoughts, and all that bosh. You never see a poet on the stage that he's not made fun of. I've lost my coat-room check at Palebrook, that's all. I didn't mind the joke just for a few days among ourselves, but if it's going to be public property——Why, my God!" he shouted, appalled, "I shall be pointed at in the streets. I'll be thought balmy!"

She felt sorry for him, and came and put her arm round his shoulders. "Try to bear up, William," she purred soothingly. "If you show the white feather now the whole thing is lost. We'll see it through between us if you'll only pull yourself together. After all, it's not so terrible. You recited splendidly yesterday."

"Oh, before you! That's not a mob."

"Well, all I can say is that everything with Sabina depends on to-night. Stephen is giving her a horseback lesson this morning, and you must do something striking to counteract the effect. Try to take a brace, there's a dear boy."

"It's come so suddenly," said William. "That's the main thing I object to." But he began to feel better.

In the evening she arranged that she would take William by herself in the carriage, and sent Mr. Burger ahead with Sabina. As soon as they were gone, she called her nephew into the dining-room.

"Well, are you ready? Come here and let me see how you look."

She glanced over the tall, thin young man, and on the whole felt satisfied. He was too tall, his nose was too long, his eyes too small, his feet too big; he had an expression of assurance which might annoy some people; but on the other side, he had thick fair hair, he was fresh-coloured, and he was healthy. Altogether, she thought he looked very nice. She straightened his tie, put a flower in his coat, patted him here and there.

"Oh, stop it, Aunt Laura! You're making me more nervous than I am already."

"I want you to make a good impression." She went to the table and poured out a glass of champagne. "You had better drink this," she said. "It will rouse the lion in you."

"You are sure you know your pieces?" she asked when they were in the carriage.

"What do you think?" At present he was feeling rather lively. "Anyhow, I've got them all written out in case of accident."

"How clever of you to hit upon that!"

"Yes. Now, look here. While I'm spouting, you're not to look at me. You're to keep your head turned away. Do you understand?"

"All right," she laughed. "I'll study my toes. And now let me give you a tip: Don't talk much, and look as serious as you can."

Chapter VII

THE COMPANY ASSEMBLED IN the high rooms of Mr. Parry's Georgian house, many of whom had never seen William, felt at liberty to scrutinize him without concealment. His reputation had preceded him; they had heard a poet would be on view; but they had no formed idea of what poets were like. He might resemble anything, from the cloaked and slouch-hatted villain of the stage, to the poor idiot who on fine days sat sunning on the quay. What they were not prepared for was the ordinary—someone like themselves; and many looking at William—the girls who had speculated vaguely; the young men who had cut the jokes of British farce about poets; the elders for whom a poet ranked with the organ-grinder and the billiard-marker—felt a trifle disappointed. They were only not absolutely revolted, saved from an unholy sensation that a trick had been put upon them, by the sight of William's pallor, his corrugated brow, a general air of defiance in his bearing.

The truth is that the young man felt he was in the position of an advertised fool. In him the characteristic which could be constantly relied upon was his eagerness to secure the applause of people whose judgments he thought counted, and among these he numbered the society of Palebrook and the country round about. Whatever free airs he might assume, there was always working in him an eager reference to the opinions of such people and an abject fear of their criticism. His dignity lay prone at a mocking smile; his serenity was at the mercy of a whisper; and the assurance of his carriage could be marred by the raising of an eyebrow. No greater sting could have been devised for his vanity than to introduce him thus publicly in the melancholy and contemptible character of a poet, which isolated him as completely from his surroundings as the clown in the circus-ring is isolated from the spectators. No character was more remote from the kind of men he admired than the character of a poet. If he had been asked to choose between coming as a nigger-minstrel or a poet, he would have chosen the former with infinite gusto. Or a boxer, or a step-dancer, or a jockey! Those were occupations which people respected. But a poet! …

No wonder he looked haggard. It was impossible for him to mix in, to feel at ease, because everybody who spoke to him spoke, as it were, on stilts. If he drew near a group, the laughter hushed. Girls said to him gravely that they supposed he found them too frivolous. The elders were even more insupportable. They patronized him as they might patronize some youth who is not what is called "all there."

"Well, Mr. Spring," sang out old Parry, as the young man wandered disconsolately into the card-room. "Mooning, I suppose—always mooning! What fellows you poets are!"

That is a specimen of what he had to bear. Sabina came to him now and then, but her visits, he felt, were inspired by respect, by duty, and she would soon move away again to Ruggles, with whom she seemed to be perfectly happy. William had never liked Ruggles since the day he first met him; what he felt now was hatred. What did a man of that age want at an evening party? If he came, why didn't he stay with the old men and women? Why wasn't he married? Why should he monopolize all the young women, who were probably laughing at him?—though as William tried to think this he had an abominable conviction that they were really laughing with the lawyer and perhaps at him—William— the poet—the guy! It was all on account of Ruggles' money, of course: nobody would tolerate him if he wasn't rich. And this was the man regarded as a rival for Sabina by Aunt Laura!

His aunt, meanwhile, had deserted him completely, and with sup- pressed fury he watched her, florid and bland, talking and laughing without apparent concern at the other side of the room. He would make her pay for that! More than once he was assailed by a temptation to cut the whole show and go home; it was only the thought of distant Ibed's which helped him to stand his ground. And he had to do some standing, for eleven o'clock had struck before Miss Parry asked him to perform.

All the guests gathered round in varying moods, with barefaced curiosity obviously on top. William, standing, saw his uncle looking at him with an odd mixture of encouragement and pity, and on the fringe of the crowd he caught sight of his aunt's well-dressed head bent down. She had remembered that then! He passed his hand across his fevered brow, a natural, necessary gesture which was, however, condemned as an affectation.

> *"Asleep or waking is it? for her neck*
> *Kissed over close, wears yet a purple speck*
>   *Wherein the pained blood falters and goes out;*
> *Soft, and stung softly—fairer for a fleck."*

He rolled out the great music in a strong voice, and his inflexions would have told a listener familiar with verse that he attached little meaning to the words. Shrinking from the labour of learning all the long poem, he had chosen the stanzas at haphazard; and this still more darkened the meaning for the audience, none too expert, as it was, in following poetry.

> *"Ah, yet would God this flesh of mine might be*
> *Where air might wash and long leaves cover me,*
>   *Where tides of grass break into foam of flowers,*
> *Or where the wind's feet shine along the sea."*

For all their preventions, their scoffings at poets and poetry, there was not a person in the room, except deaf old cousin Parry, who was not moved by the exquisite periods; so true is it that there is something in the nature of man which responds to poetry, as it responds to a fine day, and that there are chords, rusty from disuse, deep in the breasts of the most earthy which poetry and music can still make vibrate momentarily, faintly, like the strings of an old, old harpsichord whose heart died ages ago and lies buried in dust.

> *"I seal myself upon thee with my might,*
> *Abiding alway out of all men's sight*
>   *Until God loosen over sea and land*
> *The thunder of the trumpets of the night."*

… It was finished. There was a slight pause as William sat down, mopping his brow, and then a murmur of admiration. How clever! The women with moist eyes and lips crowded round this young man who could think of such wonderful things, who must have so much passion, so much feeling! And the men too looked on him with a new respect when they thought of the difficulty of tagging all those rhymes, a form of skill which they were generous enough to put almost on a level with bringing down a rocketing pheasant. He had had to wait; the time had been sore and long; but now was his hour of triumph. Sabina's eyes shone as she stood before him. Aunt Laura, flushed and handsome, looked as one celebrating the successful outcome of a doubtful scheme. On all sides were congratulations. Questions poured in. Did it take him long to compose it? Had he anything else ready? Oh yes; it was his hour of triumph.

That is to say, with all but one. Stephen Ruggles stood a little apart, perplexed.

> "Until God loosen over sea and land
> The thunder of the trumpets of the night."

Where had he heard that before? That he had heard it before was certain. Not that he had a wider knowledge of verse than anyone else in the room. It might even be said that he had less. Two or three were there who had read the Church hymns out of church; *The Christian Year*; possibly a little Longfellow. In a community whose reading wants were sufficiently supplied by some middle-aged novels provided by a badly oiled lending library at the chemist's, he was, in this matter at all events, not exceptional. At Palebrook the classical British poets were as little known as they are, I suppose, in Nigeria. If the prose-writers had few acquaintances, how should the poets be recognized? It is hardly necessary to add that this infrequentation of the classics was in no wise incompatible with the fact that the town boasted of two ladies and a gentleman who contributed occasionally to the magazines.

But the case of Ruggles was of another kind altogether. He had never written anything except legal papers and letters, and he had read very few books besides law books. This memory of lingering verse that haunted him was due to an invalid sister, dead now some years, who was fond of reading poetry aloud, to which he used to pretend to listen merely to humour the sick woman, without really paying much attention. Yet those two lines had stuck in his head. He had no acquaintance whatever with poets in the flesh, but the blond, self-satisfied William did not seem to him to suit the part. However little he might know about poetry, he understood at least that the sombre, magnificent stanzas which the young man had just recited as his own were the result of some tremendous effort of an astonishing genius; and to his shrewd eyes, trained to gauge men, William seemed the most ordinary of mortals. Of course there were cases of the baffling exterior, concealing in some measure a man's real powers; but he felt certain that all William was there before his eyes, on the surface. Given stable conditions in that young man's life, and he could predict his career to a certainty. He had seen hundreds like him; not a few had passed through his professional hands.

Still, although he judged William to be the kind of man he did not care about or value, he knew him too little to dislike him. His feelings however in this matter were given a sharper edge than they might otherwise have had by his discovery of the machinations of the Burgers to throw Sabina and her fortune into their nephew's arms, for he had almost made up his mind to marry Sabina himself.

He moved over to where William stood, walled by admirers.

"That was a very great poem you gave us," he said in his cold, incisive voice. "If it is your own, I congratulate you."

William gave a surly nod and half turned away. He did not see why he should be civil to Ruggles.

"The reason I say that," pursued the other, "is because there are some lines in it which remind me of a poem I know already."

This was too much! William's eyes blazed. What! After his untold labours, was he to be robbed of his gains in the very moment of triumph by this six-and-eightpenny blighter? He glanced over Ruggles, noted the well-brushed hair, and the evident attention to details of dress.

"Oh indeed! Is there anything about an old buck in it?" he asked as offensively as he could.

"Or about an old maid?" cried the delightful voice of Aunt Laura, who feared a storm.

Ruggles had far too much usage of the County Court not to have perfect control of his temper. He went on musing as if the other had not spoken.

"It's very singular. I know the lines, but I can't for the life of me remember the poem or the author."

"Oh, that's very likely," William sneered. "I've always heard that as we get old things don't come back to us quite so easily."

And he walked off to supper. He was now become such a personage that several of the younger guests, especially the girls, thought his reply extremely witty. Among the elderly it was not quite so much relished:

they felt it reflected a little on themselves. One of these came up and took the poet affectionately by the arm. It was old Smalt, the vicar.

"Now you mustn't be too hard on us oldsters, my boy," said he, looking at the youth in his odd way. "I'm old—sixty-seven—but I like youth myself. You have a great head; splendid sense of rhythm, language, and so on. I never read anything myself except the Latin authors, theology, and the *Times*; but I'll buy a copy of your poems any day you like. And a word in your ear." He drew closer to him. "Never mention marriage in your love-poems by way of making them respectable. Whatever else poetry should be, it should never be respectable." And with that he went off chuckling.

"Old beast!" thought William, distressfully. "I wonder how many more of them I'll have to stand."

Watchful Aunt Laura saw he was unnerved, and gathering up her Throgmorton and Sabina, made a move for home. When they got there, Sabina, who was generally so still and undemonstrative, ran up to William with enthusiasm.

"Mr. Spring, I want to tell you I never heard anything so noble. I didn't quite follow it all, but the way you spoke was beautiful. I shall hardly be able to sleep for thinking of it. You are a great man."

She was breathless, her eyes were moist, and Aunt Laura thought she detected in her accent something more than respect. In fact, this lady was confident enough, on her way to bed, to give her opinion to her husband that it was a sure thing between William and Sabina.

Chapter VIII

"Until God loosen over sea and land
The thunder of the trumpets of the night."

FOR DAYS THE VERSES were in his head—an obsession. Where did they come from?' He was more certain than ever that he had heard them before: the trumpets of the night bellowing out suddenly over the melancholy ocean had left a definite furrow in his memory. Where did the lines come from? He would drop to a halt at corners, fall into a brown study over his meals, start from his sleep thinking he had caught them.

His sister's books had drifted away after her death, but there were a few eighteenth-century poets in the house—old, dust-laden editions of Beattie, Cowper, *The Vanity of Human Wishes*. These he searched patiently line for line: he had hardly realized there was so much poetry in the world. In addition to this stock, all the poetry he was able to borrow in Palebrook was a copy of *Evangeline*, which one of the Ford girls had received as a school prize. And yet if he had only the key to those two lines in his hand, he could brain William with it! In a sense, they stood between him and four thousand a year.

This fact, he thought one morning as he journeyed along in the train, was becoming more evident day by day. Since that night of poetry the manner of Sabina had changed a little to him; in Palebrook society, where everybody knew what everybody else was doing, it was currently reported that she was showing an unmistakable preference for William. If Ruggles had been in love with Sabina this report would have made him angry: as he saw in her simply a more or less amiable little woman—amiable, that is to say, when she was feeling well and had not been crossed—who would make an advantageous match, what he took from the Palebrook report was an encouragement to be wary. He had almost too much contempt for William to bear him any malice on the personal score; but he found the youth in his way, and he meant, as he put it, to side-track him once for all. William, he thought, would look rather better when the grass was growing round his arrested wheels.

He left the train at Southampton, where he had a bankruptcy case to look after; and as soon as his work in court was ended he made his way to the large shop of a bookseller and stationer. There he sent in his name to the manager, who presently appeared.

"Good morning, Mr. Malkin. I want you to try to help me. I am looking for a poetry-book which has these lines."

And a little embarrassed for so imperturbable a person, Ruggles, first looking around to see that the shop was empty of customers, started declaiming:

> "Until God loosen over sea and land
> The thunder of the trumpets of the night."

The manager pursed his lips, put his finger to his brow, appeared to consider. Then he shook his head.

"N—no," he said slowly, "no, I can't say I remember them. They sound a little like Tennyson. You wouldn't care to buy a volume of Tennyson and look it through? We have a nice cheap edition."

A young lady standing behind the stationery counter here interposed:

"Excuse me, Mr. Malkin, I can inform you where the lines occur which the gentleman just said. They are in Swinburne's Laws Veneerus. I know much of it by heart."

Ruggles looked at her admiringly.

"Swinburne!" cried the manager. "Bless me, so they are. How stupid of me not to think of it! We have all Swinburne's works, I think. Just get down the right volume, will you, miss?" And in a moment he presented *Poems and Ballads*. "Nine shillings."

"Nine shillings for a book of poetry!" repeated Ruggles in dismay. His estimation of poetry as a means of acquiring a fortune went up considerably. "However does it sell?"

"Oh, we get it; we get it, I assure you," said the bookseller; while the young lady, taking the volume from the lawyer's hand, opened it at a certain place. And there in cold print was the poem William had recited as his own. It was well worth the money.

"Miss Sacheverel," said the manager, as soon as Ruggles had gone out of the shop, "you must leave the stationery and fancy goods after to-morrow and go into the book department. And I'll see about raising your salary."

As for Ruggles, seated in the train on his way home, while others around him read the sporting papers, the fashion papers, or the novel cheap and light, like the claret provided by a well-known wine merchant, he read the "Laus Veneris." Then he closed his book and set his fancy volving and revolving by what device he would blast William in Palebrook. He had him there to squeeze between the covers of the book, but he must contrive to do it cleanly. It would not be to his interest, nor had he the least desire, to mortify the Burgers through their nephew. All he wanted was to sweep the youth definitely out of Sabina's way, and incidentally to make him smart in the process. Sabina in her new-found enthusiasm for the arts, was attracted by the poet: expose the sham, and William must became as good as dead to her, for she did not care for William himself. So he reasoned, planning out his game at his ease as a player who holds most of the trumps scans smilingly his hand, or as your boxer who has got his man well licked postpones the blow which will give him his quietus from mere pleasure in exercising his science. Sometimes both of them are beaten, with the very taste of victory in their mouths.

Chapter IX

ONE MORNING, WHEN HE had been about two weeks at "The Firs," William, upon coming down to breakfast, found a letter. He knew that writing, based on the standard model, altered by the writing of German, and set off by certain sweeps and flourishes which seemed not spontaneous, but proceeding rather from a desire to write a different hand from other people, to achieve something personal. He tore the envelope hastily. "Dearest Will"; and further down a sentence about Palebrook. "Oh, my God!" He stuffed the letter in his pocket and made a feint at breakfasting.

Sabina with anxious eyes noted his pallor. William first maintained vehemently that there was nothing the matter, then, driven to find excuses, he muttered about disturbed sleep, bad dreams. Sabina had a picture of the poet wrestling like Jacob with the angel through the watches of the night, and she said aloud, in a tone which expressed more than the words, that the practice of composing poetry must be bad for the health in the long run. Uncle Herbert agreed with her. Privately, he thought that he had nothing to say against the poetry dodge since it had done the business with Sabina, but he was the kind of man who called it all damned skittles. He offered to make his nephew a brandy-cocktail from an excellent prescription given him by the steward of an American yacht. "It will buck you up like half-past six." William could hear the groaning of his heart.

As soon as he was able, he hastened to a retired corner of the grounds, and with a stiff face began reading the letter.

"58 PESHAWUR TERRACE,

"DEAREST WILL,—Why have you not written? Since we had a telegram from you two weeks ago saying you were all right nothing has come, though I have watched the post anxiously every day. Of course I am glad to hear you are all right, but mother thinks you might have asked about us, and also sent your address. As we were getting so anxious about you, fearing you might be ill or something, I went around to your lodgings, and Mrs. Benn told me she had heard from you only yesterday, asking her to forward some things, saying that you thought you wouldn't be coming back to London for some time. She seemed surprised that we did not know where you were. My classes finish to-morrow, thank goodness! and what do you think we have decided to do? We are going to spend our holiday at Palebrook. We have looked it up on the map, and the sea-air will be just the thing to counteract the effects of mother's cigarette-smoking. Besides, mother thinks we should make the acquaintance of your relations. So please look out lodgings for us (mother says, not too dear, but not stuffy, poky little rooms either) and meet us at the station to-morrow afternoon, 5.38. Don't forget. Dear old Will, what good times we shall have. We'll go on a regular bust up!

"Affectionately yrs.,
"Penelope Hazard.

"P.S.—Mother says that in case you cannot find decent lodgings at once, we shall go to the hotel advertised in the A B C for a few days. But it must not be for long. Awful rush for the post.   P. H."

Men who contemplate suicide, it may be surmised, do not hate the even tenor of the world. The sunshine warms their hearts out on the open road far from the haunts of man; here no troubles press; and could this continue all would be well. But they know that night is coming inexorably on, and with the night, hands to pluck at them out of the darkness. Since William had come into the country and fallen to work out his aunt's plan for his advancement, he had always had Penelope at the back of his head, and entertained her there without uneasiness. As long as she was not at Palebrook, or likely to be, he could contemplate her with equanimity, persuade himself that he intended no change in his relations with her, and place their connexion among that number of other things which one lets run on to see how they will turn out. He liked Penelope so; she did not bother; he had her always to fall back upon.

He had been engaged to her for over a year, though he wore his ligaments easily. He thought he loved her, and he did like her on the whole better than Sabina. During the last few weeks, since he had been much with Sabina, he had sometimes caught himself thinking that it would be brisker with Pen. Not that he had any violent passion for her either; and such passion as there was had stagnated considerably since the day he asked her to marry him—a step he had often since considered rather precipitate, though he remembered it to Pen's credit that since then she had always been willing to lend him money when she had any in hand. Still, she had shown him some astonishing paces in the way of fickleness, fretfulness, and arbitrary humours. After such agitating experience, he found Sabina a relief, mainly because she was different. She, too, had her moods, and he suspected that she might have her sulks; but he thought it hopeless to find any woman in the world without these incommodities. What pleased him in Sabina, besides the respect she paid him as a genius, was her unassertiveness, her good manners. Pen might have a better manner than Sabina, but Sabina had better manners. You could be certain that Sabina would never make a violent scene, or do any of those other unpleasant things which reveal a temperament. She had, moreover, that indefinable air of sureness and— small as she was—of command, that air of one who never dreams that her orders may be disputed, which accompanies great wealth; and of all this Pen had never a vestige. It takes a good deal of money from the cradle up to make what is called a lady. Then there was of course the money itself, always dangling like a monstrous yellow fruit before his eyes. Still, he thought that he liked Penelope best.

That is, in the distance. At Palebrook she was simply fatal. Far off, she might be taken for the secure wayside under the sun; here, she was the night, and suicidal vision of hands clutching from the darkness. There was no use in trying to put the visitation off: the mother was too indolent to change a plan she had already decided upon, and the daughter would suspect a ruse and come all the faster. Although her letter was evidently written in two moods—it was so like her to change her mood in the space of time it takes to write a letter—it was only too plain from the name signed in full that the mood belligerent predominated. He would have to give up Sabina; he would have to go back and drudge at Ibed's till he had a good enough salary to marry Penelope. Nor will it surprise anyone who has reflected a little on the inconsistency of mankind that his most poignant regret out of all this was that he would never be in a position to go and swagger before Ibed's clerks. And all because of the impetuosity of a headstrong girl! She loved him, he supposed—nay, he believed it thoroughly; but the thought, at other times comfortable to his vanity, was no consolation. She had simply ruined him.

Other visions surged, created by his heat-oppressed brain. He could see Ruggles and the other Palebrookites, but especially Ruggles, nudging and winking when they heard of the engagement. So that was the end of all the poetry and stuff! The heiress would go to Ruggles. From the despair engendered by this thought sprang half a resolution to confide the whole story to his aunt. She was good-natured; she might sympathize with him. After all, there was nothing to be ashamed of in it. But no—he dared not. However good-natured she might be, she would not see her plan brought to ruin with equanimity. She might even blame his deceit—women were so unpractical and ridiculous! She was capable of asking him to pack his bag, and there would be the end of his glory! Still, he would have to tell her something; and he plunged his hands deep in his pockets, frowning down on the common mother and bedfellow of us all with the face of a man whom wanton gods tormented for their sport.

He caught her in the little sitting-room just after lunch. She was writing letters, and turned round cheerfully.

"Come in, William. Have you brought some poetry to try over?"

William felt anything but merry, and when he was in trouble he always lost his off-hand manner, and his naturally harsh voice took on a whining tone, combining the reproach, the grumble, and the apology in about equal quantities—a voice which shewed as well as anything else the kind of man he would be later.

"Really, Aunt Laura," he droned, "you never seem to be serious about anything. I never saw anyone like you."

"Oh, William dear, don't do that! It ages you dreadfully. I'll be as serious as you like. What has been broken?"

"Broken? Nothing that I know of. Why should anything be broken? The fact is, Aunt Laura, I had a letter this morning from some friends of mine. They asked me to look them out lodgings in Palebrook."

"Oh, how nice! You had better send them to Mrs. Wrench's in the High Street. She has really good rooms. Her husband used to be one of the servants at Palebrook Court, so he knows all about men's things. I shall be driving by there this afternoon and I'll let the Wrenches know, if you like. What kind of men are they?"

William gulped. "They're not exactly men, Aunt Laura. In fact they're two ladies—a Mrs. Hazard and her daughter. Quite nice people. Mr. Hazard was an architect before he died. I've known them some time. They live near me in London. Mrs. Hazard has two sons, so I go in occasionally of an evening. You get so lonely in lodgings by yourself after a hard day in the City. There are always a good many people there and it passes the time."

Aunt Laura nibbled her pen. "Oh yes," she said slowly. "I see perfectly. But what an extraordinary thing to pick out a little place like Palebrook! However, I hope they'll enjoy it, I'm sure. I'll call, of course, and we'll do what we can to brighten it up for them. Wouldn't they care for the hotel? It is not at all a bad place. Of course it would be dearer than lodgings. But I suppose your friends are fairly well-to-do?"

"Well, they're not paupers, if that's what you mean. They are not millionaires either." Then he thought it advisable to bring out some of the truth. "Penelope Hazard gives lessons in drawing and painting sometimes. She's awfully clever. She's been a lot abroad. You're sure to like her."

He was overdoing it.

Aunt Laura mused again, staring at her desk. "Yes; I see it all from here. They will find it very nice at the Wrenches' and not at all expensive. Penelope, did you say? What a pretty name! She's not married or anything like that?" she asked, looking up.

"No," replied William. "Not that I know of."

"Oh. And she is pretty?"

"Well, not what you call——." His headshake was depreciating.

Chapter X

NO, NOT PRETTY, SHE decided, as she came away after her visit—not at all pretty. The girl was something less than that; she was also considerably more. Judged by the Palebrook standard of beauty she was deficient. Put her beside Jessie Bartlet, Vera Ford, or the other recognized beauties of the neighbourhood—broad-shouldered, firm, well-moulded, strong, with the vivid complexions of perfect health—and there was not a man thereabouts who would have preferred her. But Aunt Laura's perceptions were not organically provincial, and it occurred to her that in some sophisticated, tense societies, where people lived on their nerves, where the senses were rather jaded, where the perceptions were so sharpened that only the exotic, the out-of-the-way, could rouse any interest—well, among such people, Pen's languid mortal charm, so remote from acknowledged types, with her unfathomable, even dimly treacherous smile, might stir the deadliest passions. Such strange poisonous beauty as arises from a lone miasmal tarn lying blood-shot under a westering sun, or from some monstrous pharmaceutical garden where the plants in the twilight breathe forth odours so heavy that the soul of one who walks therein is torn with sobs; aspects of the night of fire, of bloody flagellations, of a cruelty that ever smiles, and of the chamber of death—all, all could be seen, by one who had eyes to see, in Pen's wan countenance and lithe, panther-like grace.

Aunt Laura had her limitations of vision, but in certain atmospheres she could see much farther than many people in Hampshire, or possibly in other counties. And watching Pen as she stood before her, tall and fragile, a veritable tower of ivory, in Mrs. Wrench's low-ceilinged parlour, she felt, with an odd seizure not altogether pleasant, that here was in the flesh one of those dangerous women whom one reads or hears about but never meets—one of those women who spread anger and quarrel and lamentation, often disaster and ruin, where they pass. Such as this was she under whose kiss King Solomon died to pleasure, and such as this she who watched with inscrutable eyes the ships drifting into Troy and the pinnacles of Ilium burning. To love her not at all were possible and easy; but he who did love her would be drunk with love; and to feel her lips clinging to his, her amber hair brushing his face, and her long arms about his neck, would sink to the nether end of Hell content. ...

All this Aunt Laura stated to herself in her own terms, of course, of the worldly-wise woman, but with immense conviction. She was trying to be fair about it, for Pen was not the kind of person that she herself liked, although she acknowledged that many women might like her. She thought her too tall and too thin; the abstract lines of her face were ordinary, and her colour too wan. The mouth looked peevish, dissatisfied, even bitter at times, and the curved nose narrowed in profile all the other features. Her abrupt disconnected manner revealed that she was at the mercy of her impulses, and those not very stable ones. A little petulant, a little defiant, and withal a little timid, she gave the general impression of one who was rather badly treated. The serene lady who was discreetly studying her while she chatted about Palebrook, suspected that storms of hysterical temper often swept over that face, followed by long fits of brooding and dolorous tears. And how old was she?

Pen had gone out of the room to get some music, and her mother replied that she was twenty-five. Aunt Laura said she looked younger, and thought she looked older. Now that she knew her age, she fancied that Pen suffered from indigestion and neurasthenia, and that when she woke in the morning her nose would be reddish. Few unmarried girls arrived at that age with equable tempers and perfect digestions unless they developed grave interests in life, or exercised themselves continually at open-air sports; and Pen did not look as if she did either. The obsession of the future husband, never at rest in girls such as Pen, was unnerving; and even when he did turn up, the long engagement was demoralizing, and made for anaemia, moods, sourness. But she acknowledged, when Pen at a certain moment looked at her full in the face, that she possibly exaggerated the ill-natured side of the girl's character, for she had hitherto failed to take note of the soft eyes, wherein there lurked a kind of latent and continual reproach. ...

"The mother is a cypher," she said to Sabina, to whom she was giving an off-hand account of these friends of her nephew.

She had, in fact, without shewing the least curiosity, found out all she wanted to know. These were people who revealed themselves with a little encouragement. Aunt Laura was in possession of the small house in Peshawur Terrace, the occasional difficulties with tradesmen, the lessons Pen gave, and hated to give, in drawing, painting, and languages. The mother was there, flaccid, fatigued-looking, meagre, will-less, turning to her daughter for support whenever she went so far as to assert anything. With plenty of money and no worries she might still have had a certain attraction; but the sordid grind of narrow means in London had taken the life out of her. She was dressed in some hot-looking black stuff, spectacles bridged her nose, and she wore a "false front" which left no room for illusion. Beneath it her forehead showed dry and seamed. And from what she heard, the visitor concluded that when the poor woman was not tyrannized over by her daughter, she was bullied by her two sons, one a lawyer's clerk, and the other in the employ of a tram-car company.

"Mother smokes too much, I'm afraid," said Penelope. "Do you smoke?"

Aunt Laura smiled. "We haven't yet got beyond doing that in secret at Palebrook."

"Really?" Pen glided on. "How funny to make a secret of it! Why, in Spain, where I was for two years, so many women smoke. La Marquesa de Donadio smokes as much as mother. I have seen a great deal of Europe. I was two years in Munich, two years in Brussels, and two years in Madrid for the languages. And I went about a lot, you know."

Aunt Laura knew that she herself had a beautiful speaking voice—a gift she had long been aware she was the sole possessor of among her acquaintance. But here in Pen she found she had a rival. Pen's voice was as exquisite an instrument in its way as her own; but it was utterly different. It was rather disconsolate. Then it was hesitating, wavering, due perhaps to the Tower of Babel she carried in her head. It was low, sinking often almost to a whisper, and it flowed on like the cooing of doves on summer noons, or again like the plashing of a brook in lone places, or like the wind in fir-trees on a still day. Tired, broken, a little chanting, it slowed down fatigued at the end of each phrase. ...

"My children tell me I have every vice," said Mrs. Hazard with a feeble smile. "Pen, dear, do play something. You play so well."

... "And then I came away," said Aunt Laura to Sabina, who seemed curious. "The girl is very graceful, but I think you will find she doesn't make the most of herself. When one is so peculiarly tall and thin one should have some peculiarities in dress. She dresses like all the world—all the world that don't know how to dress themselves. Her playing is just so-so—*pension* playing."

"Does she play better than me?" asked Sabina.

"My dear!—there is no comparison," cried Aunt Laura adroitly, and left Sabina to pocket the compliment.

Chapter XI

AS SOON AS THE visitor was gone, Pen ran up to her bedroom and proceeded to wash her hair. Then she stood before the little square of mirror, shaking out the thick coils of amber-coloured hair which streamed down over her bare arms and shoulders.

"I wish I was dead," she thought.

She looked around the little bedroom, sparsely and cheaply furnished, disgustfully. The bed was an iron cot without tester or valance, covered with a coarse, parti-coloured quilt. A much-used carpet was spread over the middle of the floor, and at the sides the boards were polished. Two flimsy yellow cane-bottomed chairs, a wooden washstand painted yellow, the dressing-table with Pen's brushes and manicure-case and bottles upon it: that was about all. A cheap lace curtain fluttered before the little window. The humble trophies of Mrs. Wrench's taste on the wall, texts in narrow gilt frames for the most part, roused the girl's scorn. "Remember thy Creator in the days of thy youth," was one of them.

"That would be a good joke if an old woman of eighty took the room."

She smiled at herself in the glass, and this reminded her to spread out her lips and inspect her small even teeth. And her thoughts ran on.

"I wonder how much longer this is going to last. I have no luck. I suppose I must go on teaching, teaching to the end of the chapter. I see nothing else. I hate teaching. I loathe and detest poverty. I should like heaps of money to buy all the dresses and jewels I want. I've only got a few rotten little things. Perhaps I might have done better if I had agreed to what Luis proposed in Spain. I'm sure he loved me. He was jolly well worked up. But then there was his wife. It would have been a sin, I suppose. Still, if you think like that you never get anything. The heaps of presents I might have had if I had only——. I should like to have all the money that woman has who was here just now. William's aunt. She's awfully rich. But William won't get any of it. If I marry William it will be just the same old grind, only worse, in a filthy little house where the smell of the dinner cooking knocks you down when you open the front door. I suppose I must marry William. I suppose I'm fond of him. He didn't seem any too anxious to see me. He's up in a big house, with heaps of servants, enjoying himself now, and I'm in a lodging. Heigh-ho! Never mind."

She shifted a little, put her elbows on the table and rested her chin in her hands—her long thin hands, fragile and morbid as the hands of saints and princesses who fold them naively in old church windows. And staring at her face in the glass, aureoled with that cloak of amber-coloured hair which seemed as if powdered with dark gold, she continued her incoherent meditations. They were the etchings of her awkward character, which no adequate steering-gear governed: of its unexpected jerks forward and bolts at furious speed; its vertiginous twists, turns; and then, sudden arrest, followed often by wreckage. She oscillated between the song-and-dance theatre and the Nonconformist chapel, and lately she had thought much of turning Roman Catholic, though she knew little or nothing of this religion. But among her pupils were one or two in convent schools, and she had with them sometimes attended the services, finding that the gloom, the lights, the mysterious vested priests, the scent of incense and flowers, and the long white chants—the very cry of yearning of the soul, of her soul, from the undefined to the unseen—stirred in her corresponding harmonies. After all that, she would go home saying to herself (unless she had somebody by her to say it to): "I am going to be really good, I am going to think of nothing but my salvation"; and she would sit for an hour frowning over the *Vie Dévote* of St. Francis de Sales which a nun had lent her.

But those who were most in her company saw that the main result of all this religiosity showed in extraordinary outbreaks of perversity, in which she tortured herself, tortured others, with the subtle devisements of the sufferer from hysteria. As she thought her health much worse than it was, and as she was, in fact, not seldom undone by her nerves, the fear of Hell had many a chance to sound its lurid note, creating the fiercest discords with the music of the mount of Venus by which she was often ravished. That was her native air, and she would have been happy if she could have allowed herself to breathe it freely. Love in a gold frame, a splendid excitement, high revel untarnished by the sense of sin, of remorse—that is the way her nature, unwarped, uncompressed, would have worked itself out. But during her girlhood her father had gone from loose Anglicanism to strict Wesleyanism, tinctured with gloomy mysticism; and each of his changes had reverberated in her impressionable soul. The consequence was that her body was ever agitated by wrestling bouts between her nature and training, neither of which she was absolutely for or against. No decided choice was on her face. And so this wave of religiosity having twisted instead of remoulding her nature, it may well be said that it had spoiled her and was the cause of her worst caprices. Hers was one of those spirits, the despair of all guides to the spiritual life, for whom religion, breaking out sporadically, in sudden squalls, in fierce emotional spells, and as suddenly subsiding, is no benefit, but rather a poison.

It was, she remembered, during one of these spells at Munich, coming home from the Maundy Thursday service at the Frauenkirche, all her nerves saturated with flowers, and white vestments, and organ music, and the sympathetic devotion of a great crowd, that she suddenly rounded on a German lieutenant whom she had hitherto encouraged to the utmost, accused him publicly of insulting her, and embroiled him with his family. When she thought over this episode now she considered it rather bad style. It was rather too like the adventuresses who frequent *table-d'hôtes*. She remembered him with his strong face and blue eyes so full of love for her—that desperate love impossible to mistake—and wondered where he was.

"He ought to have proposed to me and I would have married him. He was the nicest man I ever met; and as for brains, the others are fools to him."

Most likely he would have done so if she had not smashed the matter so suddenly. Why had she? What possessed her? Well, Frida had been scoffing about the lengths English girls would go in flirting; and then she felt so good that day coming from church, and the lieutenant had chosen his moment badly to look at her with dreaming eyes. And oh!—altogether it was something of which she could never render a satisfactory account to herself, though she had defended herself again and again to others; something over which she had not complete control, which she would not do if it were to do again.

The air, rippling through the window ajar, puffed out the curtain, and a brush fell on the floor. She picked it up and flung it across the room.

"Damn you! Blast you!"

Then she called herself an idiot, and decided to go downstairs and blow off steam on her mother. She felt a need to do that. If there was one thing about her more remarkable than another, it was that she had no inner life. Never was any one less self-contained. All the windows of her soul she tossed up, flung the furniture out of doors, and summoned the passengers to look on. Nor had this anything to do with frankness, unless there be frankness in a leaky bucket. She was not in the least frank: her mode of action was often oblique; she gave the impression, in fact, that everyday intercourse with her was rather unsafe. Her expansiveness was simply an irrepressible need to have others troubling about what troubled her. Sages have found that the best sauce to some things is discretion, and the enclosed garden has enticed many. Pen's garden was common land trampled over by a thousand alien feet that she invited within the palings. Her mother was in possession of the minutest details of her love affairs—not only her mother. She told them to her brothers, to her friends, to anybody with whom she grew a little familiar.

She slipped on a terra-cotta dressing-gown and plaited her hair in two long coils. Possibly from her frequentation of convents, she had acquired a little of the look of the nun when she was standing pre-occupied, a little of the nun's demurity and pensiveness, and her hands fell together below her waist nun-like. As she stood a moment thus, with her well-moulded neck bare and her pale head delicately poised upon it, she seemed like one of those tall lilies sick of their virginity which deck the altars of churches on festivals.

She found her mother smoking a cigarette and reading *What Every Woman Ought to Know*—Mrs. Hazard's sole occupations, save checking tradesmen's bills when she was at home. Pen took a cigarette and sat down with her elbows on her knees, staring at the grate. She was in her blackest mood; and her mother, who was afraid of her, and whom dire experience had made weather-wise, forbore to speak.

After about a quarter of an hour Pen looked up. "Did you like that woman who was here this afternoon?"

"Yes, dear, I thought she was very nice."

Pen bounded. "Oh, you think everybody is very nice. You can't see through people at all. I hated her. She came here simply to examine us—anyone could see that. There was no nice feeling about it. You could see she knew we were poor and she was patronizing us all the time. And when you think that I'm engaged to her nephew! I call it insolent. I vote we don't call."

"But she doesn't know about the engagement," put in the mother.

"Simply because William said it would be better if he explained it himself. I'm sorry I agreed to that now. It seems low. After all, I'm not so anxious to marry her nephew. It's no honour for us. We're as good as all the Springs and Burgers that ever existed. These people have got more money, that's all. If they hadn't money they would be nothing. Father's father was a Lord Mayor, wasn't he? Why didn't you bring that out to her?"

"I hadn't a chance, my dear. How could I begin talking about Lord Mayors! Besides, I thought you liked her, and I thought you were fond of William. I never know where I am with you."

Pen blew out a long puff of smoke and deliberately picked a shred of tobacco from her lip. "I don't see why not," she said, with concentrated nastiness. "I'm above-board enough. As for William, of course I'm fond of him, but I think he's acting like a cad. I don't care whether I marry him or not. We may be engaged, but I don't care. *Je m'en fiche pas mal!*"—she cried this out with amazing vehemence—"*je m'en fiche pas mal!* I never had anything from William except a rotten little ring worth about three pounds. Jack said he was sure it wasn't worth more, and as he's your son, I suppose you'll believe him. I don't know what you want to force me into marrying William for. I think it's most undignified of you. William goes swaggering round like a song and chorus—*Ach Gott!*—and do you know what he really is? He's one of the *à peu près.* Don't you think so?"

"I don't know half what you're talking about. You use so many foreign words. Oh, Pen, you make me so tired. I wish you would give me my cup of cocoa and let me go to bed."

Pen examined the little yellow-labelled tin. "There are only about two spoonfuls left, and I shan't be able to sleep a wink unless I have a cup." Then she relented. "You don't mind, do you, mother dear? You can have it if you like."

The mother made haste to reject the sacrifice.

Pen subsided into a better humour. "I don't mind that woman so much," she said airily. "Did you notice her gown? It looks simple, but it couldn't have cost a penny under fifty pounds. She reminds me rather of that Señora Espantoso at Seville I told you about. She's an awfully rich woman, too, and awfully common. You can't expect much else: her husband was a manufacturer. But she's really good fun. She's vulgar, you know, but not in the way that makes you angry. She told me that the day she was married——" Pen launched out on a story, and ended in fits of laughter. "There's nothing bad in that."

"My dear, it's quite bad enough," remonstrated the mother.

Chapter XII

AUNT LAURA WAS HABITUALLY so serene that the least cloud passing across her face was noteworthy.

"Of course," she said, "you will do as you like."

William was not at all at his ease. "But you can't object to my seeing them since they are here? I must pay them some attention."

"I don't object at all. Far from it. I rather like the Hazards; the daughter seems a nice unhealthy sort of girl. Remember to ask them to come to my party on Friday evening. I have been thinking that your holidays will soon be over, and then you must bid us all good-bye and go back to Ibed's." She paused to let this sink in. "Sabina is having another horseback lesson to-day from Stephen. They seem to be getting very fond of each other's company. Unless you have lost all interest in her, how would it do to give us some more poetry on Friday night? I could bring it in quite naturally."

But William turned pale. "For God's sake, Aunt Laura, don't do that!"

How could he give himself out as a poet before Pen? He saw her listening, supercilious. She was capable of throwing doubts publicly on his claims, out of sheer envy at his attracting more attention than she did.

Aunt Laura took note of his agitation and put it down to the wrong account. "Miss Hazard doesn't strike me as a girl who would make a very useful wife for a poor man," she remarked in a detached tone.

And with that she turned back to the house.

❧

He had not been five minutes in Mrs. Wrench's parlour before he was thinking that Miss Hazard would not make a useful wife for any kind of man, except a professional wife-beater. Pen had on exhibition her special brand of sulks, and sat mute while Mrs. Hazard and William struggled in embarrassed conversation. At last the mother, exhausted, suggested that William should take Pen for a walk. Although the girl heard this proposition, she waited till William had repeated it with an air of spontaneity which came rather tardily off.

"I may as well do that as sit here," she said, rising.

He tried to steer her to the unfrequented quay. She insisted on going through the town, and they encountered the Fords, the Bartlets, the Corders, the Parrys—the whole of Palebrook. For a man and a woman to be strolling together in manifest sulks reveals such a degree of intimacy between them that those who met the pair concluded that young Spring and the tall girl were engaged, if not secretly married; while certain who guessed Aunt Laura's hopes about Sabina felt sorry or amused, in accordance with their feelings to the amiable lady. And three or four men who prided themselves on knowing the world, stood in a group eyeing, when she had passed, Pen's filmy, provoking, and, on the whole, charming and desirable appearance, and decided that you had not exhausted the alternatives when you said engagement or secret marriage. You see, Pen was a stranger in Palebrook, and it is always wise to expect the worst from strangers. William was accepted into the fold on account of his relationship to the Burgers; but this girl, from Heaven knows where, with rather a foreign look, living in lodgings with her mother, who, they said, smoked and drank spirits—"Well, you know, Major, it is easy to put two and two together, though, mind you, I don't say anything. ..."

No sooner was the melancholy promenade over and the two returned to Mrs. Wrench's parlour, than Pen plucked off her hat and sent it spinning across the room.

"Why didn't those people stop and talk that we met? You know them all, and you went by them with your head hung down as if you were walking with a servant."

"I suppose they didn't want to stop," mumbled William. He tried to be as authoritative as he was with his mother and aunt, with Sabina too, but he was considerably cowed.

"I suppose you're ashamed of me." She was now striding to and fro in the room with an odd spasmodic lurch, twining her fingers together, and on her well-curved mouth was an ugly twist as she shot the words out. "*You* ashamed of *me!* Ha, that's good. It ought to be the other way about. I don't want to marry you. Do I, mother? You think I do? You think you can take me up and put me down when you like? I'm not good enough for your great friends? *Je suis une femme de trop, n'est-ce pas?—Ah, mais non à la fin!* It is I who do the kicking out. I simply hate you and loathe you. I've told mother a hundred times that I was sick of you."

"Then what did you want to follow me here for?" William plucked up spirits to ask.

She was momentarily staggered, less by the charge itself than by his audacity in making it. "Follow you!" her voice became almost guttural. "How dare you say that to me! It's you that ought to follow me, I should think. I suppose I can go where I like. England is a free country, isn't it? If we came here, it was just to see what kind of relations you had got. We've seen them now—the relations. *Oh, là là!* Why, I don't care twopence for your relations. Mother and I wouldn't be seen speaking to them again, would we, mother? They tried to cold-shoulder us at the tennis party the other afternoon to show their friends we weren't good enough."

William was stung by the injustice of this. "I'm sure they didn't. Everybody was nice to you as they could be. It's you who made all the bother, because you went about with your nose in the air as if you didn't want to be spoken to."

Pen was rather fond of giving people the lie. She did it now, and slapped the table with her delicate hand. And as usual she appealed to her mother for support.

"Pen, dear, what is the good of all this excitement?" said the mother, calmly lighting a cigarette. She had weathered this kind of hurricane many times before.

So had William a few times. Although flustered, he took up his straw hat with a certain shew of dignity. "I suppose you know," he ventured, "that the woman of the house and her husband can hear every word you say?"

It was a fortunate shot. Pen quieted down at once. As with many another in like case, she could control her outbursts if any inducement strong enough offered.

"It's lunch-time. I'm off," said William, looking at his watch. "My aunt told me to ask you both to her evening party on Friday, but perhaps Pen thinks we're too common to go near."

As Pen made no reply to this gamesome stroke, Mrs. Hazard, who did not much care whether she went or not, thought she was interpreting her daughter's sentiment, and in fact taking the wisest course, by desiring William to tell his aunt they would be glad to come.

Pen started up again. "Tell her nothing of the kind," she exclaimed. "Tell her we shall think about it."

"But I can't tell my aunt you'll think about it," remonstrated William from the doorstep.

"Then tell her nothing at all!" cried Pen, and slammed the door to underline it.

Chapter XIII

WILLIAM WALKED AWAY WITH his hands behind his back, dejected. The heteroclite character of this girl was like a malady. Whoever would think that she had hours of laughter and gaiety? How could he have guessed she would be like this when he proposed to her? Before that, she had for him a uniform demeanour; since, he had never seen her twice in succession in the same mood. It did not occur to him to ask whether all this might not be due to the fact that neither of them cared much for the other. Instead, his sullen musings induced him to an immense condemnation of all women. What was the good of them? They all made a puddle of men's lives.

But as a man fond of the bottle, upon waking with a headache vows he will drink no more, and then, when he sees the red wine winking in the glass and has swallowed a mouthful or two, tosses with contempt his resolution to the winds; or as one who experiences the discomforts of the rolling ship, resolves within himself nevermore to attempt the sea, but the moment past, the haven won, is ready, after a sufficient interval, to embark again—so William, upon emerging into a long road bordered with elms called The Avenue, and seeing Sabina with Ruggles slowly progressing at the far end of it, felt his indifference to womankind blown out of his head like a feather. A groom was leading away their horses, and the two, dawdling along, were chatting and laughing with a great appearance of friendliness. William regarded them in fury—the fury of a man who sees a game he has lost by his own foolishness calmly won by another. He could have stood any other man, he thought, but Ruggles. The pain in fact became intolerable, the pain of the young cock who sees the mature rooster monopolizing the attention of the hens. And as he was not much exercised in resisting his impulses, he fetched a run which soon brought him alongside of the pair.

They both looked behind them in astonishment at hearing his rapid feet; and when they saw him arrive thus panting and disordered, they wondered what calamity had befallen.

"I was only taking a little walk," explained William.

"It sounded to us like a little run," said Ruggles dryly. "Is that how you generally stroll about on a hot day? Is that how you compose your poetry?"

William looked at him and loathed him. He thought the lawyer was trying to degrade him before Sabina. And so convinced was he of the ignorance of Ruggles and of the rest of the world, except perhaps schoolmasters, on the subject of poetry, that he replied with assurance: "Never mind how I compose it. The thing is, has your memory improved?"

Ruggles wondered to see him thus brazen it out. "No," he said, "I'm afraid my memory is just where it was."

William gave an ugly laugh. "Very likely," he retorted. "We can only be young once." And with that he addressed Sabina. "We shall be late for lunch if we don't hurry. You know Uncle Herbert says he wouldn't wait for the King."

Sabina turned to Ruggles with that look of helplessness by which a woman between two men, neither of whom she wishes to offend, conveys to the one who is deserted the impression that she is being dragged off against her will.

Ruggles smiled at William. "You have all the good fortune. We saw you in the distance this morning shewing Miss Hazard the sights. Ah, you poets!" And with this body-blow he turned away.

"How can you stand that fellow?" cried William, before they were out of earshot.

There was an impulsiveness, a note of warmth in this, an arrogation, as it were, of some right to control her, which sounded like the jealousy of a lover, and Sabina looked up surprised and not displeased.

"Mr. Ruggles? I think he is hugely nice. He lends me a horse and does lots of things. Don't you like him?"

"I think he's rather a rotter," said William simply.

He proceeded to explain the kind of man he did like, the picture, as it might perhaps with most of us, bearing a close resemblance to himself. How restful Sabina was after his experience that morning! How calm, well-bred, safe! No danger of a scene from her.

And Sabina listened contentedly. Seldom a woman is seriously annoyed at finding that two men are ready to cut each other's throats about her. But it might be as well to know where she was, and she flung out a sounding-line.

"I liked what I saw of Miss Hazard the other day, but she seems rather silent. Or perhaps she found me stupid. I don't understand many of her foreign allusions, though I have travelled abroad a good deal—but only with father, you know, as a tourist. Miss Hazard told me that tourists never know anything about the countries they visit. Of course, I've never studied languages and that. I'm sorry; it must be so interesting. I'm afraid I'm not clever. Now you are so clever with your poetry and so on, you must have heaps of things in common with her?"

William had formed his own opinion about Pen's mental powers, but he kept it to himself. Instead, he said what he had determined would be the safest thing to tell his aunt, that the Hazards were coming on Friday evening.

"Then I may get to know her better. I hope so. It will be so nice if they are staying at Palebrook as long as I am."

How sweet Sabina was!

"Though I know them fairly well," said William in the most careless tone he could find, "I really"—here he switched off the head of a tall weed with his stick—"know very little about their plans."

He was on the point of proposing to Sabina there and then. After all, Penelope had given him "the chuck" that very morning. But prudence reminded him that she attached very little importance to these "chucks," which were not infrequent, and unless he had it in black and white under her hand it was better to play warily.

A few hours later he had reason to congratulate himself on his restraint, when a note sent up from Palebrook was put into his hand.

> *"Mother thinks we should go to 'The Firs' on Friday evening, because she says that she is not going to have me in this shameful position any longer, and unless you tell your aunt of our engagement on Friday evening, she will."*

William set a match to this paper and held it between his thumb and finger till it burned out. What trouble a woman could bring on a man without any fault of his own! And Friday evening, instead of the exhilarating festival to which he had been looking forward not without pleasure—an evening of social intercourse unblurred by poetry—became as the date of some abominable assize.

Nor, if he had known it, was this the only terror preparing for him. Ruggles, after standing a while in the Avenue watching the other two out of sight, turned into his house and sat musing alone. The room in which he sat was precisely as it appeared in the eighteenth century—one of those white light parlours, the secret of the English eighteenth century, fragrant of lavender and rose-leaves, where the sun-light dances so gaily, and the whole aspect of the room is like a ripple of laughter—a little self-conscious, a little insincere, verily a little hard, a little cruel, but so charming! Small paintings, originals or good copies of some eighteenth-century masters—Greuze, Boucher, Fragonard—hung on the white walls; a spinet stood in one corner; porcelain bowls and jars, that happy blue and white spaced ware, were filled with flowers, a little bee droning around them; and bright flowered poplin curtains stirred in the small wind of the summer day. Just as the room looked now must it have looked to the Mrs. Ruggles of the period, when she brought the contemporary Lady Wednesbury and a few other friends, hooped and powdered in the town fashion, back from the gazebo where they had been watching the traffic on the London road to a dish of tea or a syllabub, and a game of ombre or quadrille. And glancing out of the window at exactly the same view as the lawyer had now before his eyes, the Court ladies swung their painted fans while they discussed the virtues of tar-water, and nightgowns with mody sleeves, bone-laced caps, or sacques, and velvet patches *à la Grecque*.

He was not insensible to the graciousness of the room this clear day, for he was always influenced by his surroundings; and his eyes dwelt with a preoccupied complaisance upon the long stretches of lawn— among the best in the county—and the espalier roses nodding in the sunshine on the old grey wall which bordered one side of it. Only the assiduous tenderness of generations of the same family, living in peace, discharged from anxiety, could have brought this place to its ineffable perfection of detail. But the thoughts of the owner were at present not in the house at all; they were following those other two down the Avenue. He said to himself that he was rather sick of William; he had had enough of him; it was time to put the lid on. He had always found him objectionable to connect with since his arrival at Palebrook; still, you could always minimize the connecting points, or at worst, switch off the connexion altogether. But when William began to make love to Sabina Moll, to endanger the chance of the four thousand a year, he became more than a nuisance—a menace.

Then there was that Hazard girl, between whom and William he felt certain some tie existed; and with the instinct of the lawyer, always on the lookout for embarrassing and possibly criminal secrets, he would have given a good deal to learn just what the tie was. Perhaps he could get it out of the Hazard people themselves if he took an opportunity; or they might have talked to Mrs. Wrench, and Mrs. Wrench, upon whose house he had held a mortgage in a friendly way for years, would tell him anything. Meanwhile he had a bomb over there on the table which had cost him nine shillings, and he meant to explode that bomb at once. It was William's reputation as a poet which gave him his pull with Sabina; take that away and she would consider him as she did at first: an undesirable kind of animal.

Stephen's own feeling for Sabina was lukewarm: if she had not her four thousand a year it is unlikely that he would ever have thought of her at all; but girdled with that she was an acceptable, she was, in fact, the indicated wife. With four thousand a year added to his income, besides what might be expected to fall to an only daughter when her father died, he would be quite a rich man. He could allow himself the luxuries of a house in London and a yacht. And was he going to allow such an essential matter as his life to be kicked out of shape by the clumsy boot of an ass of a London clerk of no importance whatever in the world? He walked from the room with his thin face set hard—the kind of face he often wore in court when he was bringing one of his cases to a successful issue. He would blow William sky-high on Friday evening.

And on that night, accordingly, when he arrived at "The Firs," he had the bomb in the pocket of his overcoat. William, he supposed, would be asked to recite, and he would see to it that the performer was pressed to recite the "Laus Veneris." So, taking a favourable time as the evening wore on, he began mooting this here and there among the numerous company. William heard him, white with fury and apprehension. For Penelope and her mother were present, after all.

"I could strangle that brute," thought William. "What's his game in trying to get me to recite? I'd like to spout because it makes him so jolly small, though he doesn't seem to know it. But how can I recite before Pen?"

Pen, staring straight in front of her, sat with her most forbidding air, speaking hardly at all. She was dressed in dove-grey and silver—a costume which happened to suit her perfectly, though her clothes hardly ever did. On her long fingers shone a dull bluish opal and a long emerald set in gold. The skilful eye of Aunt Laura, running over the tall thin girl, had no fault to find with her appearance, from her amber-coloured hair wreathing over the forehead like sunset clouds, to the thin, close-fitting skirt and silver-buckled shoe which cased her long, well-shaped foot with the high instep—the foot of a dancer. She only thought it a pity that Pen had not more control of her temperament, was not able to suppress her awkward moods for the benefit of other people. Still, as she agreed fully that we all live longer, or at least happier, by doing what we like, she preferred to leave Pen to get through the evening as she chose, without any futile attempts on her part to make the girl find enjoyment where she was evidently determined not to find any.

Besides, she noted with considerable annoyance that William was in marked and remarkable attendance on the Hazards, mother and daughter, though the arrangement did not seem to make for their gaiety or his own. The mother, indeed, clad in black, her spectacles dropping over her nose, her "false front" a little askew, antiquated by her daughter's will before her time, with the deprecatory look on her face of one who is habitually snubbed and suppressed, was rather ashamed of her daughter's behaviour. She herself understood that such behaviour was due more to Pen's shyness, and an excessively morbid sense of her poverty and the uncertainty of her position, than to sheer devilment and sour temper; but others could not know this, and might well object to a girl, a stranger too in Palebrook, appearing there among hospitalities, deliberately unpleasant, almost surly. Accordingly, she did her best to cover her daughter's moodiness by conciliatory words and smiles on her own part. But she was not able to make much headway under her daughter's frowns, and William was far too anxious to give her any assistance. His compromising and embarrassed conduct, in fact, made it certain for Aunt Laura that a secret tie united those three which ended her plan about Sabina. She shrugged her shoulders and went on smiling: she had done her best. It has been said that women are never philosophers; but if it be philosophy to take the rebuffs of life without agitation, then certainly she was one.

She was not alone in seeing the behaviour of William and Pen; everybody, even old Parry and the vicar, noticed it. It had a far worse effect than if they had been laughing and talking together, to see them there side by side morose. The fact is that Pen had come to the house that night determined to placard herself publicly with William, and she succeeded. Sabina noticed it; Ruggles noticed it.

If up to half-past ten Sabina had found herself for a few minutes alone with the lawyer, he would have proposed to her and she would have accepted him. But she was occupied elsewhere—at first playing and singing, and then taking a hand at cards, of which she was rather fond. Ruggles, meanwhile, considered Pen from time to time. She did not attract him at all by her looks, his only interest in her being the interest we take in an instrument which puts the game into our hands. He had spoken to her at the tennis party some days before, and he had not liked her. He thought her stupid and pretentious, the odious type of professional female who is always explaining or hinting that she is more important than she seems, and gives herself out as the intimate friend of the people who have employed her. Expert as he was both by nature and by his practice as a lawyer in summing up men and women, he knew exactly where Penelope fitted in the social scale, and her tall talk simply amused until it tired him. This it soon did: he found her polyglot conversation too much of a reminder of the feast of Pentecost or a Soho *table d'hôte*. He thought her too tall, too thin, and her long face quite plain; wayward, extravagant, lightly ballasted, utterly treacherous, with a disposition which in a horse would be called "vicious"—and there was the end of her so far as he was concerned.

But she might be as false and as fickle and as brain-sickly as she pleased—that was Spring's lookout, who, judging from present appearances, would have the pleasure of housing her after she was married. What concerned Ruggles and what he knew—he read it in Sabina's face over there—was that the Hazard girl had done the best part of his work for him. The finishing touch he would add in half an hour or so when the poetry began; the bomb was outside there in his overcoat pocket. On the whole, it seemed likely that those three—mother and daughter and Spring—would depart without reluctance from Palebrook by an early train and never return.

It was now half-past ten, and Penelope, who was ready to cry with boredom and temper, turned to William.

"Do you know Mr. Ruggles well?"

In William, a long evening spent in watching others following enjoyments of which he was forcibly deprived had started a condition of ferocity the worse because it must be concealed, and the name of Ruggles was like salt in a wound. He answered with great bitterness that he did not. "What's more, I don't want to."

"He is rich, isn't he?"

"Rotten," said William succinctly. "I think he's an awful-looking beast, don't you?"

Pen examined the lawyer, who was almost in a line with her at the other side of the room. "No, I don't. I think he is very distinguished. He reminds me of the Count Gomez Torrijos, whom I met at Madrid. Why can't you bring him over to talk to me?"

This was about the last thing that William desired, but he was glad of an excuse to move, and lounged off ostensibly on the errand. Pen, following him with her eyes, saw that he never went near Ruggles, and after waiting some ten minutes, she determined to act herself.

Stephen was just then standing alone in a French window which gave on the garden and was wide open to the sultry night. Pen crossed the room and made as if to pass by into the garden, but in doing so she pressed against him. A subtle heady perfume enveloped him; her hair, he thought, touched his face. She turned and said in her low, sweet voice, "I am sorry."

Was this the same creature he had been criticizing as she sat over there with William? Her face was suffused with the glamour of mystery and dream, a half-smile parted her lips tenderly, and her eyes, shy and caressing, smiled too. It was Venus, the irresistible Venus in action, who lures men whither she wills to their happiness or to their undoing. Rare enough is her apparition, for in most of those who inspire love she is not manifest; but when she does appear and puts forth her power, who can resist her?

Certainly Stephen did not. He surrendered at once. His whole being was thrilling as if he had been electrified.

"Were you going out?" he said in an unsteady voice. "I believe there are some chairs out there. Shall I find you one? Do you care to sit out a little?"

"Yes," said Pen. "Let us. The house is stifling, don't you think?"

What a voice she had, so low now that it was almost a whisper, charging her commonplace words with secret intentions, blending into harmony with the breath of the flowers on the summer night, and the soft breeze.

"Do you think I might smoke?" said Pen. "I'm simply mad for a cigarette."

Stephen produced his case and lit her cigarette, and as he did so he touched her slim fingers. She sat half-lit by the light behind, lounging back in the deep chair with her long legs crossed under her thin gown. Everything she did, her least gesture, seemed to him a marvel of grace. The very ordinary act of smoking a cigarette became invested with a strange seduction. She looked up at him standing over her and laughed a still, intimate laugh, and the light behind illumined her creamy face.

Thirty-five years with an eye kept exclusively on his own interest had tempered him; various and many had been his dealings with women, he always keeping the master-hand; but now he was swept off his feet. What had he been thinking of since Penelope Hazard had been at Palebrook? Where had his eyes been? What a stodgy fool he had been in the house there only half an hour ago!

He dropped into a chair by her and they talked. By chance Penelope had hit upon one of the men to whom her appeal was strongest—coming and waiting for an answer—the right answer—like the cry of a dryad in a wood. She was like certain poems, or pieces of music, or pictures, which leave a few wan and troubled, while the general wonder what there is to admire. It was extraordinary how many subjects—or rather how many sensations—they had in common. How unlike she was to the mob of women one met about the county! From her residence in France and Spain she had absorbed some of the Latin captivation. Whatever she said now seemed to him miraculously right. How interesting she was about her foreign experiences; how just her comparisons were; how heartening her mirth!

"Do you sing?" he asked.

"No, alas!"

"Your speech in itself is a song."

When she rose to go in, he suggested that she should play some music, because he remembered that the piano stood apart in an alcove and he would still have her to himself. The crimson shades of the lights encrimsoned her face and hair, and she played softly, as if for him only, Schubert's Serenade, lingering on the notes with her sensuous touch. Oh, William and his poetry were well forgotten! He might claim now to be the author of *Hamlet*, if he liked.

Pen's cheeks were flushed, and her eyes sparkled as she put on her cloak. Even those who disliked her appearance noticed her so far as to say that she was looking much better than usual. William tried to avoid her, but he was obliged to pass near, and he paused sheepishly.

"I'm sorry," he said, hesitating, "that I've not had a chance to speak to Aunt Laura yet. I suppose——"

Chapter XIV

Mrs. Hazard turned up the lamp and sank into a chair in Mrs. Wrench's parlour.

"Oh, I'm glad this evening is over. I'm so tired!" She thought it good tactics to be first in the field with her complaints.

Pen hummed as she squirted the siphon-water into the whisky.

"Didn't you like it? I thought it was awfully nice. I enjoyed myself thoroughly." She sipped her whisky, lighted a cigarette, and pulling her gown up over her knees, sat down. "I feel awfully well, mother. I'd like to go out and walk for miles and miles. You see, I'm happy, and I always feel well when I'm happy."

"That's right, dear," said the mother, surprised and relieved. "I told you that you might like it if you went. I'm sure I enjoyed my game of bezique with that Miss Ford myself. It was nice of her to propose it, seeing me sitting alone. Isn't that the girl Mrs. Wrench told us of whom the man who is always playing billiards at the hotel and betting on races is in love with? I can't think of his name. Oh, Pen, you never ordered the cigarettes to-day, and there are only two more in the tin."

Pen was lost in thought. She stood up and looked at herself in the distorting mirror over the fire-place. "I rather like myself in this dress. It's better style altogether than the mixy-mauvey things most of those other girls had on. Mr. Ruggles thinks I'm handsome—at least, he didn't say it in so many words, but he did indirectly. Now I shouldn't call myself handsome, would you?"

"My dear, I think you're very attractive," said the mother, trying to keep her interest alive enough to say the right thing.

"I'll tell you what a person—well, a man—I've told you about him before—said to me once. He said, 'You're not handsome, you're worse.'" Pen clapped her hands on her hips, flung back her head, and laughed at herself in the mirror. "Ruggles found that to-night. He was jolly well captured." She laughed again with pleasure. "I think he's rather nice-looking, don't you?"

The mother was baffled. "I'm not sure that I know who he is, Pen. Which was Ruggles? There were so many of them."

"The man with the clean-shaven face and black hair. Do you mean to say you didn't see us together? William did; he was wild with jealousy. It was too killing. William was awfully dull. He's such a boy. I don't care about boys."

She went to bed in high spirits; but her night must have been troubled, for in the morning she had breakfast in bed, and it was between eleven and twelve before she appeared downstairs, clad in a dressing-gown and looking white and listless.

"I have a frightful headache. I couldn't eat any breakfast."

"Poor Pen!" sympathized the mother, who had heard the reverse from Mrs. Wrench.

"I've been thinking over the conduct of that man last night. It was rather insulting. I let him go too far, don't you think?"

"Oh no, my dear, I shouldn't think so," said the mother, who had not the faintest notion what man it was or how far he had gone.

"He tried to squeeze my hand—at least he touched it two or three times, and I know it wasn't by accident. He did it on purpose. He must think I'm pretty free-and-easy if I overlook that in a man I've only met twice. Then his looks were—well, suggestive."

"Were they?" Mrs. Hazard murmured pacifically. "He probably didn't mean anything."

"Didn't mean anything!" Pen began to pace up and down and the mother saw the storm was inevitable. She only hoped it would be short. "Didn't mean anything! Really, mother, I can't make you out. You don't seem to care twopence what becomes of your children. It is all one to you whether your daughter is grossly insulted or not. Do you mean to say you are willing to sit there and let that man Ruggles think he can take any liberties with me he chooses? You say he didn't mean anything! I know what he meant: I'm not a child. Would you like to have a daughter who let any man who comes along make love to her? I say his behaviour was insulting, and if you won't take it up I shall simply write to Jack or Cyril about it. As it is, I shall tell William the moment he comes."

"Pen, dear! How can you be so silly?" exclaimed the mother, roused at length. If her daughter did bring down her sons, on whose common sense she had no reliance whatever, she would assuredly be placed in a disagreeable and ridiculous position. "You can't want a scandal in this place about nothing, can you? What did the man do to you to cause all this fuss?"

"I know what he did. I saw it. It is so horribly unfair to William, too, who is breaking his heart about me."

"But did you tell him you were engaged to William?"

"How could I tell him, after promising William not to? I wonder you don't take a little more interest."

"Oh, Pen, I really won't stand these continual scenes any longer!" cried the mother. "I wish you'd get married and have done with it. What do you want me to do now? Do you want me to go to Mr. Ruggles, and tell him you're engaged to William, and ask him to explain his conduct?"

But Pen was not prepared for direct action of this kind. "It wouldn't do much good if you did. I know that kind of man. He's not the honest John Bull like William. He'd tell a lie to your face as soon as look at you. He'd say he didn't know what you were talking about. And as there's no proof——"

At this point a box and a great bunch of flowers were brought in. They had been left by Mr. Ruggles' servant with his master's compliments.

Pen frowned at the offerings. "I vote we send them back," she said, after waiting till the maid had left the room. "I hate his attentions."

"I don't think I should do anything quite so marked," replied Mrs. Hazard, humouring her.

"At any rate, we shan't open the cigarette-box till I've spoken to William," decided the daughter. "As for the flowers, you can do what you like with them. They haven't cost him much. He has miles of glass-houses."

And when William turned up a little later, the first thing she did was to tell him that Mr. Ruggles had sent her a huge box of cigarettes.

William stared, utterly puzzled. "Ruggles? To your mother, you mean," he brought out at length.

"No, I mean to me." She tapped with her foot impatiently. Now that William was there before her eyes, her emotions turned chill. No, there was no doubt about it: as a lover William was decidedly inferior to the other.

But William's amazement grew. "What on earth should Ruggles want to send cigarettes to you for?" he blurted.

It must be explained that he saw hardly any physical charm in Pen. He had indeed become engaged to her, and he could never give a very lucid account to himself of that event. Her generosity in lending money might have had something to do with it, but certainly it had not happened because he thought her handsome, or even pretty. He had never heard those of his friends upon whose judgment he was disposed to rely in these subjects approve of anything about her except her height, and even then they hedged by saying she was too thin. Therefore, that the lawyer would send things to Pen out of disinterested admiration was the very last explanation to occur to him; and as his speculations never moved very far from the centre, he could see in the action nothing else but an ironical cut at him and his flirtation with Sabina. He hated the lawyer more than ever, but he could not very well give his real reason to Penelope; and as he had not the least glimmering of jealousy where she was concerned, he did not think of bringing that into play as a motive.

"Very generous of the old buck," he sneered; but Pen's ear was not to be misled in such matters, and she perceived that whatever else the sneer implied, it did not imply jealousy.

She fingered the box. "Then you think it's all right?" she asked detachedly, to satisfy her scruples.

"What's all right?"

"Mother seemed to think I ought to send them back."

William gave a loud guffaw. "Send back five hundred expensive cigarettes! She must be crazy. What on earth for?"

Pen sliced open the box, took a cigarette, and shoved the box over to William.

"Will you have one?"

"Rather," said William.

Chapter XV

"WILLIAM, DEAR," SAID AUNT Laura casually, "you might go sailing with your uncle and Sabina this afternoon."

"I thought she was riding."

"Yes, but Stephen has sent up a note to say that the horse she rides has gone lame. It's rather tiresome: I'm so sorry for Sabina. So your uncle is going to take her on the water, and I fancied that you might go too. But I suppose you are engaged with the Hazards."

She spoke as one who shouts victory in the shadow of defeat. She had now only a fragment of hope that the affair of her nephew and

Sabina would unravel as she wished. Still, it is well to act as if what you desire is certain.

"No," said William, "I've nothing to do." He added after due reflection, for he was a young man of extreme caution in his utterances: "By the way, Ruggles has taken them up for all he's worth."

"The Hazards?"

William nodded. "He sent them a lot of flowers and cigarettes this morning."

This did give her a shock: it was about the last thing she expected to hear. That Stephen, of all men, should go out of his way to pay marked attention to people like the Hazards, who had no importance and scarcely a foothold anywhere, was what she could hardly believe. She cast about for motives, but could find none beyond the daughter's attractiveness—seeing that, indeed, much plainer than William, but still with an eye altogether unenthralled, which estimated the attractiveness as being on the whole moderate.

"You know all about the Hazards, don't you?"

"Yes," replied William. "All there is to be known."

"They have no important relations, or anything like that?"

William made the mistake of thinking that this remark was levelled at himself. "Oh, I don't know so much about that," he grumbled. "Their grandfather or something was a Lord Mayor."

Aunt Laura smiled pensively with her forefinger pressed on her cheek. She did not think this ancestral Mayor would cut much of a figure with the lawyer. No, it must be the girl; and if so, all sorts of possibilities opened up. Sabina, for one thing, would be rather neglected, and the lame nag struck her for the first time in the shape of a lame excuse.

"Be sure you're awfully nice to Sabina!" she cried with heightened courage.

The day was not altogether lost; the ground had shifted to her advantage. If Stephen was really serious about Penelope, which seemed too good and too untoward to be true, Aunt Laura did not think that in view of the large opulent life opened out before her, the Hazard girl was the kind of girl to let any affection she might feel for a mere clerk at Ibed's stand in her way.

And Sabina, resenting his desertion, would concentrate her wavering sympathies on William. Luckily, Sabina was no longer a young girl;

she must be well over twenty-five; and Aunt Laura thought she knew that women when they reach that age make a great case of youth in men. She reflected with complacency that Ruggles as a rival to William would be much more dangerous with a younger girl than with Sabina. Ruggles, she thought, cold and self-contained as he was, had some touch in him of the romantic lover, of the man who would venture desperate issues for love if once he were deeply engaged, and William certainly had not; but then, on a final analysis, neither Ruggles nor William, unless her tests were all wrong, was in love with Sabina. In a word, after unprejudiced study of the weights, age, and state of the course, it seemed pretty safe to bet that, if the weather held good, William would arrive in first.

Chapter XVI

PENELOPE CAME DOWN FROM her bedroom to the parlour about four o'clock. She had not been out of doors all day. The parlour was empty: her mother was at the back of the house gossiping with Mrs. Wrench. Pen wore a gown of myrtle green *crêpe de Chine* pulled up by the long loop of her girdle. It left her neck bare, and the long light sleeves called attention to her lithe hands. She took up a magazine, sat down by the half-open window and crossed her legs, and her patent-leather shoes with silver buckles emphasized her poppy-coloured open-work stockings.

A gentle sun penetrated through the room, and on the chimney-piece the bunch of fresh-gathered flowers which had come that morning glowed. From time to time Pen shoved back the curtain a little and threw a look into the street as if she were expecting some one; then she glanced at the clock, a smile glided over her lips, and nonchalantly, with her long frail hand on which there were three rings she arranged the loose hair on her forehead.

"Will he come?" she thought. She remembered his words, still more his looks of the night before, and she thought it likely he would. He had sent the flowers and cigarettes with sufficient promptitude. The flowers added an unexpected touch, like a caress, which indicated certainly that he had her saliently in his mind. The impression she had made, then, had out-lasted the night; would it be still strong enough to send him here this afternoon? She herself had developed, on top of her resentment of this morning, a strong desire to see him again, which arose partly, no doubt, from the vanity of having a man in her power and the wish to gratify it still more by seeing him there in front of her to play upon, but also because she was really attracted to him by the profound differences as well as by certain astonishing coincidences of their characters.

In fact, if Stephen were anxious to be received well by her, he could not find a better moment to walk in. The inevitable reaction from her scruples of the morning was in full force. William's indifference, she considered, was enough to exonerate her if she went to any lengths she pleased; and into the bargain she was rather piqued by his obvious lack of jealousy.

"What a fool I am," she thought, "to mind about William or any one else in these matters. I'd make love to the devil if I felt like it," she added wantonly, stretching out her arms.

In fact, from the moment William went out of the house, till now, she had given herself full rein to consider Stephen as a possible lover, and to debate what form her response would take. At present she was decided that she would respond if he gave her the least invitation. Although with Pen revulsion generally was at the heels of desire, still her desires had an immense vitality in their changeableness; for the imaginative conception of another pleasure more attractive, more perfect, reanimated them suddenly. Then were they born again, rapid as the thunder, irresistible, ardent, more vast, stretching from point to point till the very frame of possibility was broken. They had the charm of sweetening, for some few hours at all events, the bitterness of a thousand shocks to her self-esteem. They ran towards the unknown, towards the impossible, braving satiety in the continual search for a new sensation, for the pleasure which would be supreme and ideal. Then suddenly they collapsed, smashed by their very violence, worn out by the sterility of their efforts.

However, at this moment she was at the top of the wave. She continued to contemplate for nearly an hour, in a solitude which nobody came to break, the new horizon which had suddenly appeared to her. Indeed, she had worked herself into such a state of confidence that the sound of feet in the passage made her start, and when the door-handle rattled, a fugitive colour crept into her cheeks. But it was her mother who entered.

"Ah!" cried Pen, horribly disappointed. "It's you!"

"Yes, it's me." She sat down and lit a cigarette. "How good these cigarettes are that man sent. I'm smoking them all." She examined her daughter inattentively. "You've changed your frock, haven't you? Are you expecting any one?"

This question irritated Pen.

"Good heavens, mother, you seem always in a dream lately! I believe you smoke too much. Who is there for me to expect in this rotten little town? You know they don't call on us—or at least they haven't up to now, except William's aunt, who condescended so far. I changed my dress because I had nothing else to do. I'm bored to death."

She said all that with her most exasperating smile, and in a tone of raillery which presaged nothing good.

"I thought," said Mrs. Hazard, taking it lightly, "that you said you had a number of things to do this afternoon."

"Yes, so I had. But when I have a lot of things to do, I never want to do one of them."

The mother, finding nothing politic to answer, just blew out a puff of smoke. Pen glanced again at the clock; it was too late for him to come now. She listened, but hearing no sound in the house she rose abruptly.

"Blow it all!" she cried passionately.

She banged down the window to close out the noises of the street, and flung herself at full length upon an old horse-hair sofa in the last quarter of its life, drawn up near the fire-place in which a small fire agonized. She lay flat on her back staring at the ceiling, the poor, wasted, poppy-coloured stockings showing in all their garishness, with such an expression of dumb revolt on her face that her mother dared not speak. Nothing at all had happened; things were where they had been all day; and yet it seemed to Pen as if she had just been the victim of some definite calamity which had made a ruin of her life. And she pondered desperately on her present state, and the future which awaited her. A field spread before her vast and dreary. It was the field of regrets, of vain aspirations, of insatiable desires which could never be realized.

A sense of tedium without limits overwhelmed the girl. In her mind, in her heart, she could find only emptiness, an immense vacuity, the aridity of an infinite Sahara.

"What have I ever had to enjoy since I was born? My childhood went by without any pleasure, and I had all the miseries and mortifications of a poor girl at a boarding-school who has to refuse to join in the plans of the others because her people don't send her any money. As for love, all my flirts have turned out badly either through my own silliness, or through the kind of men I took up with. Now I'm engaged to William, and he's like the others. He's no help; a life with him isn't exactly gay to look forward to. I may even have to take pupils to help out expenses. I've only met one man I really loved and whom I could have lived with happily, poor or rich; and I fought with him. As for the rest, they're all about the same price. All? … Well, perhaps——"

She pulled up one of the cushions which were on the sofa, turned on her side with her back to her mother, and covered her face with her hands the better to concentrate her thought.

"There is this Mr. Ruggles. I'm not in love with him—not in the least—but I think I could like him awfully. He looks a bit hard, but what a lot of will there is in his face! If that man fell in love—really in love—he oughtn't to be like the others. I'm certain he hasn't the everyday young-man-at-the-tennis-party sentiments and silly conceit and self-importance of William Spring. He looks as if he was able to get what he wants done, instead of talking about the fine things he can do. And if he married, he would know how to be master of his wife, and in case of a struggle to break her and bring her to his feet, without her ceasing to love him a single minute."

At this thought Pen flung herself round on the couch with a look of admiration in her gleaming eyes, swimming in the vast sea of her fantasy with no other pilot than her caprice, and fearing only to touch land. …

Her mother, plunged in an absorbing page of *What Every Woman Ought to Know*, thought she was asleep, but chancing to look up, and seeing her daughter lying there with eyes staring into vacancy, she took this very inopportune moment to remark:

"Perhaps William will look in by and by."

Pen came to herself with a jerk.

"William," she repeated.

She considered her mother with an indefinable look: her eyes had that composite expression which must be called sphinx-like, but the dominating sentiment was a rather contemptuous pity.

"Whatever makes you want to force William on me? It's not as if he was a great catch. He's no catch at all. Did you ever realize what my life with William will be? It will be the same as home, only worse. And I detest it, I'm sick of it, and loathe it."

She was whipping herself into a state of violent excitement. Her complexion of an olive pallor became suddenly coloured, the light in her eyes was like fever, the blood pounded in her veins, and she struck the sofa with her open hand.

"You must remember," said the mother, coolly wiping her spectacles, "that he was your own choice. I had nothing to do with it. You and the boys arranged it between you."

"Yes," agreed Pen, "that's all right. And I suppose I'll marry him. I may and I may not. I suppose it's more of an advantage in some ways for a woman to be married than single. But if you think that I'm looking forward to marrying a junior clerk in Ibed's! Why, it will be everything I hate. The wretched smelly little flat; William going every morning to the office, and coming home every evening from the office. And I'll have to sit facing him every night in the little room with the stained tablecloth after the supper is cleared away; and we'll treat ourselves to the half-crown seats at the theatre every three months; and we'll have no money for jewellery and frocks and hats—no money for anything outside the house. That's what marrying William means, and I abominate all that. I detest the *tous les jours*. Do you see me the wife of a little clerk? And to be patronized by Aunt Laura, who thinks she does us so much honour by asking us to her house because she's rich and we're not any more, and who will send her nephew's wife presents of her old frocks, and a turkey at Christmas!—Oh, no—not that part of it for me!—Never!"

She ended almost on a shout, her melodious voice piteously jangled, her face sombre, her mouth bitter and awry, her fingers twitching.

"I feel stifling," she said, putting her hand on her side. "My head is on fire. I've got neuralgia all over and I don't care twopence."

She jumped from the sofa and threw open the window to breathe some air and try to recover a little calm. Just at that moment a man on horseback was passing at foot-pace before the house.

"Mr. Ruggles!" she murmured.

She flung at him such a look of fever and invitation and perversity that a magnetic current was established between them, and during a few seconds they remained as if fascinated by one another. He pulled up his horse.

"Wait a minute. I'll come in if I may," he said.

There was an inn a few yards below on the opposite side of the street. She saw him dismount and hand over his horse to the yard-man.

"Mr. Ruggles is coming, mother," cried Pen.

"Oh, is he?" said Mrs. Hazard, straightening her "false front." Her daughter had suddenly become radiant, so she judged that the visitor was to be welcomed. From where she sat she had intercepted the incandescent look—eyes and eyebrows and lips all together in it—which Pen had given the lawyer, and recalling the tirades of this morning, she thought that if Pen had used that sort of lure the night before, no man could be blamed for any liberties he took. But she was a woman not without sense, and having found that her daughter's temperament was there for good, she had long ago ceased to interfere even with its most disconcerting manifestations.

Chapter XVII

IT WAS THE LOOK from the window that did the business for Stephen. He had admired Penelope the evening before, he had even been profoundly stirred by her; but he was very far from considering her in any light which could affect his designs. He thought he knew her character, and it was one of those characters which the wise man who seeks not occasions of annoyance, or perhaps disaster, deals with sparingly. He felt he would be glad to see her again should an unforced opportunity occur; but if not—well, not. His resolution to marry Sabina was not in the least altered; the lame horse, so far from being an excuse, as Aunt Laura imagined, was standing there with his leg bandaged in the stable; and indeed at the very moment he rode down the street, he was thinking that he had been a fool to give William a second life. Then he met her look, and William and Sabina and everybody else became to him as unimportant as clouds drifting across the stars.

As he crossed the street he hit upon an excuse to cover his appearance, and this, once in the room, he brought out to Mrs. Hazard, offering her the use of one of his motors in case she felt disposed to explore the neighbourhood.

"You have only to send up Mrs. Wrench's boy with a message whenever you want it. My driver knows the country like the palm of his hand."

Mrs. Hazard said her thanks, and if she had not been so used to take most things as a matter of course, she might have been surprised at this offer from a man she hardly knew. But in Pen it reached its right address, and when she gave him a quick, tender glance which was like a promissory note, he blessed himself for his lucky thought.

He had come into the full benefit of the reaction. Very animated, Pen was using all the resources of her temperament, and revealed a subtle kind of witchery that her mother, who had always seen her disdainful or moody with the men who came to their house, never dreamed she had at command. And she thought it must have been with her present manner that her daughter had attracted all those foreign men she was for ever talking about, whose infatuation Mrs. Hazard had hitherto found it difficult to understand.

The fact is that Stephen's offer, which to some will appear paltry enough, was just the kind of thing to make Pen reverberate. It seemed to her large, considerate, generous, the act of a man indifferent to what other people said, and above the smallnesses of life. She liked to meet with a man who could walk in and hand over a motor-car and driver in a breath; it was a pleasant change from those eternal men in London who thought they were cutting quite a figure if they took you in a taxi-cab. Her ruling snobbery—her only one really—was the snobbery of position; and this is easily understood if you consider that she had generally found herself situated in direct inferiority to other people, whether to her pupils and their parents as governess, or as here now at Palebrook, where for all her boasting and scoffing, for all the ancestral Lord Mayor, she felt in her heart of hearts that she was an outsider, a waif, almost an adventuress (this word used to send a shudder down her spine), as contrasted with the rigid line of the well-to-do families in the place. To revert to Pascal's maxim, she had now been long enough in Palebrook to mind the opinion of the inhabitants.

And of all these people in Palebrook, here, sitting in front of her, was the unquestioned chief. Whoever else rode loosely at their anchors, he was infallibly harboured. He was one who had all the guarantees, who might pass confident, as much as anyone could, in the obscure chaos of hours to be lived, of which we know no more the number than we can count the smiles and the tears.

So, looking at him through half-closed eyes, Pen laughed her low, gurgling laugh, with all the melody of her voice and all the whiteness of her teeth. To Stephen she seemed adorable thus, with her head thrown back, her firmly moulded throat quivering in this joyous outburst which shook her long frame, and her hair rather disordered from lying on the sofa—a Bacchante, he thought, in lodgings.

He forgot the time, and might have sat on for hours if Mrs. Wrench's little maid had not come bustling in with the tablecloth. Pen gave her a petrifying look, but the spell was broken, and Stephen remembered he was to dine at Palebrook Court. In the passage, Mrs. Wrench herself stood timidly to pay her respects to the great man.

"Good evening, Mrs. Wrench," he said. "I hope you are making these ladies comfortable."

It was as good as a command, and Pen, delighted, saw from the look on Mrs. Wrench's face that her opinion of her lodgers had gone up with a bound. If the great Mr. Ruggles came and sat with them for nearly an hour, and took an interest in their well-being, they must be more important people than the landlady had fancied. "There's a man!" thought Pen, and she watched his back down the street with admiring eyes. He had done by chance the one thing he could have done to please her most. The landlady's sudden obsequiousness was balm of Gilead upon all the tiny wounds to her self-esteem she had suffered since she came to Palebrook. She thought of the ineffectual William, and of his aunt, who was apparently so anxious to make it clear that they were just acquaintances, and she almost loved Ruggles.

"Don't you like him, mother?" she asked, coming back into the room.

"Gertie has just been telling me that he's the great man here." Mrs. Hazard was lighting a cigarette. "He seems very nice. Very quiet and easy and all that."

"He's a darling!" cried Pen enthusiastically. She leant out of the window to get another glimpse of him, and was just in time to see him run into a railway porter, who was perhaps dreaming of collisions. Pen felt quite indignant with the porter.

"Why couldn't the stupid lout get out of the way?—But if he"—this was not the porter—"walks without taking notice he must be thinking, and I'll bet he's thinking of me."

Then, later, when the implements of supper were gone, "Mother," said Pen, "I am going to cut the cards and see what my fortune says."

"A dark man is thinking of me," quoth she, after a moment.

"I thought as much," said the mother to herself.

Oh yes, her dark man was thinking of her right enough. He thought of her through Lady Wednesbury's disquisitions on music—she played the violin—and through her husband's criticism of the Government's finances and Army Bill. Afterwards, as he strolled homeward through the park in the summer moonlight, he was thinking of her still. But his thoughts ran in cross-currents; they made by no means the steady stream of tendency in her direction which Pen saw as she lay on her back in bed down there at Palebrook, dreaming … dreaming. …

"If I don't look out," he was saying to himself, "I shall be utterly in love with that girl. I'm three-quarters in love with her already. I wonder does she care for me? Her looks say a good deal, but she has evidently seen a lot of a kind of life which our girls here in Palebrook never see. Who was it was telling me she took drugs?—I forget; I was not interested in her then and I paid no attention. The question is, am I going to throw away four thousand a year and more for five feet ten of nerves and hysteria?"

He pictured to himself with extreme lucidity life in common with Penelope: her moods, her whims, which he had seen; her sulks and scruples, which he suspected. But such as she was, he wanted her at this instant more than he wanted anything—the tall, phantasmic tower of ivory. He saw her as intensely as if she were there on the road before him, smiling that ambiguous smile of hers, with the eyes half-closed, the head thrown back, the tongue just showing between the little teeth. No girl in Palebrook could smile like that. It was the result of a special education, the most complex influences, a sounding of the most emotional mysticism and (he felt almost inclined to say) the most audacious depravity. A smile from her meant less than a smile, say, from Jessie Bartlet or the other Palebrook prettinesses; but it also meant more. …

"I wonder just where she is with that man Spring? I know where he is with her—that is, where he is now, not where he has been."

He looked hard at this, and beneath his scrutiny one aspect of the affair emerged. Stephen had more than once thought himself in love, but comparing what he could remember of his past sensations with what he felt for Pen, they seemed like the flicker of a few matches to a burning city. And yet in this case, no more than in some others, were love and the purpose of marriage paragenic: with a man of his experience, used by profession to having the seamy side of things presented to him, it would have been strange if they were. He was not more strait-hearted and selfish than most of his fellows, and a good deal less than some; but he was what is called a man of the world, and your man of the world is given to look for shabby motives in actions apparently gener-ous, and to distrust the first movements of his heart.

What he saw was a girl who did not look a neophyte, who looked in fact as if she had already shared a variegated experience and was prepared for more, dropping out of a cloudy past on Palebrook, accompanied by a person who might be her mother, and again who might not, for they bore no resemblance to each other. And this girl arrived shortly after a young man to whom she was tied in some way which could not be publicly avowed, and whom she treated, and by whom she was treated, in a manner which betokened a passion at its lees rather than love honestly come by and rejoicing. Her gestures, things she let slip, a thousand trifles which others—Aunt Laura, for instance—let pass unheeded, but which the trained observation of the lawyer carefully noted, betrayed one who had not lived—say, like Sabina, secluded and barricaded; but one who had thrown herself into life as a graceful swimmer in to a river, who had been free with the world, and with whom possibly the world had been free. Sabina looked single, almost a spinster, to the most unpractised eye; a shop-boy would call her "miss"; but Pen was one of those girls who set stran-gers betting whether they are single or married, with odds on married. Stephen liked her the better for all this; in fact, the type of Sabina did not appeal to him at all and the type of Pen most powerfully did. In his eyes, Sabina was just a nice little girl; and Pen was the siren, the goddess, what you like, who captures mortals by the magic of her eyes and voice and the knots of her hair. But then in the world's eyes Pen was at best a nobody, and at worst, as it might turn out, too well known a body; while Sabina, flanked by great interests, had four thousand a year. He loved Pen—there was no doubt about that; but from manifold reasons, social and personal, he was not prepared to marry her. And he asked himself if he could not gain his ends without marriage.

He was now come to his own gate, and he leant on the bars looking at the sweet old house basking in the moonlight among the flowers. In the thin haze which overhung the sward, phantoms of his ances-tors, whose hand had been felt so long on Palebrook, moved fantasti-cally, white-faced and dishevelled. And he asked himself if he could not gain his ends without marriage. Possibly he could. With Spring, whatever he counted for, got out of the way by being given a clear run with Sabina, Pen, seeing her character, would probably veer definitely round to him if he showed himself assiduous and generous. But even as he figured this, he saw it was not what he wanted. If he did take a step which made his relations closer with Pen, he could never bear life apart from her. His jealousy of Spring might warn him of the unsupportable obsessions which would in that case ensue. Pen living apart from her lover would make the ambiguity of her position an excuse to take all the liberties, and that would mean atrocious suffering and a break. Even if it did not come quite to that—think of the continual scenes, accusations, regrets! No, if he had her at all, it must be to sit with him in yonder house, to go about with him publicly. It must be marriage or nothing. So the matter narrowed down to this: Was he enough in love with Pen to marry her, and shoulder the various consequences, some of them disagreeable enough, of such an act?

He came to the conclusion, as he walked up the drive, that he was not.

Chapter XVIII

WITH THE INEVITABLENESS OF everything else in Palebrook, where life followed the hour with an unvarying result, Ruggles used to motor over every Tuesday and Friday to Gillingford, where he had another office. Pen's mind had been full of him since his visit, and as was always the case with her, she felt an imperious need to talk about what was in her mind. She talked about him to her mother till the mother ceased even to pretend an interest, and then she fell back on Mrs. Wrench, who admired and respected the lawyer more than any man on earth. Mrs. Wrench gave her the information about Gillingford.

For the last four days Pen had been in a turmoil, restless, feverish, eating badly, and, in spite of her drugs, lying awake long hours at night. She even gave up her drugs one night, preferring, she said, to lie awake so that she could think. And the burthen of her thoughts was: Is he in love with me?

She had not much to go on; since his visit she had not seen him again; but all the same, she thought he was. Her instinct, as she put it, told her he was. Love, where both parties are interested, can get on with wonderfully little signalling. Suppose he were to marry her, what a change in her life! And her eyes wide open in the twilight of the flickering night-light, her pulses beating, she dreamed of this triumphant refutation of her past. No more cruel lessons to unruly or stupid children, no more insolence from parents, no more journeys by omnibus, and bedraggled skirts on wet days. Instead, she would be the first woman in Palebrook, and a good second anywhere else. Oh, Heaven, what an outcome! And, as ever in her visions, she looked beyond the mark, neglecting such realities as came between.

When at length she recalled her engagement to William, she dropped down out of the blue like a spent lark. Did she love William? It didn't matter; she had to be loyal to him—at least she supposed so. For the matter of that, did she love the other man?

"Do you think I'm in love with him, mother?"

"No, my dear, I shouldn't think so." The answer was perfunctory. "You can't very well be, can you?"

"I don't know so much about that. He's just the kind of man I always wanted, even when I was a kid. Oh, I know what you think. You think it wouldn't be fair to William. But I don't see why I should always consider William. I'll marry him, I suppose, as I promised to, but I can't help my thoughts, can I?"

"No, of course not," murmured Mrs. Hazard, who was reading a chapter on the treatment of crying babies in *What Every Woman Ought to Know*, which absorbed her far more than her daughter's love affairs. It would be time enough to think about them when they did begin to look like marriage.

But if Pen considered herself bound to be loyal to William, she was not in the least disposed to let him overlook the sacrifice. Whenever the young man presented himself she was either snappish or contemptuous. She was always mentally comparing him to Stephen, and to his disadvantage. She was bound to him, she knew that, and she meant to stick to him, but there was surely no harm in being alive to his faults. She herself hardly mentioned Ruggles; but for William the lawyer had the same fascination as whatever we abhor or fear has for most of us. When, standing with his back to the empty fire-place in his favourite attitude, hands deep in trouser pockets and long legs wide apart, William started to exercise his wit on Ruggles, Pen took the offensive. Somebody—an actor she knew—had told her Swift's saying, that nobody but a fool ever wished he were younger; the phrase had struck her and she had treasured it for future use. She used it now.

"Oh, that's all right," laughed William in his easiest style. "Some old blokes have seen a bit of life, I expect. I should prefer my uncle, myself."

"You know, William," said Pen, speaking in the candid tone of one who is obliged against her will to state an unpleasant fact—the best tone she could have pitched upon to annoy him, "you will be a horrible man when you are thirty. I can picture you now."

Mrs. Hazard managed to smooth him down, and he made some excuse and hurried away.

For the rest, he paid little attention just at this time to the things Pen said, and abbreviated the opportunities for saying them. No doubt he would marry her ultimately; he had to be loyal to her—at least he supposed so. Meanwhile, he was employed elsewhere. In those days he was, so to speak, laying up treasure in Manchester. Sabina was on his hands; for Ruggles, who had hitherto shared with him that weight, seemed to be during the last week so multifariously engaged that he was regarded from "The Firs" as having tired of the tourney and abandoned the field. This at least was the opinion of Mr. Burger—no mean judge in such matters, so the Palebrook Club thought. In that establishment they were punting heavily on the result, and showed an indecent anxiety for "tips."

Sabina did not seem to mind about Stephen's remissness, and when Pen saw her on Tuesday with a numerous party, William among them, going down to the quay, evidently on a boating expedition, she appeared in what might pass, in so very minor-keyed a little person, for high spirits.

The sight of Sabina counted no more for Pen than that of any other passer in the street; but William's presence in the company was not without influence on her actions. She came down at about half-past two this same Tuesday afternoon dressed for walking. Mrs. Hazard rose to get ready.

"You needn't come unless you like, mother. I'd much prefer to be alone."

Her mother looked at her with astonishment, for since they had been in Palebrook the daughter had refused to stir a step out of doors without the mother tagged to her side. And when she heard that Pen might be absent as long as two hours she was also relieved; it was so much time gained for her book, her cigarettes, possibly sleep, certainly peace.

Penelope had decided to walk out of Palebrook on the Gillingford road. It was Tuesday: she might meet him returning. Of course there was a very good chance she might not; be might stay late, or he might be returned earlier; and she served herself with this uncertainty to silence her scruples. Then the thought of William with the boating-party definitely strangled them.

"He goes about enjoying himself without thinking of me. I don't see why I should always consider him. He's frightfully selfish."

She walked on faster with her loping, graceful walk. In a mirror which stood in a shop-window she caught sight of herself and she thought she looked handsome, in spite of the nervous fatigue in which she had lived during the last few days. A few people turned to look at her, but it was the strangeness, the foreignness of her appearance which took their eye rather than her beauty, which, as has been said, was not of a kind to appeal to the majority; and this was made plain by the fact that as many women looked after her as men.

The Gillingford road was straight and dusty and full of traffic. Motors and char-à-bancs, traps and bicycles, coming most of them from a well-known seaside town, a resort of summer tourists, some distance off, passed her in quick succession. She walked on for about two miles: then, hot and weary, choked with dust, she gave up in despair.

"He won't come," she thought, and she turned back.

All her spirits were gone. It served her right, she told herself; she had done wrong. She had been unfaithful to William. After all, he was going to marry her; why should she be running after another man? And even putting William aside, why should she be running after a man?

Stephen's motor was coming along behind her. His man was driving, and he was gazing down the unattractive roadway, thinking of her. He watched a tall woman ahead who walked as if she was tired. She reminded him of Pen. The car shot by in a cloud of dust and then stopped. It was Pen.

"You go on home, Dodd," said Stephen. "I shall walk the rest of the way."

They met face to face, and the surprise on his side, and the reaction from disappointment on hers, had the effect of making the meeting much more warm than it otherwise would have been. If there was any ice left to be broken, this meeting broke it. These two, who had not seen each other more than three times in their lives, met with the openness and familiarity of lovers, or of those who share a secret. They laughed in each other's eyes; they seemed to be resuming a conversation. She gave him her hand; he held it a little and she did not seem even surprised.

As they rambled, he called her attention to various features of the country in sight. What she saw was the keen, unflinching eyes of the man beside her; the temples with the veins showing, on one of which a strip of bleached hair about the breadth of a finger shot with singular effect among the black; the rather full lips and steady chin; and a certain air of distinction, of quality and importance, which he owed to a fairly long line of ancestors who had managed to get things their own way and keep them there.

"Haven't you been to Gillingford?" he was asking. She turned to him laughing happily, and he was captivated by the sudden coloration of this pale countenance under the lightest, most fugitive impression. He loved the occasional audacity of her look, and the capacity for passionate love (arising from cerebral and nervous instigation, self-suggestion, more than from any germinal instinct), revealed by the slightest gestures of the girl, by her whole attitude, by the incessant neurotic agitation which might be inferred from her sensitive face.

"Gillingford is worth seeing. There is a fine old church, ruins of an abbey, one or two other sights. The streets are very quaint and picturesque. Why not come over on Friday?"

An insect had lit on her neck and she did not seem able to get rid of it. She stopped in the road smiling distressfully, her fingers groping about her throat.

"I can't get it off," she said.

She felt his long fingers touching her neck, his face was very near her own. Then the fly was captured, and they walked on rather silent, till they came to the first houses of Palebrook.

"Why not come on Friday?" he repeated.

"Well. ..." She hesitated and kicked a stone along the road. Then she turned, smiling. "I don't know that it would be quite what they call the thing, would it? "

She said that to say something. At this moment she was resolved to go.

"Oh, the thing!" He looked at her persuasively. "I tell you what you've got to do. If you're afraid the Palebrookites will think we're eloping, just stroll along the road and I'll pick you up as I pass. Most natural thing in the world."

The touch of intrigue appealed to her. "Don't count on me," she said, still smiling.

"Of course not!" he protested. "About eleven on Friday morning, you know." And upon that they separated.

Pen hurried back, and burst into Mrs. Wrench's parlour. "Oh, mother darling, I do hope you haven't missed me."

"Royal marriage," said William.

He was sitting there in flannels playing bezique with her mother. He had evidently come straight up from the boating-party. Pen's heart smote her. While she was with another man—yes, and arranging a tryst with him, William had been thinking of her all the time in the midst of his pleasures. He must love her furiously. She would have to marry him, after all. From this evening, good-bye, Ruggles!

"Have you been anywhere special?" asked the young man.

Had he seen her? Was this the voice of suspicion? Pen was a little confused, and pretended to be setting her hair straight before the glass.

"Only a general canter. Why do you ask?"

William had not the least notion why he had asked, so he did not answer.

"Mother, I met Mr. Ruggles," Pen brought out. This was to salve her conscience with William.

"He's your great friend, isn't he?" asked William, but in a tone that no vanity, however acute, could distinguish from the flaccid accents in which he was declaring his cards. "He has given ours the shake. Aunt Laura thought he was in London."

Aunt Laura's name generally affected Pen like a scrubbing-brush on a tender skin, and if anything could increase her admiration for Ruggles it was to hear of his slight to the Burger connexion. But alas! that was all over. Poor old William—there he was pining for her, so much in love with her that he quitted the elements of gaiety to come and play bezique with her mother, in restless anxiety for her appearance. He might seem harsh, bouncing, over-bearing, but what a heart of gold! She covered the young man with attentions; she listened submissively, and acquiesced when he laid down his opinions on matters which she thought she knew as much about as he did, and perhaps more; she actually embarrassed him with her tendernesses.

"I must be off," he said. "It's as much as my life is worth to be late for dinner. I shan't have many more days of good dinners. My time is nearly up. I suppose you'll be going back to London too?"

As soon as he said it he saw his error. Of course she would insist on their engagement being declared before they left Palebrook. He waited for her to say it. But she said nothing of the kind.

Far from it! The one thing she wanted now was to keep the engagement dark. What would Stephen think of her when he learned that all this time she had been engaged? Oh, thrice cursed engagement! Oh, folly! Oh, spiteful fortune! And she had been calmly planning to go to Gillingford. She must be mad. If William only didn't love her! She watched his back up the street, the lovelorn man. It occurred to her that she had watched the other like that. ...

But William was striding through the town, panic-stricken. "She's madly in love with me. She gave the whole show away just now. She'll never give up the engagement of her own accord. Oh, damn it all! If she had only stayed in London! But in this hole she has no one to think of but me, and that has made her worse. Oh, damn it all! I shall have to marry her just the same. Good-bye, Sabina."

And Pen sat staring at her shoes. "Mother," she said after a bit, "you know Ruggles?"

"Yes, dear; I have heard you mention him once or twice."

"Well, we met on purpose this afternoon. I've been with him alone for over an hour!"

"So that's what kept you out! I was wondering what you had found to do."

When a man prepares a bomb with incredible skill and patience, and then anxiously explodes it, and after a most successful explosion, when the dust has settled, the operator hears the person his bomb was intended to blow through the roof remark sleepily: "I thought I heard a door bang somewhere in the house, but I may be mistaken"—the exploder may be excused if he feels a little hurt. Pen had put all her energy into what seemed to her a most startling announcement, a congeries of her scruples, and her mother sat on placid, soporific.

"You don't seem to understand," she insisted. "I've been with him alone."

"Yes; I know I wasn't with you."

"A fly got on my neck. I could have got it off if I'd liked, but I wanted him to help. And he did. Was there any harm in that?"

"No, I shouldn't think so." The mother looked more and more sleepy. "The fly had to be got off somehow."

"Yes. I should have thought a lot about it if I hadn't told you at once. Even when it was going on, I meant to tell you. Now I feel all right about it. But I don't think you quite realize the rest. I often wonder I'm your daughter. We're not a bit alike, are we? He wants me to motor to Gillingford with him on Friday. How does that strike you?"

The mother judged this worth looking at with some degree of seriousness. "Well, perhaps it might be better not. William mightn't like it."

"H'm. That's just what I thought." Pen kissed her mother. "You are a darling. Can I do anything for you, mother? Shall I bring you a cup of warm milk when you are in bed? I'm not a bit tired."

"She means to go," thought the mother. She had long ago found that whenever Pen intended to ignore her advice, or was acting against her in any way, she was always particularly sweet with her.

For the next two days this amiability overflowed upon everybody. Mrs. Wrench, the slavey, even Mrs. Wrench's boy, whom Pen had hitherto treated in a way that people who have not experienced the uppishness of niggers in the coloured zone call "like a nigger," were delighted with her consideration and benevolence. Pen was living in a kind of tormented happiness. She turned over and over in her mind the incidents of her walk on Tuesday. She was haunted by the memory of Stephen. Still, she did not mean to go to Gillingford—at least she thought not. But she knew that at their last meeting he had quitted her upon a sort of understanding that she would meet him.

On Wednesday night she lay awake for hours debating. The nightlight shed phantoms on the walls and ceiling. She could hear the heavy breathing of some one who slept in the next room. Foot-falls sounded in the street, becoming fewer and fewer, till at last the steps of one person walking struck sharply; a laugh, a far-off call, the scream of a railway whistle, a dog barking, a door banged—and then the little town sank to rest, with nothing to stir the silence but the church clock tolling the hours. Once a motor whizzed by: could it be his? She got out of bed and looked through the window. Nothing but the blank faces of the houses; that melancholy sight, shops closed in a benighted town with all the apparatus of custom, signs and posters, still conveying a message which nobody is there to heed; a flickering gas-lamp throwing a pool of light on the roadway. It was like seeing a body without a soul, or the household goods of one who is dead. She crept back into the blankets and longed for the morning—for life. She would not go to Gillingford. Stephen loved her; she was sure he loved her. Perhaps he would suffer terribly when he found she was not at the trysting-place. And this thought filled her eyes with tears.

On Thursday night she took three of her soporific tablets and slept a stifled sleep. When Mrs. Wrench brought her breakfast, she heard it was raining and rather cold. Then of course she could not go. He would not even expect her.

At about half-past ten she decided to take a walk out on the Gillingford road. That could do no harm, and she felt the need of fresh air. She would take an umbrella, but no coat, so even if she met the motor she could not go in it.

"I shall be back soon," she said to her mother.

"Then you are not going to Gillingford?"

"Of course not. I told you I should not go."

The mother raised her eyebrows and looked at the fire which had been lighted.

"Mother, how horrid of you! I believe you think I am going."

"No," said the mother. "But I'll expect you when I see you."

Pen left the house indignant. She had a good mind to go back to the room and sit there all day to prove that her mother was wrong; and it says much for the attraction Stephen exercised that she did not yield to this suggestion of perverse self-torture, so consonant with her nature. Out on the Gillingford road, the wind, swooping across the plain, bent her umbrella and thrust her skirt between her legs, and progress was difficult. The rain plashed down with a different sound as the wind blew or lulled; a soaked horse looked reproachfully over a hedge; on either side, above lonely fields, the grey rain could be seen riding on the wind. Not a soul was in sight. "He will never expect me in this weather," she thought.

Ere she had gone half a mile, a motor, going slowly, came upon her unawares from a side road, and squished up beside her in the mud. Stephen jumped out.

"That's all right!" he cried. "I had almost given you up, weather and all, you know. Get in."

She turned round, and he saw the woollen cap she wore pulled down close over her head, her hair blowing about, her face tinged with colour and wet with the rain.

"Oh, I'm not going," she said. "I can't. I have no coat."

"Nonsense. Of course you're going. I thought of the coat." And from the car he dragged a man's travelling coat.

That decided the question for Pen. If there was a coat there, already waiting for her, she must be intended to go. All her scruples evaporated as she went tearing through the country, at a rate which the long straight road encouraged, with the rain in her face.

"How lovely!" cried Pen; and Stephen, guessing she was one of those organizations which are inebriated by speed, went faster and faster, till out of the mist in the valley Gillingford steeple leaped up before them.

Pen was entrancing at Gillingford. She felt astonishingly well: she had that sort of warm content and well-being which comes to a woman who is acting in perfect harmony with her nature, and is indeed a sign that she is so acting. She cast herself on the stream of her sensations and let herself for once go freely, without a single terrified look at the hobgoblins which her imagination usually descried on the banks throwing lines to entangle her. To be in a strange town, unknown, she always found a stimulating experience; to be there with a man manifestly in love with her and of whom she was becoming fond, to be moving about by his side in the low-browed uncertain weather, their lives for the moment narrowed down to themselves, was all profit to her. And what told with her as much as anything else was the recollection that all this was momentary, a point taken in defiance of the laws of the game. It is, after all, a very elementary psychology which gives two people, whom you wish to make fall in love with each other, full liberty and opportunity, and to throw them, as the phrase is, into each other's arms; for it is in difficulty, in snatching a sip from the chalice in the teeth of fortune, that love waxes fiery. The fabulists who surrounded the enchanted princess with labyrinths and ferocious dragons, did but express this in pretty allegory. And so, when Mrs. Ford of Palebrook, who looks upon Tugg, the great cricketer, as an ineligible suitor, whisks dear Jessie round the corner when she sees him afar in the street, she is doing just what she tries to provide against; for dear Jessie's half-turn and the sympathetic fluttering of handkerchiefs between her and Tugg, do more to keep their hearts aglow than if they could be, like happier people, an hour by themselves in a garden.

At lunch at the hotel Pen revealed herself as a judge of claret. She explained that she had got used to wines on the Continent. Then they strolled forth again, lingering purposeless before shop-windows, their breaths mingling audaciously in the damp air. And where the street widened, they came upon the great church which stood black and menacing in the grey day, surrounded by its regiment of graves.

The church, never lightsome even when the sun was shining, was now gloomy and quite still. It was empty, and their voices sounded hollow under the great oak-wroughten roof. Agitated at finding himself thus alone with her, he no longer tried to conceal the love in his eyes, but studied her mobile face avidly, longing to kiss her on the lips.

"If I do," he thought, "it means marriage."

As for her, she moved along, a little self-conscious perhaps, but very self-possessed, and showed a certain interest in the monuments. Her gloved hand hung down by her side, and he took it loosely in his own. She let it be so for a moment; then she gripped his hand firmly and pulled him after her to one of the chapels.

"Let us look at this," she said.

It was an ugly florid monument of the mid-eighteenth century. By an odd chance, his own name occurred in the Latin epitaph—the name of some ancestor of his, one Catherine Ruggles, married into a burgess family of Gillingford, long extinct. Pen's eye, glancing over the monument, lighted upon the name, and she drew away her hand.

"You are on your native heath here," she said pensively, a little wistfully.

"Yes, if that's anything."

The monument, which he had forgotten all about till this minute, interested him not at all. Why had she drawn away her hand?

"You are a dear!" she cried impulsively; and right in his face she flung the daring look she had given him once before at Palebrook.

It was too much. His arm was about her waist; he was seeking her lips; she held her head back with a tantalizing smile ...

When a door banged, echoing footsteps sounded in the church, and a man coughed. It was the garage-man from the hotel, who had been ordered to bring the car round to the church at half-past three, and was now come to tell them it was outside.

They drove out of Gillingford very silent, nor did either of them try to go back on what had passed. Such little talk as they had was upon the incidents of the route.

"If it had not been for the garage-man," Ruggles was thinking, "I should have proposed to her then and there. Possibly he has handed me four thousand a year."

"If it had not been for the garage-man," Pen was thinking, "he would have proposed to me and I should have accepted him, William or no William. Possibly the garage-man has saved me a row."

When they parted at Palebrook it was with an almost imperceptible shade of constraint. Pen ran in and woke her mother out of a nap.

"Here I am back, mother," she said and kissed her. "Were you anxious?"

"Oh no. You are so used to going about. You look rather tired. Did you enjoy it?"

"I enjoyed *myself*," said Pen slowly, "which is a different thing. That doesn't happen to me often, and it may never happen to me again."

Chapter XIX

THAT EVENING, RUGGLES GAVE his career the most drastic survey it had ever received. He was a man of a determined ambition, and to this hour he had thought it a cold ambition, which steadily cleared out of the road whatever stood in its way, and of all obstacles considered love the least. In fact, whenever he estimated the forces which might hinder him, love with its satellites was not even counted in. Any man, he thought, who allowed love to get such power over him that it set his plans awry and led him to choose solutions disadvantageous, was essentially a weak man who had no business with ambition. Yet here he was now, carried so far afield by love that it was doubtful if he would ever get back to the old road again. He was staring at the wall as if he saw written on it that there were some things to his great advantage which he felt the utmost reluctance to do, because they meant that he must lose Pen.

The Electoral Committee of his party had invited him a few days before to contest the Division, upon the imminent retirement of the sitting Member to the House of Lords. He had not yet sent any reply, although he knew that these gentlemen of the Committee were await-ing it with impatience. If he remained single he might agree to stand; or if he married Sabina. If he married Pen, the expense was more than he cared to face. Of course, to be a Member of Parliament nowadays was a much cheaper thing—cheaper in all ways—than it had been in his father's time; but this was one of the expensive Divisions, bristling with subscription lists, and what was worse, crowded with well-to-do people who always out of a spirit of emulation gave large subscriptions, and the Member was expected to figure among them near the top of the lists. And there were other expenses, not only local, attached to the position when it was held by a man supposed to be rich and expected to forego the official salary for the benefit of charities in the constituency.

Nor was he sure that Pen would be of much assistance to him from a worldly point of view. He always had the power of stripping any object presented to him of all glamorous accessories which pas-sion might cast upon it, and viewing it in a hard, cold light. However much he loved and admired Pen himself, he was aware that she might not go down in Palebrook; and it was essential that his wife should go down in Palebrook. The indefiniteness of her past, the fact that she lived obscurely in London, would be against her with the Palebrookites of one kind; her manner, call it foreign or what you will—anyhow, her whole attitude and way of doing things, with the other kind, the Mrs. Wrench kind. He freely acknowledged that Pen had appeared at her worst to everybody but himself since she was here; the stupid behaviour of Spring, and the coldness of that youth's relations, placing the sensitive creature in what she was sure to look upon as an equivo-cal position, setting her on the defensive, and sterilizing social powers which were, he thought, considerable. Nay, he could discern in her a reserve power of the noble art of "getting on" with its accessories, a knack of picking out the "right people" to know, and the rest, which had not hitherto developed—or only in the wrong directions—from lack of a wide enough field to exercise in, and might be quite as for-midable as anything in that line Palebrook had to offer. But even so, however useful her gifts, she would have to fight against a serried hostility at Palebrook which it might take her years to wear down, and be the more difficult to tackle because it would not be obvious—there was nobody in Palebrook who would dare to be rude to his wife—but consist rather of things left undone than of things done.

Sabina, on the other hand, would be heartily welcomed; there was nothing about her at all to jar, and the immense wealth of her father would be of itself a letter of credit: she would be "a dear little thing" for one side, and "a nice quiet little lady" for the other. But there would be no joy in a marriage with Sabina; it would be hard business; the epithalamium would be written in a ledger. Certainly four thousand a year was a good thing; but between him and that interposed the vision of the long Pen presiding at his dinner-table with her four languages and selections from Chopin. She would be far more impressive to people in general married than single; far less restless, far more urbane and assured. True, she would always have her moods; it would always need a certain management to live with her in comfort; but Sabina, he suspected, might develop in intimacy moods far more trying than Pen's, without Pen's generous, impulsive nature to neutralize them.

The result of all this balancing was a project singularly weak for a man usually so determined and sure of himself. He had indeed struck it out as he dawdled over breakfast on Saturday morning, in complete despair of arriving at any conclusion more definite. What he thought was, that if he could have Sabina in front of him while he debated with himself, he would know better where he stood. He resolved to see her that afternoon.

Before starting, he slipped into his pocket the copy of *Poems and Ballads*. He did not quite know what use he intended to make of it, or whether he intended to make any use of it at all; but a situation might arise where it would be useful.

"The Firs," as he came up to it, had that unmistakable look of country-houses on a summer day when everybody is out. The doors and windows stood open; stillness reigned, broken only by the cooing of doves and the sound of a laugh far at the back. Instead of ringing, he strolled round to the side of the house to see if by chance anybody was on the lawn. Then, finding no one, as the long window of the drawing-room stood wide open, he passed through it, and as he did so it came upon him that it was there he had first surrendered to the witchery of Pen on a night of flowers and stars. Wherever the philtre had been brewed, in what dim hall of fate, it was on this spot it had touched his lips. And he was so profoundly moved that he walked into the middle of the room without perceiving Sabina till she called him by name.

She was dressed in white, with a black sash, and a bunch of red flowers in the sash. She was totally unoccupied, and had been either asleep or day-dreaming till he came in. She was sunk far back in the deep chair, and her shoes hung some distance above the floor like those of a child of twelve.

"I thought everybody was out," he said.

"Everybody is out," replied Sabina, "but me. Laura went out driving after lunch, Mr. Burger is gone at Southampton, and Mr. Spring is playing tennis at the Fords'. I didn't go anywhere, because we were awfully late at the Parrys' last night and I wanted to rest."

Her prim, monotonous voice had lost some of its cordiality.

"I should think Mr. Spring will be in soon," she added, colouring faintly.

Why should she colour? For a moment he wondered whether she was in love with Spring. If so, his debate was over; he had only to pick up his hat and go; Sabina and her four thousand a year could be put out of his calculations. Her next remark, however, did not seem to bear out this theory.

"You have taken to a solitary life, haven't you? You haven't been seen or heard. Laura thought you had disappeared." She spoke with some little irritation.

"Absconded with my clients' funds," said Ruggles, whose humour had a professional tinge.

"I don't know what you mean," replied Sabina, who had no humour at all. "I suppose my horse is still lame?"

"Quite lame." He thought he was not doing it well, not putting his heart into it as if he wanted to win. "I've been very much occupied of late." Then he tried to find out just where he was. "But no doubt Mr. Spring has been keeping my memory green."

Sabina raised her eyebrows and her mouth twitched a little. "Keeping your memory green?"

"I mean, he has been taking my place for the outdoor exercise. As he is in the house here he ought to be able to do that. He can't always be wrapped up in poetry."

She glanced down and began turning a bracelet round her large wrist which was out of proportion to the rest of her frame. "Mr. Spring is very nice. Everybody says he is tremendously clever."

"Do they?"

"Yes; except you, I think. But then you told me that you didn't care for poetry."

Ruggles pulled his book half out of his pocket. "I can't take it as daily bread," he laughed, "but I appreciate a good thing."

"Then you ought to like Mr. Spring's poetry. I don't profess to understand it all myself, but he's repeated it so often now that I'm getting quite into it. The vicar was telling me at dinner the other night that he considered it real genius, and that Mr. Spring ought to publish his poetry. The vicar's opinion is worth having. He's a critic. He writes for the Reviews."

Ruggles thought: "And yet he doesn't know Swinburne when he hears it"; but he kept his thought to himself. He assented vaguely, and felt for his book as a man put on his defence feels for his revolver. Now was his time to explode Spring.

"What is your book?" asked Sabina, smiling for the first time—perhaps because she noticed his agitation and put it down to the right side of the account.

"Only a book of poetry."

"Poetry? I shouldn't have thought you had the least poetry about you."

A vision of a rainy day, a gloomy church, and a tall pale girl with a white woollen cap pulled down over her amber hair standing by a monument, while her exquisite voice poured through lips which smiled triumphant love, and also a touch of love's sorrow, came before his eyes. What was he doing here, far away from her heart and the touch of her slender, imperial hands? How had he deluded himself that he could forget her?

Sabina was following some thought of her own. "Laura ought to be in soon"—she glanced at the clock—"or her nephew. By the by," she pursued, "do you know anything of those friends of Mr. Spring's, the Hazards?"

For once the lawyer's masterly self-possession was almost shaken. He actually looked a little confused.

"Oh, I know them, as you may say——" He completed the phrase with a gesture.

"My own acquaintance with them is very slight. Miss Hazard is rather an overwhelming person, I find." Sabina's blunt little face was bent down. "But I believe they are great friends of Mr. Spring. I've sometimes wondered if he and Miss Hazard were engaged."

Engaged! She engaged to Spring! Stephen could hardly contain himself. She was his! He knew it by a thousand signs. The duplicity of women was fathoms deep, but no woman could act as Pen had acted with him when she was in love with another man. That was not in nature. One thing was certain: Spring should not have her—not if he could help it. And he could help it. Spring might have Sabina and four thousand a year, or forty thousand, but he should not have Pen, by God!

He rammed the book far down in his pocket. "It is not in the least true," he said with his most incisive voice and his hard, glittering smile. "I have the best reasons for knowing there is nothing of the kind."

She looked up, rather surprised. "Really? I somehow thought—of course, if *you* know—You know everything that goes on in Palebrook, don't you? Laura will be glad. I don't think she wants her nephew to marry Miss Hazard."

"Well, he won't. She can make her mind easy on that score." And with that he rose to go away.

"Does this mean we are going to see some more of you?" said Sabina. "I'm afraid I must go home at the end of next week."

She held out her hand, and as he took it he thought, "There's four thousand a year gone!" It was a last tribute to that old life, the life devoted exclusively to his own interest, which lay dying at his feet. He was never to see it alive again.

As soon as she was alone, Sabina walked over to a mirror and stood gazing at herself. "If he was ever going to propose to me, he would have done it this afternoon. He never will now."

She sighed, because she wanted to marry. Seeing her fortune, she could have easily found many a man eager to marry her; but she wanted a man she wanted—a man, as she often said, whom she could love.

Chapter XX

RUGGLES HAD NOT BEEN gone many minutes when William came in. Sabina heard his harsh voice in the hall talking to the maid.

"They're all out, I suppose. Is there anything to drink in the house?"

"Oh, yes, sir."

"Well, I don't want any slops. Get me some hock and seltzer."

With the tumbler in his hand he came into the drawing-room. "Hullo," he cried, "I thought everybody was out. Lord, I'm thirsty."

Standing in the middle of the room, he raised the long tumbler to his lips and gurgled the contents down his throat, without pausing till he came to the last drop. Then he drew a deep breath. Sabina gazed at him in admiration. It was a fine performance.

"Pah!" said William, his ejaculation being something between a word and a snort. "I could do another of those. I never was so thirsty, ab-so-lute-ly never. I must have a fever or something."

"Did you have a good game?" Sabina inquired.

"Rotten. A rotten lot there too. How those Fords find out all the feeble slackers they get to their place, I simply can't make out. They dispute every blessed ball. It's all well enough, but—I mean, you must draw the line somewhere."

He flung himself into a chair; stuffed his hands into the pockets of his white flannel trousers, stretched out his long legs, and stood his pipe-clayed shoes on heel, with some inches of pink sock showing above them. His sun-browned neck was bare to the collar-bone; his chin was plunged down in the collar of his crimson "blazer;" a cloud rested sulkily on his handsome face. He felt himself very badly treated. He had just found a letter from Ibed's, refusing peremptorily an extension of leave he had applied for. He had, besides, seen Ruggles leaving the house as he approached. Ruggles, he supposed, was here to make love to Sabina; they might even have arranged to have the house to themselves. In that case all his trouble, his poetry and so on, was wasted.

What damnable luck was his! Why couldn't he have a shot at the four thousand a year? There were two barriers—Ruggles and Penelope. Sabina, perhaps, was in love with Ruggles; Penelope insisted upon being in love with him. He might do for Ruggles in some way; he felt himself equal to the lawyer; but what manoeuvre would avail against Penelope? It was very hard; and he stared at the carpet in a state of grave depression. He hoped Sabina would keep silent; he didn't feel equal to talking all that literary rot just now.

She on her part made no attempt to break the silence: she had far too much respect for the meditations of the poet. That his meditations were gloomy, even tragic, his face betrayed. It reminded her vaguely of portraits of Byron. She admired him thus; the eyes which she kept on his profile had some ardour; every fibre of her little body was sympathetic to the tall, muscular frame before her.

Propinquity is what counts in generating love: supposing the affections not already deeply engaged, the man on the spot has an enormous advantage. That wise woman, Aunt Laura, had probably remembered this axiom when she asked William and Sabina to her house together. Sabina had been sentimental about Ruggles, and if her sentiment had been encouraged it might well have blossomed into love; but she had never seen anything like so much of Ruggles at one time as she had seen lately of William. And then, suddenly, Ruggles had withdrawn altogether, neglecting her. This did more for William than all Aunt Laura's machinations, for it threw Sabina in a sort of pique on the nearest man she found congenial. William she found congenial; what is more, she admired him; and just there was her difficulty. She was in fact rather in awe of him. She could not imagine that towering intellect bending to the frivolities of love; still less, occupied with the little duties of the domestic relation. It would be like eating your breakfast with Solomon in all his glory. Up to now their intercourse had mainly consisted in William laying down the law on every subject broached and Sabina meekly accepting it—a situation which William found extremely flattering and agreeable and Sabina not disagreeable, for she considered herself lucky to be in the way of hearing words of wisdom from such a man, and moreover, she enjoyed looking at the sage's fresh-coloured face.

She enjoyed it now, though she was a little hurt by his prolonged silence. "He does not think me worth talking to," she thought. "He believes I am not capable of sharing his ideas." At last she said innocently: "I suppose it is at this hour that you think over your poetry?"

It was as if a wasp had stung him. "Oh bother!" he cried peevishly. "I'm sick of all that."

The moment they were spoken he wished he could recall the words. He had gone too far. Still, after all, there was not much use in keeping up the game any longer. He had to go back to Ibed's, and he was engaged to be married.

"The fact is that a man isn't always in condition for that kind of thing," he emended lamely.

He looked at Sabina with some defiance, expecting to find her shocked. On the contrary, she was radiant. She had just learned that he did not insist upon being always on the heights; he could come down to her level—nay, he was apparently willing to remain at her level if she would but allow him. She was to blame for always trying to keep their conversations up in such a rarefied atmosphere; and Heaven knows how it tried her to do so! But what longanimity he had shown! How much more intimate they might have been by now if she had only guessed that the great mind needed relaxation, and was only very glad to accommodate itself to the small things of existence.

"I should fancy it would be rather dangerous to keep it up continually," she ventured. "It is too much mental strain."

William caught at this eagerly. "You're absolutely right. That's just what it is: I've found it out myself. Too much mental strain. Supposing people were married," he added jocosely, "they couldn't go on talking poetry all day. Perfectly impossible. It would be too wearing."

Sabina coloured—she coloured for very little—and began twisting her rings. Really, she felt more at ease with him than she had ever done before; and as he dropped down from the height to which she had imaginatively hoisted him, she was able to contemplate him as the ordinary, handsome man, and his physical advantages began to appeal to her for the first time at their full value, unhindered. If Ruggles had now produced his book, the effect would have been certainly null.

"This day week I shall be in London." William brought it out dismally. "Swotting."

"And I shall be back in Manchester. How strange everything is! It seems such a coincidence."

The house was quite still; the long shadows were creeping over the grass; it was the hour of lovers, and it emboldened William.

"We have a lot in common," he said, and looked at her tenderly, though he had no definite purpose in his head beyond a little flirting to rouse her interest and assuage his baffled soul. How could he go further? He was a trammelled man.

"I have often thought that," murmured Sabina with a little sigh.

William's look of tenderness increased. She was really not half bad, he thought. She was rather pretty. "I shall miss our talks, I know that."

"Yes?" She seemed pleased. "It has been nice for me. I haven't much to look forward to at home. I don't get on there somehow, and I haven't many friends—not real friends. Nobody tries to make things pleasant for me."

William had heard from Uncle Herbert that old Moll complained bitterly that Sabina upset the house from cellar to garret when she was at home, and that everybody was glad when she decided to go on a visit. But as he had formed the lowest opinion of old Moll, he respected her for not being able to get on with her father; and he recognized that he himself must be pretty high in her favour for her to make these confidences. So he shoved his hands deeper in his pockets, looked indignant, and murmured, "Beastly shame."

"Father says——" Sabina hesitated. Then she came out with it in the tone of one relating an insult she has suffered, for which she expects condolence: "Father says that I ought to marry."

The impulse to polygamy is strong in men. It overcame William now. Forgetting Pen and his engagement, he got up and went over to Sabina. "Then why not marry me?"

She looked at him with parted lips and startled eyes. She was astonished; she had really not expected it. But William, with the admirable instinct of the unintellectual male, who perceives the inefficacy of talk as compared to contact in these matters, knelt down and took her in his arms.

That settled it. It was the first time in her experience, and she was overpowered. "I love you," whispered Sabina shyly.

"Darling!" said William, giving her a hug of such vigour that it nearly pulled her out of the chair. "There will be a devil of a row over this!" he thought.

"Do you love me, William?" she asked.

Again scorning words, he gave her another hug, and this time she found that she could maintain her position more conveniently on her feet.

"Then why do you look so sad?" She smiled softly.

"Mum, mum, mum!" William made these incoherent noises with his mouth full of some of the stuff of her blouse, which he had taken a bite of at the shoulder. "Not sad. Naughty to say sad. Not sad at all."

As Sabina could not lean her head on his shoulder in the classical attitude, she leant her head on his elbow and looked into his eyes. "Well, worried then. And I think I know why."

"If you do," thought William, "I'll be shot."

"You are afraid that father will object to you because—well, because you are a junior clerk."

It had not occurred to him before, but now that it was stated he felt it was what one might well expect from old Moll's general beastliness. A man who didn't believe in tips wouldn't be likely to know a decent son-in-law when he saw one.

"Now I'll tell you what we must do," Sabina went on prettily. "We must say you are awfully eager to work."

William's face clouded.

Sabina saw the danger and tacked. "Oh, I don't mean like you are at Ibed's. Father must find you a big position in his works. He'll do that. He's so anxious to have me married. And then you are Laura's nephew. That's a great advantage. She has heaps of influence with him. She'll talk him round."

William kissed her with the same kind of enthusiasm as that of a man who drinks a toast in plain water. His fears were not allayed by any means. But Sabina's kiss came from her soul on the lips of the handsome youth.

"I used to think," she said in a low voice, "—wasn't it silly?—that you were engaged to Miss Hazard."

He was staggered, but he countered neatly. "Oh, I say, how about you and Stephen Ruggles?"

Sabina looked into space and smiled and sighed, and then clung to the tall specimen of manhood before her. William wished she were not so small; he had really to bend almost double. ...

Then he thought of the extremely pointed letter he was now in a position to send Ibed, and he was consoled.

Two little cats, dozing in chairs, began to amuse themselves. This athletic love-making drew them from their phlegm. They had seen many things, but this scene of a very long man and a very short woman hauling each other about was exceptional. They were so curious that they drew near, and one of them humorously planted her nails in William's ankle. William kicked; the black cat fled out of the window, while the white cat rolled on the floor and laughed with her little pink mouth. ...

⁂

A few moments later, Aunt Laura stood in the window. The lovers were sitting close together. She took in the scene and judged it. Then she walked carelessly into the room.

"I'm frightfully hot," she said, "and *tired!* Sabina, dear, I hope you don't think me too rude for words not to have come back sooner. But I've been so rushed! You can't imagine what it has been."

She went on talking to give them a chance to regain their composure.

"It's not very hot," contradicted William, to cover his awkwardness. "It's rather cool."

"Isn't it?" put in Sabina, her face flushed.

"Well," said Aunt Laura, "I'm sure I am glad you find it so."

Then, without hurrying or making any excuse, still as it were keeping in contact with the conversation of the others, she picked up the white kitten and strolled away again out into the garden.

There was an odd look on her face—pleasure, tinged with a vague, charming irony.

"I've brought it off," she said to herself. "How funny!"

Chapter XXI

"I CAN'T EAT," SAID PEN, fretfully shoving her chair back from the table. "I hate cold supper."

She lit a cigarette, and stood leaning against the mantelpiece while she smoked, looking very discouraged.

"I don't seem to be able to help myself, do I, mother? I do these things simply, you know, without thinking, and then I go through torments after. But he had no right to take advantage of me." She paused and frowned. "He was trying to ruin my life."

"Oh, that's an exaggeration," said the mother impatiently. She had her querulous moods as well as her daughter, and besides, the vicar had called on her that afternoon and she was now undergoing a spasm of acute respectability. "But I warned you not to go to Gillingford. It was throwing yourself in his way. I don't call that behaviour for a girl. If a man wanted me I'd make him come and find me."

"Mother!" Pen's eyes filled with tears. "How can you say such cruel things to me!"

Probably because she was really in love, the stupid platitudes stung her like a discharge of pins. They were an appeal to that unstable religiosity, the weariness of all her youth in its most ineffectual conflict with her pagan nature, which it could only make turbid since it was not powerful enough to dam up the undercurrent of longing for a liberal life, facile and direct, without second thoughts. She took out her hand-kerchief to wipe her eyes.

Her mother looked at her relentlessly. "What are you crying about? You make me scold you because you tire me out with your eternal complaints. It never occurs to you that I have feelings as well as you. Here I've listened to nothing since last night but how that man squeezed your hand and tried to kiss you, and whether you were to blame or not. What pleasure do you think I can have in listening to all that? You wait till you have a daughter of your own and see how you'll enjoy it."

"But you told me that you liked to hear things," sobbed Pen. "I shall never tell you another word."

Mrs. Hazard picked up the poker and dabbed viciously at the small fire. "Very well; that will be so much gained. I wish to goodness if you're going to marry William that you'd hurry up and do it, instead of dawdling about after other men."

At this Pen stopped crying. "Why are you so anxious that I should marry William?" she asked fiercely. "You know well enough that we shouldn't be happy together. You often say so. And yet there's not a day passes that you don't ask me when I'm going to marry him. I can't understand you."

The mother, who did not wish to confess her genuine reason, which was simply that she was sick of having a grown-up daughter about and accordingly welcomed anybody or anything that promised to take her away, fell back on silence while she collected a plausible reply.

"One would think you didn't care whether I was happy or not," said Pen.

This drove Mrs. Hazard from crossness to positive ill-temper. "I suppose you knew what you were about when you got engaged," she cried vehemently. "You're old enough, Heaven knows! I was married when I was twenty, and here you are twenty-six and still on the shelf—and likely to be, seeing the way you go on. If I'd had my way, I should have spoken to that Mrs. Burger as soon as we came down. That's what we came down for. But of course you knew best. Now you can settle your own business. All I say is, settle it somehow and have done with it."

"Oh, you are cruel," wailed Pen, sobbing afresh. "I can never think the same of you again. I used to love you so much too. I see now that all you want is to get rid of me. I'll look out for a place as governess or secretary, and go and live by myself as soon as we get back to London."

"You can go to-morrow if you like," snapped Mrs. Hazard. She lit a cigarette and puffed at it furiously, and opened *What Every Woman Ought to Know* at the chapter on the Ideal Home.

In the lull that followed, Mrs. Wrench's maid entered. To explain the opportunity of her arrival, it should be mentioned that she had come some little time before into the passage, but hearing voices raised in dispute she had carefully applied her ear to the keyhole and kept it there while the dramatic interest was at its height. Now she came forward holding a letter between her thumb and finger.

"Please, mum," she said, "it's for miss, and Mr. Ruggles' man is waiting."

Pen flushed scarlet. No one thing could have come more unseasonably on top of the discussion—no, not even Ruggles in person.

"All right, Gertie, you needn't wait. I'll give the man the answer myself." And Pen broke open the envelope.

Then, when the maid had left the room, "Do you want to read it?" she asked.

The mother kept her eyes obstinately on her book, but curiosity got the better of her and she held out her hand. A few lines were written lengthwise across the paper:

"I must see you to-morrow. It is most important. Please send appointment by bearer.—S. R."

"H'm!" cried Mrs. Hazard, and tossed the note on the table. Her tone was a mixture of satire and contempt. "He seems pretty intimate. He doesn't even begin with your name."

"Do you think I had better make an appointment?" Pen spoke a little tremulously.

"I'm sure I can't tell you. If I mention William, you say I'm forcing him down your throat. But of course you'll see this man, say what I will."

"There you're wrong," exclaimed Pen, rising like a white flame. "I will not see him."

She snatched up Stephen's note and an envelope and swept out of the room. On the table in the passage there were a pen and ink, and she wrote across the face of his message: "I cannot. Good-bye."

As she was sticking down the envelope she paused. She had her handkerchief in her hand, a little rag of a thing damp with her tears, and after pondering a moment, she stuffed that in too. Then she gave the packet to the messenger and came back to the parlour.

"I think I shall go to bed." Her voice was husky, and she spoke with her head round the door.

"Very well," replied the mother frigidly.

"Are you very angry, mother, dear?"

"I am as well as can be expected," came the answer in a most uncompromising tone.

Pen sighed. "Good night," she said almost in a whisper.

There was no reply.

Chapter XXII

RUGGLES WAS TRYING TO prolong his dessert after dinner, when the note came. He would have been more alarmed by her message, if it had not been for the handkerchief accompanying it. This stirred in him depths of tenderness which he had never suspected. The bit of cambric was crumpled and moist—perhaps with tears shed because they must part. It had still a faint perfume which he had noticed about her when they were together. Whatever the note meant, the handkerchief was an avowal most gracious, most tender, and he pressed it to his lips.

The note might simply mean that her mother, thinking he did not contemplate marriage, had forbidden her to see more of him; but he could not believe that Pen would allow matters to come to a halt on that account if the road were otherwise clear. It might mean that the relations with Spring were deeper and more obscure than he had supposed. Or it might even mean—for what did he know of her life?—that there was some other entanglement in London or elsewhere which would make a marriage with him impossible.

This thought he found so grievous that he could not rest still in the house, and he wandered out under the moon. It was a mild, windless night, and no sound could be heard from his terrace save the bleating of a flock of sheep folded far off on the lea. With that desire common to lovers to look upon the mere walls which house the beloved, he found himself strolling down to Palebrook. The High Street on this Saturday night was filled with country people buying against the next week, and he was too well known to parade up and down in front of

Mrs. Wrench's windows. But at the back of the house there was a small garden which ran down to the canal, with a muddy lane at the foot of it. He could easily find his way in the moonlight.

※

Pen undressed and got into bed, but she could not sleep. She was like one who watches the dust arising just after a building has caved in. Her life, she thought, had sunk into ruin. She had put Stephen out of her life, and with him went her interest in life. Existence with her mother was become impossible. She would have to marry William, or as that seemed now almost beyond her power, the alternative was to begin again those deadly lessons, and live in cheap lodgings by herself. Or she might go out as a governess and be tolerated by a family. What a shame that she had only that to fall back on—she who loathed anything in the nature of an intellectual task and took no interest whatever in manifestations of the budding intelligence. Heavens, how grey and hopeless it all was! Oh, the grinding misery of being poor! And she had put Stephen out of her life. She turned on her pillow and began to cry again.

After a while she heard her mother come to bed, and some time after that the church clock struck ten. She got up and looked out of the window. The street was growing quieter. In a star-strewn sky the moon sailed gloriously through a stream of misty light. Her room seemed close, and she thought she would like to be out in the moonshine.

She remembered a back-door which led into the garden, easy to unlock. Thus she could breathe the night wind and the unwalled liberty of the night. She put on a loose dressing robe of white serge over her nightgown, and a long blue scarf which trailed down from her loosened hair. Then she lit a cigarette and descended.

The garden breathed faintly of blush pinks, honeysuckle and marjoram, and there was no sound at all in the garden. The rumour from the street came so softened as to blend into the general whisper of the night. The little wind was caressing, and Pen stretched her arms out full length, threw back her head, and breathed it in.

Now, as she stood thus, Stephen rose up from a low wall on which he had been sitting for some time, and glanced backward up the garden. He doubted the report of his eyes. It was an hallucination, a ghost in the moonshine. Then he saw a cigarette glowing in a long frail hand, with an odd, well-remembered curve of the little finger which he always used to think so personal and expressive.

He leaped from the wall and made up the lane to the wicket which opened on the garden, keeping his eyes all the time fixed on the tall, immobile white figure. Pen, hearing the click of the gate, started back and sent her gaze through the pale night. Something in her heart told her it was he, and she came forward at once with her lithe grace, laughing low in her throat she knew not why.

Of the pleasures of life, few exceed the pleasure of finding some one you love, whom you have lately parted from as you thought for years, or whom you believed to be at a distance, unexpectedly standing before you. It is one of the sweetest respites on our haggard march. At such a moment, if ever in a lifetime, the world is lost sight of with its fardels and trammels, and actions become genuine and sheer as the sunrise, or the surf rolling to the shore. It caused in these two a kind of delirium which made no case at all of the debates and prudences and hesitations they had of late found so heavy. He saw the little laugh in her eyes, the kind of glorious insouciance which the moment—one of her most splendid moments—gave her as she came down the path; and she saw the desire on his face and his arms held out. A force that she made no attempt to resist drew her towards him; and then she was in his arms, and he was kissing the creamy face and amber-coloured hair under the electric softness of the moon.

"At last!" he murmured. "How I have longed for this! I see now that this is the one thing I desired out of all the world."

"Oh!" she sighed helplessly. "Why did you come?"

"I came to ask you to marry me."

She quivered, opened her eyes and tried to get free.

"No, no," she moaned. "That is impossible. I can't."

He felt the softness of her soft garments under his arm, and held her closer.

"You can't? Ah, but you can, Pen; you must!" Thereupon a searing thought leaped through his head, but he held her still closer. "Why can't you? You are not married?"

"Oh no!" She struggled again to get free.

"Then nothing else counts," said Stephen, and he kissed her on the neck.

Pen covered his mouth with her hand. "Hush! I must go in now. I'll see you to-morrow and explain. It would be too hard to-night—after this!" She ran up the path and stood a second in the doorway, looking at him with a wonderful smile. "Darling!" she whispered, and shut the door.

On the other side of the door she paused before she went upstairs. "I wonder do I love him as much as that?" she asked herself.

When she was in bed she decided that she did.

Chapter XXIII

RUGGLES LIT A CIGAR and strolled homeward through the vacant Palebrook street. At first he thought of nothing, and he read the familiar signs on the shops. The night, he thought, was very oppressive. Then, gradually, as he neared the top of the street, he realized that there lay on his mind a vague uneasiness. It was like the awakening in the morning after some drama overnight.

By degrees his reflections hardened into shape. He was now certain to marry her: she had declared she was not married, and nothing else must stand in the way. He would not tolerate anything else in the way. He could never love any one as he loved Pen.

This, however, did not prevent him from reviewing with harrowing lucidity what a marriage with her would mean. He saw her neurasthenia, her incalculable moods, her impulse to flirt with any man who attracted her, and the tiresome scene of remorse which would inevitably follow. He saw, furthermore, that she could never be absorbed in any group known to Palebrook: it was impossible to imagine her golfing, tennis-playing, hockey-playing, like all the girls in the place, and their mothers too. People would have to make the best of her way of looking at life, for she would never come round to theirs. Once she was firmly settled, she would not care a farthing whether a thing was decreed to be done or not done by the Palebrook and county society: if she wanted to do it, do it she would. Her individuality might even tend to isolate her. Nevertheless, he felt that if he were deprived of her now, life would become without savour. Her very defects made her more dear. He lived over again that glorious passionate minute in the garden, and he vowed that to have held her thus was worth a fragment of life. To hold her again like that was surely worth a life. It would seem as if he had been struck by a ray of this wonderful moon—the kind of moon old witches choose to gather their simples under. He was lifted to summits he had never dreamed of touching in his wildest flights before. For this experience he was willing to risk a thousand disenchantments, if disenchantments must be. And he too, the hard-and-fast lawyer, knew the touch of rapture, and shared an hour with Mark Antony and the other great lovers of the world. There, in the prosaic Palebrook street, to which only the moonbeams lent a touch of romance, he found himself, somewhat to his own astonishment, asking what more is to be gained in the whole world after one has had love, the real love, the love of her for whose embrace the lover is willing to die.

As he turned into the Avenue it became somewhat darker, but still the moonlight came in great splashes through the trees. By the advantage of this unequal gleam, Ruggles caught sight of a man approaching—a man in evening dress, bareheaded and smoking a pipe.

It was William, who had also his emotions and uneasinesses, and felt the need of the cool of the night. No sooner did Stephen recognize the face than he threw aside his romance like a costume of masquerade and determined to come down to business on the spot. He stood still in the road and waited till the other came up.

"Good evening," he said. "Are you taking the air?"

"Might as well do that as anything else," replied William, with a touch of hostility. "There's nothing going on up at ours."

"Then if you are not in a hurry, we might have a talk for a few minutes. I have a question to ask you."

"If it's about poetry," said William, "I *am* in a hurry." And he made as if to pass on.

The other laid a hand on his sleeve. "It is not about poetry. Not just now, at least. It is about something which you can account for more easily. The question may seem abrupt—but would you mind telling me just where you stand with Miss Hazard?"

William's ruddy face turned as pale as the very moon. "He's a lawyer, and she's instructed him to go for me." Such was his thought, and it was sufficiently nerve-shaking. But if he weakened now he was lost, and he squared himself as well as he could for the onset.

"I don't know what right you have to interfere," he brought out morosely. "What are you mixing in for?"

To Ruggles, William's lack of surprise in front of the question was in itself a luculent proof that close relations with Pen had prevailed at some time or other; and his heart was sore. Still, that could not be helped; and if it could, it did not matter now.

"My right," he answered frigidly, "is quite simple to explain. I am going to marry Miss Hazard."

William leaped back with such force that he banged against a tree. "You!" he shouted in the night. "O my God! You!"

The relief from the tension, the dread, of the late miserable hours was so sudden, this lifting of the fog of his difficulties so sweet, that he almost broke down and cried. He began to laugh instead.

Ruggles strode up to him. "If you don't drop that," he said, "I'll smash you."

William waved his hand feebly. "No, no!" he expostulated incoherently. "It's not anything like that. Give you my word it ain't. No offence meant, and that kind of thing. But—but—look here; I'm engaged too. I may as well tell you. I'm engaged to Sabina Moll."

Ruggles received this with the famous equanimity he used to show in court when a surprise was sprung on him by the other side. But he looked at it carefully, and wondered if he had better ask any more questions. He concluded that as things were shaping it would be more for his own dignity and that of his future wife to let the matter die then and there. This engagement to Sabina put Spring out of action as a practical agent. And he would hear what Penelope had to say to-morrow.

So he congratulated William. The youth was mopping his linen cheeks and brow, still under the influence of the shock.

"No doubt you will live in Manchester?" said Ruggles, for the sake of saying something.

"Yes—no," William gulped. "That is—I mean, there's nothing settled yet. Whew! I suppose that bar at the hotel would be closed by now. I'm not very strong sometimes. I feel the need of a little refreshment."

"They'll give you what you want," said Ruggles, who missed nothing of the young man's consternation, "if you explain who you are. Mention your uncle's name. It must be the weather."

"Just so." William fanned himself with his handkerchief. "The weather—sudden change—oh Lord!"

They stood chatting a few minutes longer on indifferent subjects: the weather, the state of the roads, the latest cricket. For the first time in their acquaintance the barbed wire was stripped off. There was no more antagonism in their bearing; there was even that cordiality such as springs up between two people bent on the same enterprise. They were just two wayfarers on the perilous road of life, mindful of sympathy, grateful for a word of cheer.

Their looks were kind and friendly; their looks had something of the encouragement and pathos plain in the looks given to men who are embarking on a risky voyage. At parting they gripped hands. Neither envied the other.

"I hope she loves him well enough to forgive the Swinburne, if ever she finds it out," Ruggles thought.

And William was thinking: "I hope he'll be able to manage Pen."

They really felt very kindly to one another. So much so, that when they had gone a little way each felt the need to look at the other's receding back. William turned round and found that Ruggles was looking after him.

To cover their confusion, they waved at each other vaguely.

~

The End of a Family

*Taken from the papers of M. Chalumet-Lacluze, a well-known
Parisian lawyer, lately dead*

Chapter I

ON A HOT EVENING in August 1893, just after dinner, I was handed
a note from the Marquis de Péréfix, who desired to see me at once.

Since my grandfather's time our office had managed the affairs of
this ancient and distinguished family. They had always been what may
be called wealthy—sometimes, of course, less than at other times, but
at no time had they come down to the narrow means, and even pen-
ury, from which so many families of our old nobility have suffered.
The Péréfix of the revolutionary time was a friend of Horace Walpole,
whom he had met at Lord Hertford's, when that nobleman was ambas-
sador to France; and aided by the astute Mr. Walpole he had very profitably invested large sums in English securities, so that when he returned
to France in the last years of the Empire he returned in no equivocal
position. During the Restoration, and again under Louis-Philippe, the
Péréfixes accepted diplomatic and military posts which they occupied
worthily enough. After the *coup d'état* they retired altogether from
public affairs, regarding the various forms of government which followed that event with impatient disapproval. A few of them served in
the army: one lost his life at Wörth. The father of my present client was
an influential member of the Jockey Club, and divided his time about
equally between racehorses and dancers at the opera. He was notorious
in Paris on account of his waistcoats. "M. le Marquis de Péréfix wore
another of his amazing waistcoats," the journalists would write when
they reported some function of the fashionable world. "A man must be
celebrated for something," he used to say to my father with his pinched
little smile, which insinuated a vague irony.

His son, the present Marquis, Caspar Joachim Marie Jean, Marquis
de Péréfix, lord of Sauxillanges and of other places, was now forty-
eight years old. During his minority he had led rather a nomad and
expensive life, and had borrowed large sums on his prospects. Upon
the death of his father, it had been my duty to arrange these debts and

to put his affairs generally in order; and ever since I had been in constant intercourse with him, though I saw him rarely, and knew really very little of his way of life.

Accordingly, as I sauntered through the hot air of the evening to the rue Barbet-de-Jouy, where he lived, I was unable to imagine what he wanted to see me about. All I knew was that nothing in the ordinary course of business would be the subject of our interview, for his affairs were in perfect order, thanks in part to my excellent management, and also to a more regular and regulated expenditure of funds which he himself had adopted of late years. So, as I paced gravely through streets at first full of provincials and foreigners, and then, as I drew near the river, almost empty, I had an opportunity to exercise what little imagination I have. Possibly it was owing to this vacuity of mind that my thoughts, which I endeavour to keep cold and precise as my written or spoken statements, became agreeably, and what I suppose might be called poetically affected, as I crossed the bridge, by the full moon casting unequal splashes of light on the river water and unshadowing fantastically the cathedral towers—a sight I had been familiar with any time these sixty years and never before noticed particularly. That is why I mention it here, for it has no bearing on my narrative, and the impression was dissipated long before I reached the quiet street where the Marquis dwelt.

The house itself was old, like all those in that street, but his apartments were furnished in the modern style with considerable taste and luxury. I found him in the dining-room. He had evidently dined in company, but he was now sitting alone at the table smoking. He greeted me with more exuberant cordiality than he usually showed; his eyes glittered and his face was a little flushed; and from these indications I concluded he had drunk rather too much wine.

The Marquis de Péréfix had always seemed to me an extremely handsome man, and as he got older the distinction of his features increased. He stood well, with the supple, well-knit frame of a man who spends much of his time in violent exercise. His dark clear-cut face was relieved by brindled hair somewhat thin at the temples, and by black eyebrows which in their turn overshadowed very expressive eyes, with that look of profound melancholy which is often seen in the eyes of our French nobility even when their present fortunes seem happiest. I speak here, of course, of the genuine French nobility, those who date back authentically to Louis XV at least. These, deprived as they are of political power, seem to me to have as a body an air of greater charm and distinction than any other nobility in Europe. This may be in part owing to the great sufferings which the ancestors of many of them endured, and also, no doubt, to the strictness with which marriages in most cases have been limited till very lately to unions among themselves—a custom which has preserved the type at the expense of certain physiological advantages.

As it turned out, it was of his own marriage that the Marquis wished to speak to me. Such an obvious business for a lawyer I had left out when I was considering in the street the reasons for my summons, because he had repeatedly declared to me, upon my frequent remonstrances, that he had the strongest objection to marry.

"I am very glad," I said. "As I have often remarked, it is a pity to let the old family die out. For a family that has had at one time or another so many branches, you are singularly extinct. Except for you——"

"That's just the point," he interrupted eagerly. "I have no relations that count, nobody to consider in this matter but myself. Consequently I can marry whom I choose."

He poured out and shoved over to me some champagne—a wine I detest. Then he went on, bringing out his words with the emphasis of one who expects a dispute and has prepared in advance:

"I intend to marry Elizabeth—Mlle. Elizabeth Kymars."

I knew of this lady. She was a circus-rider—not one of the kind who wear tights and jump through hoops, but of the other kind who in top-hat and habit perform seriously the evolutions of the *haute-école*. She had lived under the "protection," as it is called, of the Marquis for over two years, and it had fallen among my duties to pay large bills for her to jewellers, dressmakers, and other tradespeople. And as all such bills were paid with my cheques, I am afraid I incurred some unjust reproach among certain respectable tradesmen who happened to have my personal custom as well as that of Mlle. Kymars; for comparing the modest purchases I made for my wife and daughter with the large bills I paid on behalf of the circus-rider, they could hardly fail to draw conclusions to my detriment as a husband and father.

The Marquis examined me narrowly as he lit a cigarette, and having apparently satisfied himself that there was little opposition to be feared, he went on talking in his even and rather nasal voice.

"I have a thousand reasons for this step, and two or three are excellent ones. I like Mlle. Kymars; I am very fond of her indeed. In some months she will be the mother of my child."

"Really!" I cried, very much startled.

The Marquis nodded with the satisfaction of one who witnesses the success of a premeditated effect. "Now, here is the point. This child, boy or girl, will be my heir and will inherit in a very short time."

"Nonsense, nonsense."

"It is not nonsense," said the Marquis testily. "I know what I am talking about. I was examined by Budmose-Cladel lately, and he hardly gives me three years to live."

I was confounded, but I made a show of spirits. "One doctor is not enough for a decision of that kind," I said. "Who else have you seen?"

"Who else? Nobody else. I don't want to ask all the doctors in Paris how soon I am going to die. It's a blow, but there it is. It would be a blow if I were ninety. What's the use? Besides, I know I'm done for. My heart is all wrong. I've never been the same man since I got that sunstroke in the Sahara."

He blew out a great puff of smoke.

"It's a serious moment for me," he pursued gravely. "It's a serious moment for anybody who thinks as a Christian. I dare say I haven't lived a very Christian life, but I intend to set myself in order to die like one. By the rules of the Church, I must either regulate my position with Elizabeth or separate from her altogether. Now this last is quite out of the question. I'm not going to separate from Elizabeth. So you see——"

He waved his hand to show that further argument was useless. I perceived that this was indeed the case, and so I took my part at once.

"When you give me your instructions I will draw up the necessary papers," I said. "As you say, you have nobody's feelings to consult in this matter but your own. There are only your relatives, the Princess San Rossore in Italy, and the Countess of Southmead in England. I suppose you will notify them?"

"Quite useless," he replied. "It is not their business. They are sure to get to hear of it somehow or other. Besides——"

At this moment the door was opened cautiously. I expected to see the circus-rider, the future marchioness, enter, but it was in fact an apparition much more disquieting.

"Come in, Isidor," said the Marquis to a burly man who stood hesitating on the threshold. "This is M. Chalumet-Lacluze, who has been kind enough to come and see me." And he introduced Mr. Isidor Lorty, one of the ringmasters at the Nouveau Cirque.

This man's profession explained his presence. His familiarity and swaggering assurance, as he drew a chair to the table and poured out a glass of wine, were also accounted for by a remark which the Marquis let drop to the effect that Isidor was a cousin of the bride. I am bound to say I was not prepossessed favourably by Isidor. He seemed a low type of *rastaquouère*. He was a big and obviously very strong man, with heavy rounded shoulders like a labourer, oily black hair plastered down over his narrow forehead, small cunning black eyes, a conquering moustache, and a thick neck. He wore some diamond rings on his fingers, which were hairy and not very clean. He had an expansive smile which showed his strong white teeth, but this did not nullify the unpleasant effect of his manner, which was that of a man uneasy and servile trying to assert himself by swaggering in the company of his betters. The Marquis, however, seemed to like him.

"I got sick of playing dice with Elizabeth, so I thought I'd come in," he remarked, and shot a furtive look at me out of his little black eyes as if to gather whether I was a friend or an enemy. He spoke French well, but he was certainly not French. It was hard to say exactly what he was: Servian possibly, or Roumanian, or some species of Tzigany.

The Marquis rose. "Let us go into the drawing-room," he said. "We shall find Elizabeth there."

I had never seen this lady before, and I could not help admiring her appearance, without being in the least captivated by it. She had in fact the kind of beauty that many men would coldly admire, but only a few would love. As we entered she was leaning against the mantelpiece, and a rather close-fitting gown revealed the perfection of her muscular figure, used, one could see, to hard training from childhood. Her face had a curious pearl-like pallor which threw into brilliant relief her enigmatic black eyes and black hair. But the most extraordinary thing about her face was the look of indomitable pride settled there. For a trained observer like myself, it was easy to make out that this was not an affectation of a person accustomed to show herself as a spectacle: it was innate. Nor was it the look of disdain and superiority of the tamer of horses, often called upon to risk her life, though there was something

of that in it too. No; this was the look of the natally proud soul pierc-
ing the face and influencing the carriage—proud too, as such souls are,
without warrant, without any reference to what they are or what they
have done in the world—which often, when the surroundings happen
to be mean, exposes them to the hushed gibes of onlookers.

Certainly any gibes uttered at the expense of Mlle. Kymars would
have been very hushed indeed. For here was one of the women who
can give a look which cuts like a whip, and whose own arm would be
quick to avenge an affront. In truth she was the personification of the
haughty aristocrat dear to novelists and actresses; though the haughty
expression of countenance is not often in reality found among families
of some antiquity. The Marquis de Péréfix, for instance, whose ancestors, some of them, were in the Crusades, and another received Henry
VIII on the Field of the Cloth of Gold, looked melancholy, resigned,
unassertive, and almost ordinary, in comparison with this little circus-
rider, sprung from Heaven knows where.

She received me amiably enough, and talked with much more connexion and sense than I had anticipated. She too was certainly not
French, nor had she the distinguishing marks of any nation. Like her
cousin, she was probably some kind of gypsy, at least in part. I sat there
doing my best till the three fell into a vehement discussion over horses,
whereupon I took my leave.

A short time after, the marriage was celebrated privately in one of
the chapels of St. Clotilde.

Chapter II

O**N THE NIGHT OF** the 11th of December, 1903, I received a telegram, handed in at the office of the chief town of Puy-de-Dôme,
the department in which the château of the Marquis de Péréfix was
situated, asking for my presence in most urgent terms. This telegram
was unsigned and afforded no explanation as to what I was wanted for.
It was too late to go that night, but the next morning I caught a very
early train to Clermont-Ferrand.

During the long, cold journey towards the mountains, I had leisure
to spend some thought on this client of mine, whom I had not thought
of with any particularity for a long time. Notwithstanding the predic-
tion of the doctor, he had survived these ten years. About two months

after his marriage he had retired to his country estate, and had never since left it. There in due season a son was born, the only child of the pair. I had every reason to suppose the Marquis happy in his odd marriage, for if he had not been I should infallibly have been consulted, and I never was. In fact, my relation to the Marquis was become merely that of a Paris agent whose aid is rarely needed, and, as I say, I had got to think but seldom of a man for whom the services I performed were almost mechanical.

It was the parting of the day and night when I arrived at Clermont-Ferrand. The evening was cold and rough, and just as I left the station a fine snow began to fall. The château of the Marquis was some eight miles away over mountain roads, and at the Hôtel Poste I found the landlord very reluctant to send out horses in this wild weather. His wife proposed to me a comfortable room for the night, clinching her offer with the assurance that a man of my years would certainly catch his death on such a night journey, either by a fall, or just by cold and snow. However, I waved these sinister prophecies aside, and what with the bribe of a good sum, and the promise that horses and driver could be quartered on the Marquis till they were fit to return, I obtained at length a carriage. After I had eaten a good meal we started. I remember having been somewhat amused at the look I caught on the face of the landlady, an odd confusion of pity and terror, as standing under a great lamp in the snow, she watched us clattering across the *Place* with much cracking of whip.

But scarcely had we cleared the town than I was nearer sharing than laughing at the good woman's dismay. It was a pitch-black night as we struck into the uneven roads, and the wind came with such force that I thought it would send the carriage on its side. I sat inside holding on to the arm-rests to keep my balance, while through the glass I could see the broad back of the driver, crusted with snow, as he sat in the shine of the lamps bellowing at the stock Auvergne horses. Fortunately the snow left off after we had been going about half an hour, but the darkness and the rugged way were still a sufficient cause for anxiety—and, no doubt, more to me, who knew not where I was going, than to the driver, familiar with these roads from childhood. At last, after we had been travelling very slowly for some hours, the carriage stopped. It was now about eleven o'clock.

The driver dismounted. I let down the glass, put my head out, and saw him examining the feet of the steaming horses.

"Are we at the house?" I cried.

He came slowly back to me, and stood by the front wheel in the lamplight.

"There," he said, pointing with his whip, "is the château."

I peered into the direction he indicated, but could see nothing that looked like a house. A drizzling snow had again begun to fall. After a while I made out a haze of yellow light at a certain distance, which seemed to rise from far below the level of the road.

"Do you mean where the light is?"

He nodded. "The château lies deep in the glen. It will be a hard pull to get down."

He mounted again, turned sharp to the right, and a descent began, with sliding of wheels and scrunching of brakes, which lasted more than a quarter of an hour. Then we passed through an archway, struck a good level road, and in a few minutes came before the house. It seemed to be a large building, and lights shone from many of the windows.

The grave man clad in black, by whom I was received, led me through wide stone passages to a large high room, comfortably though rather stiffly furnished, and having the walls dressed with portraits in heavy frames. A great fire blazed at the far end, and near it was drawn a small table laid for supper with shining napery and silver.

"Very sad about the young Count, sir," said the man.

"Has anything happened to him?"

"He died suddenly two days ago. His body is still in the house. The Marquis himself," added the man, "is dying. He is not expected to live through the night. He had the Sacraments this afternoon. What a series of misfortunes!"

"You may well say that!" I answered, feeling colder than ever I did on the road. "And where is her ladyship?"

"Her ladyship never leaves the sick-room, except for a few hours' rest. She has nursed the Marquis ever since he became seriously ill. We all say she looks ill enough herself. I had orders to bring you to the Marquis as soon as you arrived, but perhaps you would like some food first?"

"No, I will go at once."

The man, walking ahead with a lamp, led me a considerable distance through several winding corridors. The house—a part of it, at all events—was evidently of some antiquity, and had escaped destruction during the revolutionary time, possibly on account of its secluded position, lying as it did in a hollow between hills and quite invisible from the main road.

At a certain door he stopped, opened it a little, and whispered to one inside. Then he made me a sign to enter.

A large screen standing at some distance from the door blocked a sight of the room till I had passed round it. Then, indeed, I had before me a lugubrious scene. The room was wide and lofty, with an uneven floor of polished oak, mostly covered with rugs. Candles in branched silver candlesticks cast a sad and unequal light. A large curtained bed stood in the corner, and red curtains were drawn across the vast windows. One side of the room was very curiously painted and had the words of a Latin psalm in antique characters upon it: the other walls were covered with tapestry. Altogether the effect of the room was sombre and depressing, and exhaled that heavy odour of mortality which pervades rooms where some one lies at the point of death.

Near a great carven fire-place in which the logs glowed, in a deep chair propped with pillows, the Marquis sat with vacant eyes, breathing stertorously. The doctor, a fat, clever-looking little man, stood by him, and as I entered was taking his pulse. Near by, a Sister of Charity in her white hood and blue gown stood holding a small bowl. And leaning over the back of the chair, regarding the dying man with an indescribable look of yearning and devotion such as I was startled to see on that proud impassive face, was the ex-circus-rider, the Marchioness de Péréfix.

The Sister touched her, and she pulled herself together as if startled out of a dream. Then she raised herself up, and after giving me a long, haggard look, moved away to a door which opened into a smaller room. I followed, and when I was face to face with her I saw that although she bore the stains of watching and great suffering, although she was clad in a loose white dressing robe and her hair was unbrushed and carelessly knotted, the imperious beauty of her face and carriage was as striking as ever.

"Here is a dreadful state of affairs, madam," I said. "The death of the young Count——"

"Ah, yes," she murmured; "my poor little son! Tell me—you have known the Marquis a long time—do you think he looks as if he might pull through?"

I hesitated for an instant; but seeing her composed, almost stern look, I spoke freely. "Madam, I have seen too many people die to be deceived in the signs. M. de Péréfix is very near death."

"It is a pity," she replied. "I have done all I could."

"There is one consolation," I said, after a short pause. "He does not know of the death of the young Count——"

"On the contrary," she interrupted, "he knew shortly after it happened. I told him myself."

I stared at her. "Was that quite wise, quite merciful——"

"He had to know, while there was yet time to alter his will. He did add a codicil. I have it here to give you."

With that she went to a desk and took out an envelope. In this was a paper with the following words:

> "On account of the death of my beloved son, Melchior Louis Elizabeth, Count de Sauxillanges, I desire that, with the exception of the provision for my wife and the legacies to servants mentioned in my will, all the other provisions in that document may be null and void, and my property disposed of in accordance with a memorandum I left with my lawyer in Paris, M. Chalumet-Lacluze, just before my journey into Africa, when I thought I should die childless."

This was signed with the well-known signature of the Marquis, and duly witnessed.

"We have that memorandum quite safe," I said to the Marchioness. "There will be no difficulty."

She made a vague gesture with her hand which I took to mean that nothing could possibly interest her less, and actually had the resolution to ask me some questions about my adventures on the road, though I saw that she was not thinking of me personally any more than of a piece of furniture. I regarded her with uneasiness and some indignation. I resented her calmness and self-control before her husband dying in one room, and the yet unburied body of her only child in the other. Her devotion to her husband appeared genuine; but why had she afflicted his last hours with the miserable news that his son was dead and his race ended? For it was unnecessary; as things were, the codicil of the Marquis was of little importance. Ah, the bohemian, the child of the circus, was well seen in such an action!—without feeling and tactless, eager to secure herself at all hazards, and perfectly unable to comprehend the anguish of a man of family who learns that his ancient race is finished.

A new silence fell between us, while the storm lashed the windows. She broke in by inquiring whether I had eaten, and upon my reply that I had not, made that an excuse to put an end to the interview, and glided back to the sick-room. I followed, and when I was come up to the Marquis I took his hand which lay idle on the arm of his chair.

"Marquis de Péréfix," I said, in a solemn voice, "how is it with you, sir? Here is your old friend Chalumet-Lacluze. Be of good cheer."

I know not whether he heard me, for he made no kind of motion. Then I released his hand and left the room, in a sorrow intensified by the reflection that the nearest friend to the dying man was an old lawyer from Paris whom he had scarcely seen in ten years.

I found a good supper on the table by the fire, but I drew in my chair to it with a very faint appetite. Hard and dry as I am supposed to be, and as perhaps I am, I could almost have wept as I thought of the sad end of this distinguished family with which my own had been so long connected.

When I had as good as finished the meal, the door opened and the doctor came in.

"I thought I would allow you to get your supper over before I broke in on you," he observed, and brought up a chair. "I can do no good to the Marquis by staying up there in his room. He may last till morning."

"I suppose he is certain to die?"

The doctor nodded as he lit a cigar. "It is a question of hours. He has not been a strong man for some years, and in my opinion he would have been dead long ago if it had not been for the extreme care of his wife."

"Really?"

"Yes. I practise at Mont-Dore during the season, but in the winter I am here, and he has been under my observation for some years. Her attention to him has been extraordinary. You will think me fanciful for a man who prides himself on being scientific, but I do sometimes think she has kept him alive by her force of will. Now you are going to laugh."

"Oh no, I don't feel like laughing. She has a very singular and powerful character, I think."

"She has. She will need all of it to-morrow or next day to stand the facer we are obliged to give her."

I stared at him. "You mean——"

The doctor bent across the table. "I mean that the young Count de Sauxillanges did not die a natural death. He was poisoned."

"Good Heavens!" I was so horrified that I could hardly speak. "Wasn't the boy ill?"

"He had a bronchial cold—nothing at all to worry about. He was a robust lad, fond of the open air. Then between the morning and night he collapsed and died with every symptom of poisoning."

I pushed my chair back from the table. "But who would poison the boy in his father's house? There must be some mistake."

"Oh, it is not only my opinion, though I may say I am not usually mistaken in such matters. Le Cateau of Clermont-Ferrand had been called into consultation about the Marquis, and was present at the lad's death. It was in fact owing to the fuss he made that I—most unwillingly, I assure you—took any steps."

"And pray what steps have you taken?" I asked. "I hope you don't intend to cause any scandal in this distinguished family? I must remind you that though the line of the Marquis is at this moment practically ended, he has relations, both in France and abroad, very highly placed—very highly placed——"

I broke off. I was so shocked that I hardly knew what I was saying.

"I don't think we have caused any scandal so far," replied the doctor, "and I don't know that we intend to. But I can only speak for myself. Some scandal is inevitable if Dr. Le Cateau insists on a public examination, as he threatens. Le Cateau is a Radical-Socialist in politics, and the feelings of noble families don't weigh much with him. But what it was possible to do I have done. Nobody up to the present has heard a word of this affair except yourself, myself, Le Cateau, and one other person. This is the Sub-prefect of Police of Clermont-Ferrand."

"What!" I exclaimed. "You have already put the matter in the hands of the police?"

"I saw no way to avoid having an investigation in the house. All that was left was to have it done in the quietest way possible. I persuaded the Sub-prefect to come out here on the pretence of examining into a fire which luckily happened at a farm near by some nights ago. He lodges here in the château, which seems very natural, for the Marquis has often put him up when he had business in the district. Then I got permission from the Marchioness to wire to you, putting my request to her on the ground of her husband's illness, which appeared reasonable enough."

"And what," I inquired, "has this police officer discovered?"

"He had better tell you himself," answered the doctor, rising. "He is waiting to see you. Shall I bring him in?"

The Sub-prefect of Police turned out to be an energetic kind of man, with, as I judged, a considerable natural fund of astuteness and cunning developed by police methods, and provincial police methods at that. The Prefect was away on leave of absence, he explained, so the duties had fallen upon him. He spoke with a certain emphasis as though he expected to be contradicted, and was on his guard against it, and I remarked in him what I have had often occasion to remark in the course of my professional experience, the jealousy and distrust of the provincial functionary before a Parisian.

After we had talked a little, "This is a very dark business," I said with a sigh.

"You are right in the spirit of metaphor," replied the Sub-prefect, who was rolling a cigarette, "but in the matter of fact you are wrong."

"Indeed? How is that?"

"Because," said the Sub-prefect, looking me straight in the face with a smile, "I have discovered the criminal."

I almost jumped out of my chair; but the doctor had evidently been informed already, for he only nodded in acquiescence. The Sub-prefect paused a moment, calculating his effects.

"The criminal," he resumed, "is a servant in this house. She has been nurse to the young Count for some years. Her name is Jeanne Dangu."

I took this in at first with some scepticism. "And what reasons have you for suspecting this woman?"

"I think we can satisfy you," said the Sub-prefect. "The Count, as the doctor here will tell you, was poisoned by a dose, or repeated doses, of digitalin. Now I have found an empty bottle of digitalin in this woman's room, hidden away, so as not to be noticed, among other bottles in the drawer of the washstand. Some people—I might say most people—would never have examined the bottles on the washstand, acting on the supposition that the instinct of the criminal would lead her to destroy such a damning evidence of her crime. But I make it a rule to take no chances."

"And a very good rule too," I said. "Still, there remains the alternative that the woman might have bought the bottle for her own use."

"That is impossible," put in the doctor. "I know the bottle—in fact it came out of my surgery for the Marquis. Digitalin was in his treatment for a while, but we had given it up, which is the reason the bottle wasn't missed."

"But you must have a motive," I exclaimed. "People as a rule don't commit murders by way of passing the afternoon. Now what motive can you possibly allege as likely to influence this nurse—this servant-woman—to poison a boy ten years old?"

There was no immediate reply, and I thought I had embarrassed the Sub-prefect; but I was mistaken. He was meditating, and after a few moments he threw back his head and looked at me with a significant smile.

"M. Chalumet-Lacluze," he began, "I have a theory about that which you may think good or not, but which seems adequate to me. I flatter myself upon being something of a psychologist, which helps me very considerably in criminal investigations. Well, here is what I have worked out. This woman Dangu has only been here four years. She comes from the suburbs of Paris: she is, in fact, a Parisian. Now between the character of the Parisian worker and the provincial there is a vast difference, and allowance should always be made for it. The provincial, especially in the smaller towns, is sane, saving, takes long views, has a great respect for the law and its representatives; the Parisian, on the other hand, is reckless and often thriftless, lives on excitement, and continually craves some new sensation. It follows that such people are particularly open to the worst suggestions of crime—and not the ordinary everyday crime such as you meet with in the provinces, but refinements and variations of crime. Their natures being completely demoralized, monstrous unheard-of notions rise in their heads and are harboured there."

He paused to light a cigarette and looked round at us both. We remained impassive.

"I take it," pursued the Sub-prefect, "that you agree so far. Now I come to the case before us. This woman Dangu is a Parisian: therefore, strange ideas, monstrous whims must be allowed for and even expected. She is, by profession, a nurse—what is called a nursery-governess. Her profession throws her, a poor woman, among the well-to-do class, and places under her eyes luxuries and enjoyments which she can never hope to have. Hence, even with the best disposed, envy, depression; with the demoralized, the degenerate, an impulse to crime. Now, I have noticed in nurses that they often love their charges immoderately; but they often also hate them. The first is, of course, evident enough; but the last is hidden from all but the most skilled observers, for it is obvious that a woman who wished to keep her place would do her best to conceal her hate. But in disorganized individuals there is no temperate emotion: it is either extreme love or violent hate. Arrived at that point, they are ready to commit a crime from either the hate or love which happens to sway them. Upon the hate motive I need not dwell; but I would point out that the love motive is equally potent for crime. For the love becomes sometimes so uncontrollable that a nurse, as is well known, will kidnap a child from jealousy of the child's parents—or she will kill the child. That, gentlemen," concluded the Sub-prefect, "is my version of the case."

He leaned back in his chair and looked at us both, awaiting our opinion. I in my turn looked at the doctor, but he remained obstinately silent, so I was forced to speak.

"I think your theory is plausible," I said slowly at last, picking my words so as not to offend him, "and considered as a theory even ingenious. But I have found that nothing is more dangerous in criminal cases than to apply abstract theories to particular instances. For example, as you say you are a psychologist, you must know that the best psychologists have abandoned the 'guilty look' theory as practically worthless. To apply your theory successfully in this case would require a knowledge of the character of Jeanne Dangu which none of us possesses."

"I hold to it," exclaimed the Sub-prefect confidently.

"I repeat, it is an interesting theory," I replied.

"I'm afraid the Marchioness will have to be told to-morrow," interposed the doctor in a low voice. "My colleague at Clermont-Ferrand spoke of demanding an autopsy before the funeral."

"Gentlemen," I said, rising, "you will forgive me if I talk no more to-night. I am an old man and very tired. You can share my feelings. I arrive here, all unprepared, and find my old friend dying and his son a corpse in the house—you say, most foully murdered. This is too terrible to speak of further. It is a dark business—dark and shameful. God forgive us all!"

And with that we parted for the night.

Chapter III

THE MORNING BROKE FINE after the storm. I was told by the servant who came to my bedroom that the Marquis had died about six
o'clock. Downstairs, I found the people moving about their work with
a listless air, stunned by these calamities.

Just before eleven, while I and the police functionary were having
breakfast together, Dr. Le Cateau from Clermont-Ferrand arrived. He
was a tall, spare man with a hard, positive manner, austere and even
sour, and, I think, very keen-witted. He was inclined to treat respectfully the official's view of the case. Both of these men were most earnest
with me to open the matter to the Marchioness, and the local doctor,
coming in while we were still arguing, added his persuasion to theirs.

Accordingly, I sent a message to the lady asking when it would be
convenient for her to see me. The servant came back and said her ladyship would receive me at once. So, leaving the three men together, I
went upstairs with the greatest reluctance and a heart like lead. The
servant announced me, and retired.

When I entered, the Marchioness was crouching over the fire with
her hands open to the blaze as if she were suffering from the cold, but
no sooner was I well in the room than she drew herself up erect in her
chair. Shall I ever forget that commanding, impenetrable face? Not a
quiver of a muscle betrayed emotion; the wide dark eyes were dry; and
her pallor seemed no deeper than usual. Alone, a quite irrepressible
sigh before she spoke, hardly noticeable, betrayed the sorely charged
heart.

I ventured some words of condolence, which I felt were idle enough,
and then spoke of her fatigue and advised her to rest.

"Oh, I am not tired," she said; "not tired at all. I couldn't sleep," she
added, staring at me with her parched eyes, "if I tried."

I nodded. "Yes, I can understand how you feel. But you should try. I
am told that you watched night and day by your husband."

"I have done what I could," she said.

These words, spoken in the same tone, were the words she had used
to me the night before, and I now observed for the first time that we
were in the same little room. The Marquis, then, lay dead in the next

room, with the door half open between, and all through our interview I felt his presence, as if he were paying attention to us in there.

We spoke again about the funeral; then she let a silence fall and lay in her chair staring into space, doubtless expecting me to take my leave—if, indeed, she had not forgotten me altogether.

With an immense effort I summoned my resolution and stood up before the fire.

"Madam," I began huskily, "there is one matter I am obliged to speak to you about, and believe me I never had anything so disagreeable to do in my life. It is about the death of the Count de Sauxillanges."

She was quite still. "About my poor son?"

"Yes. The doctors here—not only the local doctor, but Le Cateau from Clermont—declare his death was not natural." I hesitated, looking at her. "They say he was poisoned."

She murmured something that I did not catch, and then asked: "Deliberately poisoned?"

I assented. She seemed absolutely calm. I need not say I was rather astonished at this lack of surprise and of any emotion at receiving such a heart-breaking piece of news, but she was such a queer, cold woman that what would have appeared monstrous in others in her seemed natural enough.

"They have even," I added, "put their finger on the criminal."

This stirred her a little. "Ah!" she said. "And whom do they accuse?"

"It is not so much they who accuse, nor I either. It is the chief of police. Practically, he accuses a servant in the house, Jeanne Dangu."

To my utter stupefaction, she flung back her head and gave vent to a peal of horrible, joyless laughter which left me helpless and powerless as if I had been nailed to the floor.

"Jeanne!" exclaimed the Marchioness. "Oh, my God! Jeanne, who is crying her poor heart out and refuses to stir from the side of my dead son! There's an idea for you!"

"They found the poison bottle in her room," I stammered.

She leaned forward and fixed her beautiful, terrible eyes on me. "M. Chalumet-Lacluze," she asked earnestly, "do they mean to accuse Jeanne? Do they mean to punish her?"

I recovered myself a little at this appeal. "She will undoubtedly be under very strong suspicion, and if the matter is not cleared up, I am afraid——" I threw out my arm vaguely.

"You are afraid they will kill Jeanne?"

"Oh no, I don't say that—far from it."

Then the Marchioness stood up. "Listen, M. Chalumet-Lacluze. You must tell them not to kill Jeanne. Jeanne is a good woman. Jeanne has only loved—she has done nothing bad at all. It was I who killed my son."

If the house had been shaken to its foundations by an earthquake I could not have been more startled. But at once I had a reaction. The lady was raving, of course; her brain was turned by sorrow. I suppose she read what I thought on my face, for she answered as if I had spoken.

"I am quite in my senses, M. Chalumet-Lacluze. Jeanne must not suffer for me. Nobody must suffer for me. What I did was the best thing to do. I think it was the best thing to do. I would have kept silent—for the honour of the Marquis, you know—but I am not afraid to tell. I can explain it all so easily to you, because you know everything from the beginning."

When she had said that she did a singular thing. She went to the half-open door, and looked round it into the room where the corpse lay. Then holding the door in her hand she turned to me. "Would you prefer me to speak in there?" she said.

I can't explain why, but I was taken with a strong shudder. I could only shake my head. She left the door open and came back to her chair with her free, unhumbled movement, and no least look of shame or terror upon her indomitable marble face.

"That poor Jeanne!" she said as she dropped into her chair. "How could they accuse her, the poor woman! She came to me some nights ago for some drops to ease her raging tooth. I was so full of other things at the time that I took up the first empty bottle I found to put her drops in, without looking at the label. That is how they found the bottle in her room. But all that has no importance, as you can see. I am going to tell you about it, from the beginning."

She let her eyes fall on a point in the floor and kept them fixed there, frowning a little. She remained silent so long that at last I said: "Madam, I am waiting to hear what you have to tell."

"Yes. I am sorry; I was thinking. You know I was married only about six months before the birth of my son. It was because I was going to have a child that the Marquis married me. He thought he was going to die very soon, and he wished this child to bear his name. But the

Marquis was not the father of my child, as he thought he was. The father of the child was Isidor Lorty. You met this man the night you came to our house in Paris years ago. I don't think you liked him. He left Paris just after our marriage and I never saw him again. I have heard he was killed in America.

"At the time of my marriage I did not care much for the Marquis, and I felt no unwillingness to trick him in this way. Women brought up as I have been learn early to seize all advantages that offer over the men they have dealings with. Besides, I saw hardly anything to choose between being a wife or a mistress. I did not want to marry: I had never asked him to marry me. The only advantage I saw in it was that my son would have a smoother life than if he came on the world as the son of Lorty. That is why I married."

I was going to speak, but she held up her hand.

"Please don't interrupt me or I shan't be able to go on again. M. Chalumet-Lacluze, by the time my son was born I loved my husband—I loved him before all else in the world. I would have laid down my life for him. How did this come about? I don't know; I cannot explain. But nothing has changed me, nothing could change me. I think I may have done him some good. I hope so. The doctors gave him only three years to live. He has lived ten.

"But the boy as he grew up was a dagger in my heart. I loved him too—oh yes, I loved him well, my poor little Louis! But when I saw the pride of the Marquis over the lad, and how he used to take him everywhere, and present him as his son, and say all the great things the little Count would do when he himself was gone, and arrange everything with a view to the future of Louis—what a blade of fire in my breast! It was not that I had to tell any lies; but I had to stand by and see a huge lie acted every day and all day. And the worst was that the Marquis was always searching for resemblances to himself and his ancestors in Louis. He used to imagine he found them; but I saw well enough that the boy only resembled me, and that later he would resemble Lorty. And I saw in the future the name of Péréfix carried and all the family wealth owned by a thick man with low and brutal instincts who looked like Lorty, and who had only in his veins the blood of a bully and of a drab of a circus-rider.

"I used to lie awake for hours at night thinking what I had better do. You will say, I ought to have told the Marquis. Do you think I did not often consider that? But I did not want to kill him—no, I did not want to kill him. And it would have killed him. He might have killed me first and that would not have mattered, but he would have died himself of shame and the knowledge that I, whom he loved so much, had so shamefully tricked him. No, I could not tell him about the boy. I had not the strength. …

"So the time went on, till some weeks ago when he fell very ill. Then he began to make all kinds of arrangements for the boy's future—leaving him all his property, writing to his relations about him, and so on. It was even arranged that the boy should go for a while after his father's death to one of the relations of the family, a Princess in Italy. Then I said to myself: All this must not be. Louis must not inherit this great name, and all its riches and responsibilities: he has not the blood to bear them. He will but make a failure or, very likely, a disgrace of his life, and that will be an injury done by me to the man who has loved me so kindly.

"Then I said: It would be better if little Louis died while he is happy. The Marquis will be sorry; but if I tell the truth he will be shamed, and it is better he should go with sorrow to his grave than with shame. Then, when I had thought these things, I took the poison to little Louis and I gave it to him myself."

The low voice ceased; but what I was about to say was struck from my lips, for her iron self-control suddenly broke down and she began to sob, horrible dry sobs, staring at me meanwhile with wide, tearless eyes.

"He looked so pretty!" she said.

I am free to say I never went through such a harrowing moment. When I considered the force of will which had enabled her to carry this anguish stuffed in her bosom, and that no womanish tenderness had abated her resolution to work out her plan, she appeared to me a monster; and yet—God forgive me!—I felt as I looked at her a stir of pity. For when I thought of her wild rearing, her warped code, her dark morality, on the one hand; and then of her love and devotion and the unselfishness of her motives, she became, for the moment at all events, a kind of inverted heroine, a saint predestined to hell. She repelled and even frightened me; she filled me with abhorrence; but mingled with that was a pang of regret for an admirable force misused and lost. My feelings might be summed up in the line of the great poet Racine which I had often heard declaimed on the stage:

Ainsi que la vertu, le crime a ses degrés.

Her paroxysm was mastered in a few seconds. When she spoke again it was in the even, unemotional voice she had used all the time.

"I am sorry for that," she said. "I have been watching a good deal lately, and I am rather worn out. M. Chalumet-Lacluze, you will understand that you must tell those gentlemen downstairs what I have told you, and nothing must be done to Jeanne. If they wish to accuse me, I am of course quite ready. Only, if you could arrange to leave the matter at rest it might be better, because, you know, his memory"—she looked towards the half-open door—"would be smirched if his wife was placed in the assize court."

"Ah, his memory!" I repeated bitterly. "That ought to have been thought of before."

She looked at me with immense sadness. "You see, I did not love him then."

The strange woman! Her remorse was plainly applied only to her false dealing with the Marquis, and not at all to the taking off of her little son. And I judged that she regarded this as one of the harsh necessary acts of existence which it was useless to repent or bewail.

"I know you dislike me, M. Chalumet-Lacluze, but there is one favour you may possibly do me on account of your dead friend. If these gentlemen decide to accuse me publicly, will you give me some warning before they act?"

I saw what she meant. "You shall be warned," I replied. "Madam, I have nothing more to say to you. I am very unhappy, and no doubt you are still more unhappy."

At that she gave me a wry little smile, and as I stepped into the corridor I saw her rise from her chair and walk towards the half-open door which led into the chamber of death.

I went down and found those gentlemen, and thereupon opened the case to them as it was, and dwelt with all my resources upon the uselessness of a prosecution and the advisability of keeping the secret between us. The local doctor and, to my surprise, the police functionary came

SENTIMENT AND OTHER STORIES *Vincent O'Sullivan*

round without much difficulty to my view, but Dr. Le Cateau gave me great trouble. He poured out his fury on the Marchioness, whom he compared to Jael, Judith, and to others I have forgotten, and he even became insulting to myself, calling me the henchman of aristocrats and a screener of their vices. How I had the patience and skill to manage him, suffering as I was from the effects of the terrific blow I had just received, I know not; but I did at last bring him also to promise silence.

"Besides," I said, "justice will not have long to wait, for if ever I saw the marks of death on any face, it is on the face of that most miserable woman upstairs. Even now, unless I am mistaken, she is measuring her grave."

Two days later, in dull cold weather, the Marquis and the boy were laid together in the ancient vault of the Péréfix family. The Marchioness attended the funeral. Her lips and cheeks were faded to ashes as though they had already begun to separate from life; blue circles were under her eyes and showed up cruelly in the daylight; but she bore herself in her mourning robes through that black funeral and the sullen dirging of the choir with an air of intense suffering dignity which impressed all beholders. When the rite was ended, I felt such insuperable horror at the thought of returning to the house where the lonely woman would be lodged with her grief and sin, that I availed myself of the doctor's carriage to Clermont-Ferrand, whence I took the first train to Paris.

Chapter IV

FIVE MONTHS AFTER, SHE died. Before her death she saw no doctor, saw no priest, and by her orders was buried among the poor and outcast. The personal fortune left her by her husband was untouched, and was placed at my disposition. After some reflection, I distributed this among such institutions as particularly care for circus-people, van-dwellers, and other wanderers by the road. I hope they sometimes pray for their unknown benefactress, and that I may gain a little blessing too from their prayers.

The Mormon

Chapter I

"I S THAT ENGLAND?" AN American lady asked.

Thomas Peddar raised himself erect from the rail he was leaning against, watching the green waves cresting in the sun and the foam streaming in patches along the steamer's side, and answered with a foolish, proud smile, as if he were pointing out something of his own that he was responsible for and had reason to boast of, that the dim blue mass perceptible on the sea-line to the starboard of the ship's bow was indeed England. He was quite willing to say more, to enlighten the foreigner, to explain to her what she had to expect when she landed in England; but the lady strolled away, and he leaned once more on the rail in about as pleasant a meditation as a man can have in this world.

It was something to be able to tell people that the land was England out yonder there. England! She had been an indifferent, not to say harsh, mother to him during the time of his youth before he emigrated to America; but all through the thirty-six years spent in the retail boot-and-shoe business in Philadelphia, he had never lost the vision of her green fields and grey skies. He had always looked on America as a make-shift: he had always been the Englishman aggressively—never failing to hang a Union Jack over his shop in Peanut Street on the Sovereign's birthday and the Feast of St. George, sticking to his English habits (it became to him, for instance, a matter of principle to have his tea in the afternoon), and never failing to express his sense of the superiority of everything English, from Government down to postage-stamps, in a city not overflowing with love for the English. "You ain't got no gentry out here," was one of his constant chastening remarks in a country where every man, down to the nigger hall-boy, calls himself a gentleman. Like almost every Englishman who lives for any length of time under Republican institutions in the United States, he was become the most dogged of Tories, and gave forth his beliefs with great freedom. All this might conceivably have interfered with the prosperity of his business, if his partner, a shrewd Pennsylvanian who knew the value of Thomas Peddar as a workman, had not conciliated opinion, uprooting always where the other had sown, till their trade was no longer liable to accidents. After all, even Americans will end by sticking to a shop which sells good material, though their country is not appreciated by the proprietor. They revenged themselves by saying sometimes, "Why don't you go back there?" to which Thomas would always reply that he would be jolly glad of the chance, and was going next year. He had said that, meaning to go next year, every year for nigh on forty years. Then his partner had died, and the upheaval which followed that event had sufficient momentum to send Thomas across the Atlantic.

He had not quite decided what he would do when he got "home," as he always called England. Possibly he might stay there for good. He was not at all what would be considered rich in Philadelphia; but in little Palebrook, the sea-coast Hampshire town of his birth, he could make a considerable figure. He was nearly sixty; but one thing at least he had learned from the unloved country of his sojourn, and that was that late life is the time for youthful things. So at the back of his head he cherished an unelaborated plan to marry a pretty girl—he had vague notions of "a lady," some daughter of the well-to-do people whom he had regarded with awe when he was a boy—and to settle down with her in one of those good-sized houses on the landslip jutting out into the bay. And that terrible American atmosphere is so infectious, even for those constantly guarding against it, and does end by giving any man in the least prosperous so much assurance, that it never occurred to Thomas Peddar to doubt that the well-to-do people would smile amiably on such an arrangement. His recollection of class prejudice, really the strongest feature of English provincial life, had become blurred after forty years of Philadelphia, and no wonder! He had even forgotten how all classes take a hand in this; his own class—the class he sprang from—marking the degrees with the same precision as the rest.

Chapter II

A S OF OLD, THE little lights, visible from the station, swayed on the mast-heads of ships in the harbour, and there was something strangely poignant in the remembered skirl of the sea-wind as it swept up the narrow street from the quay. Save the lights and the north wind, there was no other welcome for Thomas Peddar upon his return to his birthplace, and in spite of his common sense, he felt disappointed.

After two years in Philadelphia he had lost all touch with Palebrook: his mother was dead before he left; his father could not write; and for his friends writing was a labour which as time went on they became increasingly unwilling to undergo for one they were never likely to see again. But somehow he had thought that there would be a knot of his old cronies hanging about the station whom the important-looking stranger would surprise by grasping cordially by the hand. Such faces as he saw at the station, and they were few at that hour of the evening, he had never seen before. A porter put his trunk on a barrow, and holding his "grip," he trudged beside the man through the dusty, ill-lit street to the King's Arms.

The landlady, who had been in the place for fifteen years, looked aggrieved when she was told by this stout man with an American accent that she was a stranger. However, he ordered largely, and she thought it worth while to give him some minutes of her company while he ate his supper. She had never heard of him, she told him frankly: the name of Peddar had disappeared from the annals of Palebrook, leaving no trace. Such names as she mentioned—the Bartlets, the Fords, the Parrys—were names of those well-to-do people who had been vaguely in his mind of late—people for whom his father and himself had worked. Old Mr. Ruggles, the lawyer and Member of Parliament, the great man of Palebrook, who had often given him a penny for holding his horse, was dead, and his son lived at the house. Some of the shops too, which had existed in his youth, still flourished under descendants of the former owners. But the lower grades, to which he himself had belonged, were covered with mist. For one name that the landlady knew, to ten she shook her head. Altogether, the landlady's account of Palebrook rather shattered the theory of the stationary condition of sleepy English towns.

"People read the papers more nowadays," said the landlady. "They won't put up with a little dead-alive place like Palebrook. They go away and you hear no more of them."

She launched into an explanation of her own residence at Palebrook, to which Peddar listened with the solemn interest of a man without resources who fears to be left alone. His interest was hardly repaid; the fact that he, Thomas Peddar, had come back to Palebrook all the way from America after thirty-six years, and able to spend a sovereign without looking twice at it—this event, so wonderful that he could hardly realize it, did not seem to impress her much. She remarked slightly that she had often Americans motoring through in the summer-time who stopped for tea.

"Better to go out there, I say, than stick in a dog-hole like this," quoth the landlady. "America is Canada, ain't it? Everybody does well there, it seems to me. Now, my husband's brother he went to New Zealand——"

By the time the New Zealander's adventures were ended, Peddar's meal was ended too, so he lit a cigar and strolled out. He was in a state of great excitement. Even if he were not recognized, it was a consummation to lounge importantly smoking a cigar through the crowded Saturday-evening market, which was just the same as when his mother used to hold him by the hand while she chaffered for a bit of fish. He had a good moment of triumph: he smiled blandly at the people, and seeing a barefoot boy near a fruit barrow, he bought him some apples.

By degrees he shook off the business part of the town, and entered the long tree-bordered road called the Avenue. About half-way down was the well-remembered gate of the Ruggles' place, and through the bars he could make out the beautiful Queen Anne house, standing serene and unchanged amid its lawns in the moonlight. Peddar would have been put to it to define the vague impulses, the half-formed intentions, which had brought him to this spot; but now that he was here, he perceived that the spirit of Palebrook—of England perhaps—had already got hold of him. He could no more go up that drive and ring that bell and present himself on terms of equality, than he could forget that he used to go up there with his mother every Christmas Eve to get their Christmas dinner. Out in America he had conversed easily on occasion with the Member of Congress for his district, the Mayor of Philadelphia, and various other people much more important than Mr. Ruggles of Palebrook; but that was somehow different. In America, the fact that any man of any significance was looked upon as a public man, living in a public house, to be devoted to the public at all hours, influenced the point of view. Besides, out there he did not care himself, and nobody else cared, what was his origin: old families in Philadelphia counted for nothing if they lost their money: the whole spirit of the country was to make him feel as good as anybody else as long as he had a solid banking account. Only the other day on the steamer he had thought it not impossible that the Marquess of Wednesbury, the chief landowner of the district, would ask him to dinner at Palebrook

Court the moment he heard of his presence in the town; that had really seemed to him quite in the ordinary course of things. And now, ere he had been a few hours in his native place, old traditions, old associations, an heredity of subservience through generations which had been only artificially overlaid, regained him with such effect that he looked with far more awe at the house of his lordship's agent than he had ever done at the residence of the Mayor of Philadelphia.

But though he was obliged to acknowledge this weakening of his American attitude, he was none the less annoyed that it should be so. And this was odd enough, for out in Philadelphia he had consistently reviled the American attitude when applied to England, and steadfastly maintained that the gentry, to say nothing of the peerage, had a right to the respect and the submission of the lower classes. Possibly this was the reason that the first breath of his native place stripped off the American garment so neatly and completely. It had always been an unnatural garment for him; he had always struggled to keep it off his back; he had never realized that any part of it had managed to get on till he left the American shore. He had never given his heart to America; he had never had the least desire to become an American. Still, expressions of class-inferiority were empty in America; they bound one to nothing; they were merely ebullitions of that British patriotism which makes it a point of honour in a foreign land to maintain that everything in England is superior to things anywhere else. In Philadelphia, to proclaim the superiority of the British peerage and landed gentry over the rest of mankind, was in no wise inconvenient; there could not possibly be any practical test of his subordination. There was no one in Peanut Street, or in Chestnut Street either, for that matter, who could exact his deference. There were any number of men far richer than he could ever hope to be, but he had no more essential respect for them on that account than he had for a man who could eat more than himself. They were not British.

But here in Palebrook, up against the real thing, his self-assurance flickered lamentably. He began to see that his marriage with "a lady," some daughter of one of the long-established, well-to-do Palebrook families, might prove a more difficult enterprise than it had seemed on the steamer. He had imagination enough to picture his reception were he to call on the Bartlets or the Fords. He would be received by one of the male members of the family; if they could recall his old father, the roadmender and "odd man," he would be congratulated on his industry and good fortune; he might be offered a drink; and then he would go out of the door and never again see the inside of those walls unless one of the servants happened to remember him and asked him to come round to the kitchen. All that was certain; and Thomas Peddar had been so long used to his importance in Peanut Street and the adjacent district that the fact was rather galling. Money no doubt could do anything; but you had to have enough money. It was conceivable that even Tom Peddar, the son of old John Peddar the roadmender, might batter down those Palebrook doors if he could set up a millionaire's establishment in his native place. With an income of some hundreds it was hopeless.

As he thought these things, he was tramping heavily back to the heart of the town. He had remembered the Swan inn, where a club of the more prosperous tradesmen used to be held on a Saturday evening. Far below as that was from his first plans, it was yet a place in which his father and himself in the old days had never dared to put a foot.

The club-room was crowded, and through a haze of tobacco smoke several faces scrutinized him with torpid speculation when he entered. Peddar sat down, and his heart tightened a little as he perceived that not one of these faces was familiar to him.

"Cold," said the man in the next chair, taking his pipe from his mouth.

Peddar assented, and then asked him to have a drink. They fell into a desultory conversation, and the rest of the company, as usually happens in communities where a stranger is a marked man, hushed their own conversation to listen attentively. It was not long before Peddar declared himself.

"My name's Peddar," he said. "I'm Tom Peddar. Just come back from America after thirty-six years."

There was no shout of recognition. There was a dead silence. To most of those in the room the name signified nothing. They were trying to sum up this fat, grey-bearded man in black broadcloth. He didn't look like one of the governing class, but he didn't look like an English tradesman either. They were balancing between a commercial traveller, and an advance agent for one of the theatrical companies which sometimes visited the town.

"America, d'ye say?" quoth the chemist with a shrewd look. "I thought there was a Yankee twang about your talk."

Few things could have surprised Peddar more. In America it used to make him proud that he was always spotted for an Englishman as soon as he opened his mouth. Was not his establishment in Peanut Street known as "the English shoe-store"? Had all his patriotism, all his waving of the Union Jack, gone for no more than this—to be called a foreigner in his own country?

"I ain't no more a Yankee than you are yourself," he replied gruffly. "I was born and brought up in Palebrook."

"I remember old Peddar when I was a boy," said Rawk, the grocer, without warmth. "Rum old codger he was too. Had only one foot—that's how I remember him. Are you young Tom Peddar that used to work in the cobbler's shop on the quay?"

Peddar said he was, and there the subject dropped. Nobody seemed to care. Old Peddar, who had passed from the workhouse to a pauper's grave about as quietly as that grim journey can be performed, was not exactly the kind of person for a prosperous tradesman to show any interest in. And besides, it was all so long ago! Hardly anybody remembered the wretched Peddars, who had lived from hand to mouth.

Peddar, disappointed and mortified, divined their feelings, and he began to brag. He jingled the money in his pocket. He could buy up the whole of Palebrook if he liked—Wednesbury, and Ruggles, and the whole lot. He didn't care a damn for your lords and marquesses: in America they put that kind of truck under the pump. Repeatedly he ordered drinks for the whole room, and a box of the sinister cigars supplied by the Swan was handed round for those who had the courage to smoke them. Just before closing time he had in champagne. And the upshot was that Thomas Peddar, who had ever been a model of sobriety in Peanut Street, signalized his arrival in his birthplace by going to bed very drunk.

Chapter III

THE NEXT MORNING THOMAS Peddar went to church. He wore a frock-coat and a top-hat, and his appearance was quite sensational. Several members of the Saturday-night club, who found themselves in the congregation, whispered to their neighbours that he was an American. At the end, knots gathered in the churchyard to watch him come out. Children did not lower their voices to shout, "Hi—i—ie! come and look at the American." But it was all the hard rind of curiosity; there was no fruit of friendliness. Nobody claimed acquaintance with him; nobody even spoke to him. Even those he had encountered the night before gave him but a distant nod as they came stiffly out of church, wives on arm. He was treated as a stranger.

This conduct had two effects on Peddar. In the first place, it drove him to rely on the bottle by way of counteracting his depression and mortification and loneliness. And in the second place, as he still clung to his idea of picking up a wife in Palebrook, and he saw no way now of meeting girls in the ordinary course, he took to winking and smiling amiably at any face which attracted him in the street. Lizzie Meed, an amiable trollop, who didn't much care whom she took up with, went for a walk with him along the foreshore on Monday afternoon. She made no bones about it on her return, rather boasted of it; said he had asked her to go to America with him, and added mysteriously that he had shewn her "papers." These, to tell the truth, were only some of those immense, inconvenient wads, full of pictures, issued as time-tables by the railroads of the United States.

But Lizzie only said vaguely that he had shewn her "papers." Now just at this time some of the newspapers were in an uproar about certain Mormons who were said to be pursuing a rather harassed apostolate in the English towns. Palebrook might be behindhand in some things, but at least it read the ha'penny press. Not a notorious crime, however monstrous, to which the newspapers gave any prominence, could be committed that the inhabitants did not suspect the like would break out in their midst, till something fresh put it out of their heads. In all popular movements it is not so much sudden action as skilful preparation that counts. At present Palebrook was discussing Mormonism. Public opinion, following the newspapers, was dead against it. Not Governor Cumming himself, when he made that memorable descent on Utah, could have been more merciless to the Latter-Day Saints. And as Mormonism is a sex-religion, apparently to the advantage of the male, the women were shrillest. Most of the men were ruminative, but those who were tied to yellow-faced, sour-mouthed shrews trounced the Mormons without mercy. They could not bear to think of those chaps out there who were able to throw a curtain over one wife when they had done with her, and turn to another. All Palebrook combined to shake a disapproving head at America. Mormons were Yankees; consequently Yankees were Mormons.

You see the pits which were opening out beneath poor Tom Peddar's feet in the town of his birth. He came from America; he had been taking a good deal of notice of girls; he had even given them—don't say it too loud—*papers*. Not the least doubt of it: he was a Mormon. The damned scoundrel!

"Ever been to this 'ere Salt Lake City?" asked the shrewd chemist on Tuesday evening at the Swan. They meant to get the truth out of him.

O vanity! Peddar said he had. As a matter of fact, he had never been farther west than Niagara Falls, whither he had once gone on a five-day excursion organized by the Sixth Street Presbyterian Church. For the rest his travels in America had been confined to a month on the New Jersey coast in the summer, in common with most other middle-class Philadelphians. Salt Lake City was as remote from him as Belgrade or Bagdad.

But he was starving for the consideration which had been so ruthlessly denied him. He caught at straws. As a traveller he might yet make his mark. And he erected a mythical Salt Lake City before the malevolent eyes of the Swan. Ah, there was a town for you! If you once saw that place, you'd never want to see Palebrook again!

People shunned him. Everyone was anxious to go home and tell his wife. Peddar was soon left alone with the landlord, who, by way of compensating himself, urged Peddar to another bout of champagne.

"You see, he pays well and it don't hurt me," the landlord explained afterwards. "My wife ain't likely to go to Salt Lake." And he sighed.

Then happened an event which placed the matter beyond conjecture.

On Wednesday evening, about seven o'clock, Kate Tidman, employed as kitchenmaid at "The Firs," was stepping over to see her aunt, Mrs. Wrench, in the High Street. It was dusky and raining, and just as Kate turned a corner she saw Tom Peddar, whom she knew very well as an object of curiosity, mooning along under an umbrella. He felt extremely bored, the poor man, and descrying a rather attractive girl, he was moved to offer her a share of his umbrella. And as Kate stood there, Peddar put her hesitation down to the right side of the account, and caught her arm gently to draw her in. Kate broke away in terror, which was partly affected, and fled to her aunt's parlour—secure to-night, at all events, of her importance and her welcome.

"Oh, aunt!" she gasped breathlessly. "That Mormon—he kept following me about—he wanted to catch hold of me." She felt delightfully happy.

But her aunt felt outraged. "He ought to be turned out of the place. And he will be—I'll see to that. I'll get your uncle to speak about it to-morrow. That old devil—with all his wives too, as I've heard tell. Sixty is what they tell me. Mormons! I've no patience with such. How any woman can take up with them I can't think. I'd rather be a Suffragette."

The husband of Mrs. Wrench often took round his own fruit and vegetables in a cart, and the next day the report of the attack on his niece by the Mormon was spread by him in all quarters of the town. During the next few days there were hostile mutterings. Peddar encountered sullen looks everywhere. Once or twice boys threw stones at him from a safe distance, and the adults standing by, although they did not actually join in, yet seemed to support the boys. His complaints were met with looks of indifference or hostility. That power which can become even formidable by dint of its very meanness and stupidity, the concentrated malice of a little town, was against him. Aware of the prejudices of the Palebrookites, who resented the presence in the town of anyone from outside a twenty-mile radius, he attributed his unpopularity to the fact that they took him for a foreigner, and he felt sore.

On Sunday came the storm. The vicar of the parish was away, and the curate-in-charge was an impulsive and energetic young man who lacked in Palebrook sufficient scope for his energies. As soon as he heard about Peddar, he was with difficulty restrained by his wife from going to the King's Arms and seizing the old miscreant by the beard. However, as various bishops had thundered with prodigious violence against Mormonism in the Press, he thought he might at least permit himself to follow in the steps of those Fathers in God, and accordingly he preached an exciting sermon at the morning service which took no count of charity among the Christian virtues it exemplified.

The people left the church in an ugly mood. They now felt that they had the governing powers to support them. About half-past three, as Tom Peddar was swaggering innocently down the High Street in his top-hat and frock-coat, a group of men lounging on the quay made a dangerous rush.

"There's the old beggar now!" they shouted. "Let's have him in the water."

A policeman caught Peddar by the shoulders and shoved him up a little alley.

"Stay here till they pass," he said hurriedly, "and then run for your life to the Arms."

❧

Late that evening, the landlady, who was beginning to fear for her own popularity if she continued to harbour Peddar, told him curtly that the police-sergeant wished to speak to him. He went down, and the policeman urged him to leave Palebrook in the morning. The people, he explained, objected to Mormons. "You had a chance to see that this afternoon," said the policeman.

"Mormon!" Peddar was dumbfounded. "I ain't no Mormon. I'm Church of England here, and Presbyterian in America. I never even saw a Mormon in my life."

The policeman took a confidential, man-of-the-world tone, as of one prepared for all human infirmities, whom few crimes could astonish.

"You may be what they allege or you may not. That's got nothin' to do with me. After the sermon this morning, your life is in danger here. I can't answer for the people: I can't keep them in check. I'll see you off by the first train. Come, you'd be wiser to go."

"Yes," said Peddar, "I'll go. I'll go back to Philadelphia. I've come to find," he added sadly, "that it ain't where you're born and bred that's home."

"No?" queried the policeman.

He was evidently interested in the question and shewed some willingness to discuss it, but old Peddar, trembling with rage and the sense of injustice, turned upstairs to pack his trunk.

~

Mrs. Turner

Chapter I

SHE LOOKED AROUND THE room. No, she had forgotten nothing; she might close her bag. She did so, and then lifting it a little found it so heavy that she wished she had sent it with her trunk as "luggage in advance." There was nobody to carry it. The arrangement was that when she left the house she was to lock the door and then leave the key with a neighbour on her way to the station. She looked out of the window, wondering if by chance some man or boy might be about willing to earn threepence; but Palebrook woke late, and there was only the steady downpour of rain on the muddy street.

"I hope to goodness I don't miss the train."

She picked up her black hat from the table and pinned it on hastily in front of the dim little mirror over the stripped chimney-piece. She scrutinized herself without mercy, and thought that on the whole she didn't look so bad. Her magnificent red hair, under the black hat, encircled her small head like a nimbus. Her deep turquoise-blue eyes, appealing and unhappy, were full of charm. The lips of her large amiable mouth were rather dry and discoloured; the skin of her face tight-drawn and waxen; but she told herself with truth that although she looked fatigued, she did not shew her age. She looked like a woman of twenty-eight or thirty who had lived worried and poor. Her black dress was quite good; so were her gloves; and her long black coat fitted her tall well-knit figure. The weak point was her boots, which were very much worn, and, what was worse, looked worn. Try all she could, she had not been able to save money to buy a new pair before going away. Still, one could keep them tucked in. ...

A railway whistle sounded far off.

"That's the train at the junction. I'm sure to miss it."

She lived too far away to hear the church clock, and she had no watch. She had pawned it a month ago to help in paying the last instalment for the house rent and furniture. The remembrance of this little fact aided to bring the bitter tears of poverty and forlornness to her eyes, and it was through tears she looked round the barren room which she never expected to see again.

"There! I'm blubbing now. I'll look a nice sight at the station."

She put her bag on the door-step and locked the door. Then she knocked at the next house.

A large woman, still young, but malformed, probably by too much child-bearing, took the key.

"Law, Mrs. Turner, I thought you'd given up going. You'll never catch it now——"

"How much time have I?"

"Not more'n five minutes, if that. My husband would carry the bag for you and welcome, but he's that poorly with his back——"

Breathless, almost sobbing with the strain, she got to the station.

"Label that for London, please."

"Now then, hurry up! Third class in front."

The train had come from Southampton and the carriage was packed. Somebody insisted on keeping both windows shut, and as the journey continued the faces of the passengers became more and more congested. Mrs. Turner looked at them very little: she looked out of the window at the rain-drenched land, and thought and thought. ...

She thought of the house she had left. She had lived there ten years. There she had come with her husband after his misdeed and punishment, and their child, a boy of twelve. The husband had died five years ago. The son, now twenty-two, had utterly deserted her. She had heard he was in a good position in Glasgow; but he never sent her any money, and it was now two years since she had even had a letter. She kept herself alive by doing work of various kinds for the well-to-do of Palebrook.

Her husband, although broken by his disaster, had yet managed to make some money as clerk to a firm of coal merchants till he got ill. He had not been a bad husband to her—poor Harry! But since his death she had gone through all the phases of misery—first, to meet the expenses of her son while he was at school, and then, after he was gone, to pay off the debts he had left in the town.

What a life had been hers! As she thought of it she nearly cried—she would have cried but for all these men in the carriage. Hardly a single day of happiness since she was eighteen. Yes—stay!—for a month she was in hospital. Since then, when she was lying awake at night and wanted to think of something pleasant in her life, she thought of her time in the hospital. All her life—all her young life she had wept, she had been hungry and humiliated. She had buried her husband. He was not a bad man, she thought, although they had put him in gaol. Sometimes at night, when he was not too tired, he would sing. The day they arrested him he had on a pair of new boots. ... Oh God!

She pretended to blow her nose, and looked hard out of the window.

The shame had killed him. ... And her son—ah, how she had loved her son! She had given him all she had, gone hungry that he might not want, to the point that if there was an egg in the larder it was he who had it. And then Mr. Ford had found him a good post, and he had gone away. He did not write any more; perhaps he was ashamed of her—the little baby whose mouth she had felt against her breast. Oh, why wasn't he little again? Then there would have been some sense in living. For him she would have slaved and begged at doors. Even now, if he wanted her, she would pardon him without a word of reproach. ...

But he didn't want her; nobody wanted her. What was the use of going through all these miseries just to keep herself alive for a few more years? And yet there were so many people happy in life. There were all those rich people she worked for. Most of them thought themselves condescending when they spoke to her. Some of them found it difficult to remember her existence. And yet how were they better than she was? She had education; she could draw, paint, play the piano as well as most of them could. But she was poor. ...

She shivered. On the way to the station the rain had soaked through her broken shoes.

"That's it! Now I'm going to get pneumonia. That's all that's wanted to make it perfect."

A man, who perhaps noticed the strained look on her face, offered her his *Daily Mail*. She thanked him, and glanced at it, but did not read it.

On the front page of the newspaper was an advertisement of the very firm she was hoping to get an engagement with—Flavour and Blades of Oxford Street. Old Mr. Parry, the banker at Palebrook, whose daughters she had worked for, had written about her to his friend Sir Lawson Flavour, and she had been asked to call to-day. So she was going to London.

Should she ever forget what had decided her to go? Mrs. Burger, of "The Firs," had left an Aberdeen terrier in her charge with precise orders to look after it well. Often, when she was lonely, she used to get in one of her neighbour's children, a little fellow of about four or five, who reminded her vaguely of her own son. One day she cooked the dog's bone and put it as usual out in the deserted street. Suddenly she heard the dog snarl and the child cry, and she rushed to the window. The child, on his hands and knees in the gutter, had taken the dog's bone.

"I'se hungry," he sobbed. "Muvver sometimes gives me bones."

Mrs. Turner took the child home and told the story.

"Well, what can I do?" said the mother. "The child's hungry. 'Tain't likely I can feed eleven o' them and my husband on eighteen bob a week. Never you mind. The dog won't miss it. He's fed better than my little Tommy, I'll be bound."

"It isn't that," said Mrs. Turner. "But that a child should have to fight with a dog for a bone! In a Christian land!"

Her friend looked at her in astonishment.

"Lor' love you, my gal, there's nothin' in that! I'd be glad if you *could* spare one of the dog's bones for little Tommy. Bless you, the dog'll never miss it. They're rich where he comes from."

Till that day she had been living on the narrowest of margins, spending one week what she earned the week before. Now she was frightened. She determined to get steady wages and put by. Perhaps she would take little Tommy to live with her.

Chapter II

THE TRAIN STOPPED. IT was necessary to change for London. A wait of half an hour.

It was close on twelve o'clock. She had not eaten all day, and she decided to risk a little money on some food. She went into the station buffet and asked for a cup of Bovril and a biscuit. When she had taken it she put down a sovereign—one of the two she had in the world.

The barmaid went to the other end of the counter, loitered a little chatting, and then came back and put down some change.

"But I gave you a sovereign," faltered Mrs. Turner.

"A sovereign? Oh no. A ten-shilling piece. I never make mistakes in change"—she drew in her breath noisily—"never!"

Mrs. Turner became very red. "But I know it was a sovereign!" She began to talk loudly. "What does this mean? I had only two pounds. I know what I had——"

The barmaid looked at her with some contempt and turned to her colleague, who was standing near.

"This person thinks her half-sovereign was a sovereign. P'raps you took notice, miss?"

The other came casually into the dispute. "I saw quite plain. It was a half-sovereign." She gave Mrs. Turner a reassuring smile.

Mrs. Turner wanted to shout reproaches, to call for the police. Then, with the instinctive fear and distrust the poor have of the law, she reflected that, like all vagabonds against organized respectability, she would get the worst of it if she did. And the delay would make her lose her appointment in London. She hurried out on the platform.

"Please, is this the Waterloo train?" she asked a boy.

"Yes," said the boy.

She got into the first carriage she came to. Her feet were like ice; something like the pendulum of a clock was going throb, throb inside her head. To lose ten shillings just when she wanted it most, and in such a silly way! If she had only had the spending of it, no matter how foolishly. Oh, it was cruel—cruel. She trembled with rage: she wanted to go back and fling a glass at those two women and make a scandal. She half rose from her seat; then she noticed that the train was running at full speed. Her ten shillings were gone. ...

She felt so futile and helpless that she wanted to cry. All the wretchedness of her life seemed to be concentrated in the loss of her ten-shilling piece. Only the thought of how it would spoil her for the coming interview with Flavour and Blades made her choke back the tears.

An inspector came along the corridor and asked for her ticket.

"You're in the wrong train," he said.

Mrs. Turner gave him a look of despair. "But that can't be! They told me it was the Waterloo train."

"The down from Waterloo—so it is. You must get out at the next stop. Let me see." He took a time-table from his pocket. "You'll have an hour to wait. Then you'll get an express."

Chapter III

ON THE PLATFORM OF the country station the rain soaked and soaked. There was no fire in the waiting-room. What with lack of food, and cold, she was beginning to lose her grasp of things in general. One thing only kept in her mind—she would be late for the interview.

"Perhaps they won't see me at all now."

Trains came and went in the dismal weather. To make sure of not being mistaken this time, she gave a porter twopence to put her in the right train. She was very wet; her head ached; and oh, her lost ten shillings!

At Waterloo she inquired about her bag, which had of course gone astray in the error about the trains. She heard it would take some time to get it out, and decided to leave it for the present. She would hurry on to Oxford Street. In the station yard she spoke to a cabman.

"How much will you charge to go to Flavour and Blades in Oxford Street?"

The man looked her up and down; then he pointed to his indicator. "It'll mark it there. Flavour and Blades, did you say? Yes, I know."

She examined herself in the little glass of the cab, and thought she looked ghastly. In truth, what with her damp clothes, her hunger, and all the tears she had kept unshed since early morning, she was hardly fit for a business interview. But the swift movement through the London streets did something to revive her. How long it was since she had driven anywhere! Years and years. She had almost forgotten how to sit in a cab. ...

"This is Flavour and Blades."

Lights were already in the streets, and the great windows of the shop were filled with light. A black crowd under umbrellas was passing. Mrs. Turner had kept a careful eye on the dial, and paid the cabman exactly what it marked. Then she hurried away to get out of the rain.

But the cabman came after her.

"Here, what d'ye call this? You might give me somethin' over. I found the place for you, didn't I?"

She had not the courage to dispute there in the street. She was too bewildered. She gave him another sixpence, and hurried through the swingdoors.

A man approached her.

"What can we have the pleasure——"

"Please, I want to see Sir Lawson Flavour himself."

The man looked at her closely and then became suddenly interested in something outside in the street.

"I'm afraid not," he said with a smile. "Sir Lawson never sees even important people without an appointment."

"But I have an appointment. Mr. Parry, the banker, of Palebrook.— Please let me see him."

And after some rummaging, she produced the letter she had received from the firm. It looked damp and not very clean. The man read it with some interest.

"Perhaps you had better step this way."

He led her to a lift, and went along with her to an upper storey. Then he brought her through various rooms to one where there were half a dozen men and women writing.

A man came forward, and the other said to him, "This—er—lady has an appointment with the chief."

He passed on the letter and departed. The other man read the letter, looked at Mrs. Turner, and then opened a large gold watch and closed it with a snap.

"You're two hours behind the time mentioned in this letter. I don't know whether Sir Lawson will see you now. Punctuality is the rule here."

"I assure you, sir, it was not my fault. The London train and the Waterloo train got mixed——"

But the gentleman didn't want her explanations. "Just take a seat and I'll find out."

He came back in a moment, beckoned to her, and preceded her into a large and expensively furnished room, where a man sat by himself lounging in an easy-chair.

"Mrs. Turner, sir."

He bowed and withdrew.

The man in the chair raised himself up slightly and looked at the tall woman in black standing before him.

"You may sit down."

Thereupon she seated herself gingerly on one of the expensive chairs. She caught sight of herself in a mirror opposite, and instinctively she put up her hand to straighten her hat and arrange her hair. Then she stopped, for Sir Lawson Flavour was staring at her.

He was a florid, handsome man about fifty-five or sixty, very neatly dressed, with well-brushed fair hair streaked with grey, a clear blue eye, and the complexion of robust health. He looked surly, dissatisfied, selfish, and domineering, but, with all that, a good deal more amiable than the two understrappers she had dealt with.

"I agreed to see you, Mrs. Turner, because my old friend, Mr. Parry, desired me to particularly. You know them?"

"Yes," said she.

"Ah, charming man. Charming family. Charming place, Palebrook. I know it well. Now, what can you do?"

She hesitated. She thought of all the things she had done in her life. But she could not explain to this big man; she felt shy and uncertain and chilled to the bone. She pitched on the first thing that came into her head. "I can design frocks."

"Well," said Sir Lawson Flavour, "if I've interviewed one woman this year who can do that, I've interviewed a hundred. They all can do it. We've really got no use for that kind of thing. Can't you do anything else?"

Mrs. Turner tried to think of an answer which would please him. She was silent.

"Come, speak out. I can't invent work for you, you know. Mr. Parry—my old friend Mr. Parry—wrote me vaguely that you were a capable woman, but we have dozens of that kind of woman coming here. Whenever people don't know what to do with their daughter they say, 'Let's find her a well-paid billet at Flavour and Blades!' I've had half the peerage in this room, male and female, trying to stick in some distant cousin. But that's not business. What I want is a woman who knows something special and knows she knows it."

She felt she was throwing away a chance—a horrible feeling—perhaps the chance of her life; but she could not speak out. There was a sort of numbness all over her as if she were drugged. Cold, lack of food, the anxiety and worry she had already gone through to-day, and also, no doubt, the irresolution of the poor before the wealthy, conspired to intimidate her.

"I've designed some dresses in Palebrook. I made them up too. They were very much liked."

Sir Lawson Flavour looked at her pityingly. "Palebrook? That's no good. Have you been at the opera lately?"

"No."

"Ah, there you are! You can't do things unless you move about. Even if you live in the country you should stir about—run up to town, and go to the opera and the smart restaurants, and decent races in the season. Also, run over to Paris. That's how you pick up ideas."

"Yes," said Mrs. Turner, and she wondered if the blond, well-fed man had the least notion of what it was to be poor—beat—down to the dregs.

"You're rather older than we like to employ women here. You must be—I should say about thirty-two, eh?"

It was the only pleasure that had happened to her that day. She threw a triumphant glance into the mirror, and at that moment the poor thing looked really handsome.

"Not quite," she replied deliberately.

"No? Well, I don't often make mistakes about people's ages."

He rose, and she rose too. She was reckless; she felt that he did not mean to hire her.

"Good-bye," she said flippantly. "Thank you so much."

Sir Lawson glanced at her, but he was talking on the telephone.

"Ask Mr. Bull to come here."

And in a moment a dark, good-looking young man appeared, evidently a Hebrew, notwithstanding his superlatively English name.

"Who did you say wanted to see me?" inquired Sir Lawson.

Mr. Bull came very near and spoke in a low voice. "It's Captain Dover. He says he has a message from your son."

Sir Lawson looked considerably annoyed. "Very well, I suppose I'll see him." His eye fell upon Mrs. Turner standing there. "By the way, Mr. Bull, you might take this lady's name and address, and if any suitable work offers, you can notify her."

In the outer office Mr. Bull shewed he had delightful manners. He encouraged Mrs. Turner very much, and accompanied her to the lift. "You may rely upon it. We'll let you know—you will probably hear from us next week. Good-bye. So very kind of you to have come."

Chapter IV

S HE WAS STANDING IN the rain scanning the buses. She wanted to find the one which would take her on the road to an address in Maida Vale given her in Palebrook. Her trunk, her "luggage in advance," had been sent on there. She was feeling relieved and gratified: she had at last got a position after all the heartbreak; probably a good one. They were so nice about it, particularly Mr. Bull. ...

A man spoke to her. "Can I help you to find your way? I saw you upstairs just now."

He was one of the clerks. She thanked him and explained where she wanted to go. "I'm so glad I am going to work here," she added, tossing her head backward in the direction of the shop.

The man looked at her dubiously and a little sadly.

"Well," he said, "I hope it is not of much importance to you. But it would be cruel to keep you in uncertainty if you set much store by it. You are not going to get anything out of Flavour and Blades."

"But Mr. Bull—Sir Lawson Flavour himself——"

She gasped. The street seemed to be sinking under her.

"Yes," said the man slowly, "I heard what Mr. Bull said. I suppose you came well recommended and they want to let you down easy. They'll keep your name before them right enough—they'll keep it before them for the next twenty years."

He looked in front of him across the street.

"When you're as old as I am, you'll know that people like our chief here, Sir Lawson Flavour, make all the nice promises themselves, and go back on them through their secretaries. This will be your bus. Good-bye—good luck."

Chapter V

S HE DID NOT TAKE the bus. She walked straight ahead towards the Marble Arch in the rain. Her body was broken with fatigue, her head on fire. She did not want to believe what the man had said; that would be too stupid. How was she to live? She had only a sovereign left. She was so terrified that she stopped and went a little way up a quiet street to make sure she had it still in her purse.

At the Marble Arch a policeman gave her some directions and put her in the right bus. There was no room inside, so she climbed to the top and sat there shuddering.

"I'm going to be ill. That's a great joke. I wonder how I can afford it?"

The bus rattled on. There was some fog. Now and then she had spasms of giddiness from lack of food. ...

She would pawn some clothes—yes, and her wedding-ring. It was rather thin, but it would fetch something. It was impossible to go back to Palebrook. She would have to look around in London to-morrow ... next day. ...

She passed some cheap eating-houses. She would have liked to stop, to get some soup, and rest. But to spend money on food when there were lodgings to be faced, fees for agencies, expenses of going about London, and only a pound in the world! "Have you been at the opera lately? You should go to the smart restaurants, run over to Paris. ..." Who said that? It seemed ages ago. She wondered if she was delirious, and cursed her nerves.

She heard the conductor call out the name of her street. She clambered down and asked him the way.

"Don't know," he said brutally. "Get off the step."

After all, it was not so far: she found it without much trouble. Bed at last and dry clothes!

Chapter VI

T HE LANDLADY WAS OLD and looked like an invalid.

"I never expected you to-night," she said. "Haven't you got any box?"

"But my trunk is here already."

"What trunk?"

The trunk had not been delivered. It had been delayed, or sent to the wrong address. She could never go back to Waterloo for her bag—she felt too cold and sick.

She followed the landlady up to the top of the house.

"You said in your letter you wanted a cheap room, my dear—the cheapest I'd got. It's all ready."

It was a small, narrow room without carpet. A camp-bedstead half filled it. Although there was no fire-place in the room, it was full of smoke so thick that Mrs. Turner began to cough.

"Have you got a penny? When you want gas you just drop a penny in this box here. That's it! Now it'll burn for a little while. You look tired, my dear. As you haven't got a box, could you let me have some money down? It's the way we do in London."

Mrs. Turner gave her last sovereign, and asked: "Could you give me some change?"

"Change?" The landlady looked at the coin. "Well, I'll see in the morning. Good night."

She went and then came back.

"I was near forgetting the key. Here, I'll put it on the inside."

Mrs. Turner listened to her heavy tread on the stairs. Somebody was singing in the street. …

Chapter VII

THE LIGHT WAS BECOMING dimmer. She remembered what the woman had said about the penny and felt in her purse, but she hadn't one left.

Then she broke down. She wept and wept. All the tears she had been keeping back all through the miserable, unlucky day poured from her eyes. All her life—all her revolt and despair.

"God knows I've never had a decent chance. … Oh, Harry, Harry, I wish I was where you are now!"

It was her dead husband, the gaol-bird, she cried to—the only human being she had really known in her lonely life. Her tears ended in a fit of coughing.

The light got lower and lower and gradually went out. She unpinned her black hat and took off her old boots. Then she pulled down the cover of the bed and flung herself into it without undressing, and lay there staring into the darkness. She was so tired that she could not sleep.

A Case of Conscience

Chapter I

HE FELT IT WAS impossible to go that afternoon. This meant that it was impossible to go anywhere, for of places to go to, her house was as satisfactory as any. But the streets were hot, and his rooms were cool and pleasant. The flowers in the room nodded in the small wind that blew through the windows; the leaves on the lime-trees whispered; the pigeons down on the road cooed drowsily. So quiet! He took a sheet of paper and wrote:

> "DEAR MRS. WALDEN,—Do forgive me for not turning up. I am simply overwhelmed with a rush of work which it would be fatal to leave."

He paused, and wondered what to say next. He liked Peggy Walden, and he was anxious not to offend her. He reflected that he had rather abandoned her of late, and she was perhaps feeling sore. He rummaged among excuses. Then he remembered that he had seen her at a distance in the Park last Tuesday week, and he was sure she had not seen him. He took up his pen again.

> "I was unlucky not to find you at home when I called last Tuesday week. When I go to you, you are out, and when you are in I can't go.—Yours ever,
>
> "RICHARD CHARTERS."

He sent the letter away, and lounged very tranquilly through the rest of the afternoon.

Chapter II

CHARTERS WAS IN BRUSSELS when he got a reply to his letter. From a bundle handed to him by the porter in the hall of the hotel he selected first an envelope with Mrs. Walden's reckless writing, and, as he was really uneasy about her mood, he stood where he was to read what she said.

> "DEAR DICKIE,—I am frightfully sorry to have missed you when you called. The servant never said a word to me about it, and I wanted to see

you most particularly. Call me up on the telephone when you get this
and tell me when you will come.—Yours,

"M. W.

"P.S.—I am getting rid of Linda, my maid, and am going to Brighton till
I can find another. So don't come to the house till you hear from me."

Charters took this in carelessly, and felt relieved that she was not
angry with him. Then, when he had read his other letters, he strolled
into the street. As he walked in the sunshine, pleasantly conscious of
the bravery and noise of the Boulevard, he was in that state of hazy
enjoyment which people often experience at moments when they have
nothing special to rejoice or trouble about. There was nothing really to
bring the postscript of Mrs. Walden's letter back to his mind. Come,
however, it did, on a corner, as he was waiting to cross the roadway. "I
am getting rid of Linda, my maid."

He was a man who possessed a conscience which had been battered
by long intercourse with the world into a serviceable hardness equal
to most campaigns, and he had never in his life been troubled by what
some call a morbid scrupulosity. Nevertheless, he found himself all at
once extremely uncomfortable about Mrs. Walden's servant. He was,
in fact, so overcome that he stood where he was on the corner, staring at the pavement. For if Mrs. Walden was discharging her maid,
it was undoubtedly on account of the careless lie he had written by
way of excuse in his letter. Mrs. Walden would blame the maid for
not telling her he had called; the maid would deny that he had called;
Mrs. Walden, of course, would never question his statement; and the
end would be just what had happened—the maid would be turned off.
She would be turned off, too, without a character.

Charters remembered her well—a tall, handsome, broad-shouldered
girl, with black eyes and a vivid complexion. He could picture no one
in the world more likely to come to grief than this girl, if she were
once thrown out of the orderly courses of life. Unprotected, desperate,
she would make but the briefest struggle against the irresistible current
which would sweep her down headlong to a sordid kind of vagabond-
age, without any pause at the half-way houses which border the route.
She would not be in a position to find the half-way houses; it would be
one swift dive. Charters felt his heart freeze as he pictured the stages
of her wretched career and its likelihoods. The streets, the hospital, the
gaol—worse—worse! And he would be the cause of it all! Of all the sin

and squalor and suffering which this unhappy soul would have to bear during her passage through the world, he would be the agent. All the metaphysics, all the arguments of fate, all the proofs of the unimportance of the individual, could not shake that black truth.

The Boulevard Anspach is not a street to aid a man with an agitated mind. He was glad to regain the large, stupid hall of his hotel, and he sat there pondering what he had better do. Should he write to Mrs. Walden and explain? But he detested explaining anything by letter, which generally, in his experience, involved another explanation. Eventually, he asked for his bill and took his ticket for London.

Chapter III

AFTER ABOUT TEN DAYS, Mrs. Walden rang him up on the telephone and asked him to come to her house that afternoon.

Once there, when the maid—the new maid—brought in tea, Charters saw his opportunity, and braced himself for his task. Now that he was in front of the explanation, he found it considerably more unpleasant and difficult than he had thought it would be.

"I see you have managed to get a new maid," he began.

"Yes," she said, "I have managed that. But I miss Linda so much. I shouldn't have minded her lie so much if she hadn't been so brazen about it."

"What lie?"

Mrs. Walden raised her eyebrows. "Dear me, you seem very interested. Oddly enough, it concerned you. You wrote me that you had called; I scolded Linda for not telling me; she swore that you had not called, and became quite troublesome. Did you get any answer when you rang that day?"

Charters did not reply at once.

"Look here," he said huskily, "I want to tell you something. I hope you won't be offended; but Linda told the truth. I never called that afternoon."

He paused, and then finding that she remained silent, he added: "It has given me a lot of worry. I'm sure I am heartily ashamed of myself."

Mrs. Walden poured out a cup of tea.

"So you ought to be," she said. "To fall to making paltry excuses with me, of all people!"

She paused, hummed a little, and then added: "However, it doesn't matter."

"Then I suppose it will be all right about Linda?"

"About Linda?" Mrs. Walden stared. "Let me see—where are we?"

"Yes. You know I was the cause of her being turned away. She had really done nothing. And on the terms she left you, she will probably have great difficulty in finding a place. I thought—that is, I was hoping you might decide to take her back."

"Take her back!" cried Mrs. Walden. "What a preposterous notion! No, indeed! I have no intention of taking her back. Besides, I could hardly find her."

"But can't you let her know," pleaded Charters, "that you will now give her a good character? At present she would not dare to refer any-one to you."

"I tell you again I don't know where she is. I am no longer interested in her."

"Then I must be interested in her," declared Charters, and he stood up. "I must find her out, and give her a sum of money, and help her in any way I can. It is my fault if she is thrown on the streets, and all the evil that happens to her will rest on my head. Can't you help me to find her?"

Mrs. Walden smoothed her skirt. "I think you are excessively mor-bid. I believe she has a mother living somewhere in London," she added coldly, "and my cook may possibly know the address. I will ring and ask. ..."

The mother, it turned out, lived at Catford; and the next day Charters, possessed of the street and number, made his way out there. It was a long, dreary street, lined with uniform little red-brick houses. About half-way down he came upon the number he wanted, and knocked.

Linda's mother was an elderly woman, apparently far gone in drop-sy. She was evidently on bad terms with her daughter, and received Charters' inquiry with considerable sourness. Another woman was sit-ting with her, and it was to her rather than to him she spoke.

"She comes swankin' in here just as I was goin' to bed, and she sez, 'Mother,' she sez, 'I've split with my lady, and I ain't goin' into service no more.' 'Oh,' I sez, 'you bad, wicked girl to come back on your mother who's so poorly.' 'Well,' she sez, pinnin' on her hat, 'I know who'll keep me if my own mother won't!' 'Mark my words, my gal,' I sez, 'men will be your downfall.' Those were my words. I 'aven't seen her since."

The friend, a much younger woman, with a face which indicated powers of gaiety and enjoyment which had never had a fair chance to develop, nodded her approval, and then winked slightly at Charters. He left some money, and went away sorrowful. He could do nothing more, and the misery and evil he had caused must go to swell the great mass of needless sin in the world.

Chapter IV

AT AIX-LES-BAINS, IN THE summer-time, the Casino is decidedly a comfortable place. There you sit in a rocking-chair on a balcony, sleepily watching the birds on the lawn, the leaves of the trees blown by the soft wind, the flowers—pansy, geranium, hyacinth, asphodel— which are about everywhere. A band, at a respectful distance, plays a slow, hushed kind of music. Cool-looking ladies, charmingly dressed, pass in and out, or sit down in groups on the balcony. There is nothing at all to do. To the left is a good restaurant, if you feel disposed to eat.

Charters was smoking a cigarette and attempting to read a novel, but for the last minute or two he had been also eyeing discreetly one of the cool-looking ladies who was seated some distance off. He was persuaded that he had seen her somewhere before, but he could not for the life of him think where. He thought over faces and places dreamily … drowsily. …

"Mr. Charters, do you remember me?"

He started broad awake, with a contented sense of the pleasant vision before him.

"Do you know, I've been trying to think for the last quarter of an hour. It is stupid of me, but I confess——"

"Oh," she explained frankly, "I am Linda."

"Linda!"

"Yes; Linda, who used to be at Mrs. Walden's three years ago. You used to often speak to me. Don't you remember me?"

"I should think I do," said Charters.

Linda! He felt as if he had been carrying a heavy weight on his back and the string had suddenly been cut. For Linda did not look as if she had suffered. She looked prosperous and handsome—a little florid. She was clad in blue muslin and old lace, and her hair was miraculously dressed.

"May I get you a chair?" faltered Charters. "There's something I have to talk to you about."

Linda sat down, and glanced round her as if in search of a subject of conversation.

"How funny to meet like this!" she found.

"Yes. Look here, I have to make a confession to you, and to ask your pardon, if you can give it to me. I am the cause of your——"

From the habit of long brooding over her supposed wretchedness he was going to say "misfortune"; but seeing Linda sitting there so placid, so obviously content with her treatment by the world, it occurred to him that "misfortune" was hardly the word for the situation.

"I am the cause of all your trouble," he went on. "I told Mrs. Walden I had called, but really I had not called. I tried to put it right with her, but it was too late. Then I went to see your mother, but she didn't know where you were. God knows I have been punished enough since. I have had a trial for manslaughter constantly going on in my breast. I can truly say that I have had no pleasure since the day you disappeared, for every pleasure has been poisoned by the thought of what I did and what you must be suffering."

He paused, wiped his face with his handkerchief, and then laughed ruefully.

Linda laughed too, but there were surprise and a shine of gratitude in her eyes.

"Oh, dear Mr. Charters, to think of your minding for me like that!" Very self-possessed, she laid her hand on his arm. "Listen. If you did that, I must owe all my good luck to you. You were the making of me. Only for you I'd still be at Mrs. Walden's, while now ..." She glanced over her frock. "Then there's mother. You saw what she was. She treated me most unkindly. But she's had a good house and garden, and a nurse, and a good doctor, and whatever she wants, all through me."

Various solutions offered, and Charters selected the one which will occur to most of those who read this. Contrary to the chances, Linda had found a half-way house! Thinking so, he was all unprepared for what followed.

"Do you remember," she asked, "that friend of Mrs. Walden's, Mr. György Dirak?"

"The Hungarian jeweller? Yes, I remember him perfectly."

"Well, he used often to be waiting while Mrs. Walden was out, and then he'd talk to me to pass the time. Only two days before the upset, he told me if I ever wanted for anything to come to him. So when mother wouldn't take me in, I went to see him at the Carlton Hotel. He was awfully kind, and he told me I must go out to Buda to look after his two daughters. Well, I did; and—and—one thing led to another, and"—she smiled and tapped the toe of her shoe with her parasol—"we were married last month."

"Good!" said Charters. He looked at her a little resentfully. "If I had only known!—my God, if I had only known! But I congratulate you. You have married a millionaire."

"Yes," assented Linda simply. "He's been awfully good to me. He has gone for a motor-run to-day, but he'll be back to-night. We're staying at the Splendide. Won't you come up and see him?"

Just then a maid approached with her wraps, and Linda sailed off with a gay little nod.

"Then I'll tell him you'll look in some time this evening," she said, over her shoulder.

That was the last time he saw her. He sent a note to the hotel offering some excuse for not turning up—"She won't put much faith in my promises," he thought grimly—and took the evening train to Chambéry.

~

Anna Vaddock's Fame

"Un bon tailleur vaut mieux que trois sculpteurs classiques."
"Begin at the end."

FUTURE PROVERBS

Chapter I

I WAS TOILING UP THE Rue de Pigalle in a June glare, pondering what that poor creature had said and wondering what I should do— very depressed in fact—when out of a *zinc*, with a packet of cigarettes in his clutch, came Heller. He hurried up to me, stood, pushed his soft hat back from his forehead, and stared fixedly with his blue northern eyes.

"Are you a Vaddockite?" he asked.

That Heller! It was noon, the street was busy, there was a general uproar of dogs, street vendors, rattling wheels, women's shouts, and a gramophone somewhere overhead squawking "The Girl of the Golden West," but he stood impavid as if he were in a bedroom. He was always possessed by his idea, that man, more than anybody I ever knew. I never saw him laugh. The most he conceded to an amuser was a transient distracted smile. At a theatre with you he would watch an act, perhaps take it in (though I doubt that too), but when the curtain fell he struck at once into his own obsession, remote as possible from the play. Arguello, the Franco-Argentine poet, had a story that one day he was knocked down by a motor and nearly run over, and as he picked himself up and stood muddy and dazed amid a vociferating crowd, up came Heller and seized him by the arm. "You've been run over?" he asked carelessly, as he might have asked if the poet had dropped a match. "Listen! I have become convinced that in writing a tale you must deposit literature. The naked idea. Telegraph language. There's art! Style?—that's the poison, my chap."

I now said to him gropingly, "Vaddockite?" I was Atlantics away.

Up a little further, a wide house-door gaped. He made for it, and under the arch he looked at me interrogatively, anxiously, while he tortured his tan beard with the nervous nicotine-stained fingers of his dead-white hand.

"Vaddock—Anna Vaddock, the Englishwoman. What a genius! A revolutionary. Crisp? Ah, my God! All the back-wash of Renoir—not to say Redon—will go down the sewer with their smudges. Have you seen her lithographs? Pastels? But, my chap," he exclaimed querulously, "you are so odd, so mysterious! You hide yourself away. You get out of step, out of rhythm. Come," he said, moving off, "you must see the great Anna's things. Only two streets to her studio."

I made a show of resistance. It was noon; I was on my way to the restaurant.

Pity came into his eyes, a shade of contempt. "Do you eat regular meals? Is your stomach a slave to clocks? All these people"—he waved his arm to comprise the street—"are now going to eat. They don't want to eat really; each one goes because the other goes. Ants! Have you ever watched ants? My chap, you don't want to eat: you are the victim of habit and the town clock and gregariousness. Art would perish so domesticated. As well have a wife and six children. Come and see Anna Vaddock. You will forget the *manger*."

Chapter II

I DID. I WAS FLABBERGASTED. The big tall woman, with the pale, sensual, treacherous face under flaming-red hair, her well-moulded form clad in a blue print gown and white apron, who moved about gracefully on high laced boots in the clear matted studio, was no more English than the Teutonic Heller himself. She was American, though she had purged all trace of accent; but I spotted her by her persistence in alluding to her ancestors. But she was an astonishing artist, not waterlogged at all by the waves of Heller's enthusiasm. The thick black lines in her drawings were as brutal as a porter's oath, as adroit as a prizefighter's punch. These people of hers, stripped to the buff, had no souls, but every ounce of their bodies was valued. Here was ale, the strong ale of art. There was no passion, no emphatic gesture; but what was there was sheer lubricity and stir, and it was truly that which made her important. Two or three of the paintings made you quiver when you approached them with their shameless colour—heady, sensual colour, provoked by touches as delicate and skilful as if she were touching flesh. When the artist gave me her cool, firm hand at parting, I took it with a certain thrill, a certain awe, and also with a feeling of thankfulness that the operations of that hand happened to be in art.

"Is she known?" I said in the street. "Has she been published, written about?"

"No more than you. Let us go and eat. It is a quarter to three. The commercials whom you imitate will have finished their digestion. In the empty restaurant, untroubled by the snouts of statesmen and millionaires, we shall organize the fame of Anna Vaddock."

"We? Who?"

"Do you know Leverly? He is an Englishman, an English correspondent. He has great influence in London, they tell me. I have an appointment with him at the restaurant at three."

The hill crested, I was for turning into the *Rat Mort*, but Heller steered me across the street and we tabled in the café on the opposite corner, which I have made up my mind was the one where the two damsels of Villiers de l'Isle-Adam's story had their dignified scene.

"You noticed how I dragged you from the *Rat Mort*, my chap," said Heller. "I never put my foot into that place before twelve at night. Other places have their ghosts in the dark, but the ghosts gather there in the daytime. Here's Leverly."

And there came up a short man with a fatigued, capacious, hair-sown head, who wore glasses upon his astonished and haggard eyes which squinted. He gave us a flaccid hand, sat down negligently, and glancing about the room emitted some opinions, mostly without interest. There was question of music and literature, of sculpture and of psychology, of feminism, of occultism, and of various other things. With the coffee Heller docked him at Anna Vaddock.

"Boom is what she needs. The loud timbrel. Noise, my chaps, that will crack old Public's eardrums. Let us form ourselves into a brass band."

But Leverly shook his head. "You are up the wrong avenue. We believe in Anna, don't we? Really and truly? Well, we don't want her to be accepted as a success, but as a genius. We don't want to make her popular, but notorious. With the examples of Whistler and Beardsley before his mind, every artist who knows his business would pledge his soul to be unpopular. Then, you see, the real duffers can come in too. They're among the neglected. It's consoling."

He took off his glasses and wiped them with the table-napkin.

"The excessive disdains of which people are victims make them interesting. What we want to do about Anna is to get her abused. Real abuse, you know, not a little sneer in a corner. All the big thunder—obscurity, vulgarity, immorality, and the rest of it."

"Something like: 'Her work is tainted by a suggestion of morbid sensuality very difficult to locate,'" offered Heller.

Leverly grinned admiration. "That's the music. And sounds true—a great advantage. It must be bellowed. After all, when a book or a play or a symphony or a picture is hooted, there is only one person really interesting, and that is the author of it. So Vaddock's pedestal will be built of the missiles hurled at her. I'll manage the British Press."

"Vienna and Munich and Dresden can be left to me," said Heller, "safely. As for you, my chap,"—he turned to my side—"you can do the praise in the little obscure papers that appear for two numbers and then collapse. You're about in tune with that sort of thing; you're not serious. Have you ever read Bergson, or William James, or that wonderful American professor—I forget his name—who writes about aesthetics? *Non, n'est-ce pas?* But there must be praise somewhere to emphasize the abuse, and praise from the little student papers will help on the big move. And it will come well from you. Nobody will take it seriously."

Leverly agreed. He raised his little glass of brandy, squinting as if he had cut a lemon. "I drink to the failure of Anna Vaddock," he said.

"Prosit!" shouted Heller.

Chapter III

I MUDDLE THINGS UP SO when I write, or I should have said before that at the time we were making our plan we knew that the great Anna had arranged for a show in London some six months later, in the gallery of a dealer supposed to be friendly to the "advanced" of all kinds. Our campaign opened a few months before the show, and, though I say it myself, it was astonishingly well done. For weeks there had been dull preparative growling. Once the doors opened all the dogs were unleashed. The big papers were incredibly scurrilous and insolent. The American correspondent, never famous for an amicable reception of the unusual, yelled. Perhaps the best of all were the caricatures of the Vaddock touch in the comic papers.

Six weeks the show was to run, and at the end of the fifth I managed to reach London. My main thought was to get a glimpse of poor Anna's things before they were packed away.

It was a bright afternoon, and as I went through the streets I fancied there would be a few people, thinking themselves very brave, in the gallery, moving about discreetly and talking in low voices, as people do in a house where there has been a scandal.

I ran into a throng of halted carriages and motor-cars. My thought, of course, was that something big and social was going on near by. But no! A crowd, a rich-looking crowd, clogged the door of the gallery. More were arriving every minute. Footmen, distracted, struggled to reach their employers. Royalty, I gathered, had either just arrived or just left. Thrown by the surge against the wall, I read on a poster—an undeniable Vaddock poster in black and red—that the show would remain open still for several weeks. My heart paused. How could one deny in the very teeth of the event? Anna Vaddock was become a success.

I don't quite remember how I got into that heated room. I know I was dishevelled bodily and mentally. The Duchess of Leamington passed, talking art with authority. Braced against a railing in a corner, to save myself from being carried away in her wash, I made out Posseback and Minster, those two critics who are always pioneers when a thing begins to look safe. In front of me, a ponderous gentleman in rough tweeds, a well-known American millionaire, came to anchor with the dealer, the founder of the feast.

"She's an honour to our great country," the millionaire decided. "You can take that from me right here. We Americans always wait for success before we take any notice. We don't encourage artists who can't make money; we don't want that kind of truck lying about. This woman is a money-getter. She is *some*—and considerably more. The Metropolitan Museum in New York will be proud to enshrine her work. I'm going to turn myself loose on Anna Vaddocks."

The dealer looked at him admiringly. "You know a good investment."

After that, I battled to the door. In the rush I just missed not seeing a man who was sauntering up and down on the opposite side of the street. I drew a breath of salvation and ran over to him. It was Heller.

"Well, how do you like it?" He smiled evilly.

"She's a public success!" I gasped. "A success first shot, too. How do you make it out?"

"How do I make it out?" He beat the kerb-stone with his stick. "I don't try to make it out. It's all up. *Fichue*, Anna Vaddock! How can you go about complaining that an artist is neglected who persists in being popular? Nothing could hold her. There must have been a flaw in her somewhere and none of us saw it. You see, my chap, there are some people born for revolt, and others who lean against the recognized lines as hard as they will bear, and one is often mistaken for the other. It's the second that win—win this sort of thing." He swept with his arm. "What can you do with a revolutionary whom all the world accepts the moment the flag is raised? You can make out the Vaddock's career from this point. Big expensive studio at Hampstead; portraits of the aristocracy, of a few safe actresses, of royalty; two pictures in the Academy regularly till old age. Great ornament to British Art. Apotheosis in the Tate Gallery. Ah. ..."

Two ladies had crossed the street from the exhibition, and were getting into a carriage which stood near us. Then they drove off.

Heller looked after them disgustfully. "Fashionable picture buyers, my chap," he muttered. "Always in the vanguard. People who are so anxious to be on the spot when the clock strikes that they don't know when it has struck. Ten years hence, if they ever let the likes of us into their houses, they'll show the Vaddocks on the wall and tell us"—he minced outrageously—"'Oh, *I* discovered Anna Vaddock when hardly anybody had a word to say for her. Don't you think I'm *rather* clever?'— Ach, Gott!" He stared gloomily at the throngs.

"How does Leverly take it?" I asked, to divert him.

"Damn him! He's the worst of all. He's going about saying, 'I told you so.' The Discoverer! Picked her out of the gutter in Paris; brought her to London; organized her show—you know the sort. The only thing he needs now is that the Vaddock would consent to die."

He stretched, affecting unconcern. "Well, I only came to watch the crowds. I'm off to Munich to-night."

~

War Declared

Chapter I

THE CLUB-ROOM WAS CROWDED and there was a great noise. Men stood in knots of four or five, shouting, gesticulating, all talking at once. Now and then, amidst the babbled nonsense, some one would say something true and important, and, a little shocked, they would all pause or a moment to consider it, like the wind lulls in a storm. Most of them had drunk too much in their excitement, and they were all very anxious; but their anxiety was different. There were those who were pale, strained, and haggard, and others red-faced, bragging, defiant. The sweat stood in little drops on the foreheads of some and shone as they leaned forward, arguing, with feverish eyes. One big man, with a fair beard, rested his back against the wall and gazed vacantly before him, repeating monotonously, "They will march … they will march. …" Nobody took any notice of him. Sometimes, somebody swinging his arms would upset a tray of glasses which a waiter was carrying, and there would be a crash which nobody heeded. The whole room was overhung by one thick blue cloud of tobacco smoke, which blurred the little balls of electric light. And meanwhile, from the street outside, we could hear troops as they passed the door—the irregular trampling of cavalry, the dull, steady thud of infantry, drums beating just two taps for step, the occasional squeal of a bugle, and cries that sounded far off.

I was sitting in a corner with the latest edition of the evening paper, and it was some time before I saw him. As usual he was talking, talking, with his air of profound conviction about the importance of what he was saying. There he was with his eternal look of a deputy-professor in a small college; his clean-shaven, priggish face—the pale, leaden face of a man who takes no exercise; his glasses on his nose, from which a thin gold chain hung down; black cut-away coat with the tails too short; a crumpled vest; trousers baggy at the knees; and elastic-sided boots not very well cleaned. His auburn hair, parted in the middle, waved naturally, and would have given a touch of distinction to most faces; but it only emphasized the nullity of his. His nose was very short, and his cheeks puffed out rather full at the ends of the mouth, as is often seen in inexhaustible talkers. He held a newspaper twisted like a club in one hand, and he brought it down now and then with a soft slap in the palm of the other. How often I had seen him do that! How well I knew his tricks!

And though he talked and talked, nobody seemed to listen to him, and he didn't seem to mind. No doubt he was saying his same old platitudes which he always brought out with so much confidence. Occasionally, with the newspaper in front of me, I heard him uttering bits of phrases which were there before my eyes in its columns.

It was getting near dinner-time, and the groups began to break up. People shook hands with some fervour and made exact arrangements to meet, guarding against the uncertainties of to-morrow. Him I saw too shaking hands in his pompous, rather condescending way, which was so ridiculous! I could feel that loose clammy pressure—I had felt it so often! He shook hands with as many as he could, gravely, as if he shared some immensely important secret. Ah, how I despised him, the wretched prig! What a bumptious, self-satisfied, absurd ass!

Chapter II

THE CLUB-ROOM WAS NEARLY empty now. The drunken man, tired of leaning against the wall, had fallen into a big chair and gone to sleep. You could hear his snores. My man stood in the middle of the room pulling on his gloves. He settled his glasses firmer on his nose and looked about, unwilling to leave if there was still anyone to talk to left. He recognized the snoring man; his face brightened; he went over to him. He called his name very loud; he even shook him. But the sleeper persisted in sleeping. Then he flung a despairing glance all round and spotted me in my corner.

"The devil!" I said to myself.

For he was coming towards me deliberately, composedly, with his stupid, affable smile, never doubting his welcome. He held out his hand.

"How are you?"

Then he gave a dry laugh. "None of us can be very well. This war——"

He swallowed something in his throat and added importantly: "If you want to know my private opinion——"

And he continued talking, talking, a lot of twaddle which nobody with an ounce of sense could value. The best of it I had just been reading in the paper. As I looked at this person with his short chin, the muddy complexion of the sedentary and housed, and his dull eyes behind the glasses, I thought I had never seen a figure less like a soldier, and the absurdity of his having any opinion at all on military matters struck me more than ever.

"I'm going home," I said, after about ten minutes of it. I spoke unamiably, hoping to discourage him, for he lived near me. But of course he was not going to miss a chance.

He held up his gloved hands and with one pointed to the other. "You see I'm just off. We'll go together, shall we?"

There was nothing else for it. As we stepped into the street he took my arm.

"If you want to know my private opinion——"

Alas! ... The streets were rather empty and not very well lighted. Squads of soldiers kept marching by in the roadway or on the footpath. I noticed the badly fitting uniforms; and one young officer, in command of a small body of men whom he was bringing along in narrow file close to the houses, looked conscious and ashamed of his coat, with the sleeves too short and crumpled breast. The officer caught my eye and frowned surlily, thinking I was turning him into ridicule.

Then, as we came to a corner and turned into the square, we saw halted under the bare trees, with the grim black mass of the church in the background, a squadron of cavalry, probably waiting for some special orders before marching. He waved his arm towards them.

"I must be going along in the rear of those fellows."

I stopped dead and stared at him, thunderstruck. "You?"

"Oh, yes." He went on in his intolerable detached voice of a lecturer demonstrating easy truths to a class of poor intelligence. "Patriotism, whether the result of instinct or education, is certainly very strong. At a time like this, when our hearths and homes are threatened, one feels the sentiment rising to the surface. ..."

He continued, ladling out his nauseous platitudes, and, as I listened to him, I was nearly blind with fury. For now I knew I should have to go. All the afternoon it had been hanging uneasily about my heart that I ought to go, and I had tried not to think of it. I didn't want to go. I had my habits, my comforts. ...

Chapter III

A N ICY WIND SQUALLED across the square, and the snow began to fall. The squadron never budged. And I saw myself marching, marching in the teeth of a death-dealing blast; marching and stumbling over uneven roads, with my hand frozen to the butt of the rifle; marching dog-tired with eyes closed. And if I changed the position of my stiff arm my gun would slip; and if I stood still, somebody would push me from behind; and if I fell, the company would trample me down. …

And I saw my room, waiting for me only a few hundred yards off, with my slippers before the snapping fire, the room warm in the glow of it, the curtains drawn, the cutter in the book, the gleam of napkins and bottles for a good dinner.

No, I didn't want to go. But this sheep, this dolt, whom I had always despised, was going! He had a mother and a wife and child; doubtless they loved him. Nobody in the world cared whether I lived or died. And his house was only three doors from mine. How could I bear to pass his door day by day and realize that he was out there marching in rain and sleet, lying hard and cold, halted behind some improvised shelter of dead horses and broken carts, while I was going comfortably to the club, the restaurant, to pay a visit … ?

Suddenly, out of the squadron, rose the tortured blare of a bugle. The bugler was perhaps cold, or a new hand, for the sound came wavering and broken, and there was something about it boding, lugubrious, even sinister, as the notes were thrown back by the wall of the great church. And I hated him for forcing me to go.

"Good-bye, good-bye!" I cried furiously.

I caught his look of astonishment and disappointment as I hurried away. I hastened along the stark street of high, dark buildings where we both lived, and when I was just at my door I saw him run across the road and overtake two men, and under a street lamp I could make out that there he was at it again, talking importantly, giving his "private opinion." …

And yet the sergeant of his company told me that the very afternoon he was killed he was saying, as he cleaned his gun, that the thing which had impressed him most in life was the real loneliness of all men.

He was killed doing something there was no great need to do, but it was a good thing, and he was not bound to do it. Part of his shoulder and neck were torn away. Yet he did not die at once. He crawled a bit, till they carried him out of the danger zone, and he died while the doctor was palping and gathering the wound.

"Who was he?" asked the doctor, as he wiped his hands, staring down at the dirty, blood-smeared face.

"I b'lieve that's him they called Samson—some joke about the jawbone."

"Well," said the doctor, "I call him a brave man," and he touched his cap. Those standing about the ambulance, in a smell of wounds and disinfectants, did the same.

~

The Dark Day

IN THAT CITY, THE hospital, the court-house, and the gaol lay hard by each other. On the wide steps before the buildings beggars sat all day. Some had no shirts, and their skin and bones showed, and their sores. Their clothes were torn in strips like grid-irons. On the faces of all, when they were looked at, came that false grimace, full of humility, of people with no means of defence who are not sure whether they have a right to live.

One of themselves was inside. ...

They talked in guttural voices about that. The women showed perhaps more protest than the men, but men and women had the vague, dim look of animals used to the whip. Men played cards on the steps with the usual muttered quarrel and oaths. Women held skeletons of infants to their shrunken breasts. They all looked bestial, ready for any crime.

Some of them talked. These wretches condemned from the cradle, that society crushes and kills, these elementary skulls, brought the world to judgment. "Is there any justice to-day?" Some of them, vague communists, would resettle the bases of social life and make all equal and fraternal—scraps of rubbish remembered from those who had befooled them for ages. Others proclaimed themselves anarchists—the propaganda by act—abrogation of the old morals. ...

Meanwhile they did nothing, and the privileged who alighted from time to time from their vehicles and moved up the steps laughed and spat at them.

A stir, it shuffling of feet, a long groan like a flock of sheep heard in the distance—it was the mother who came out, a black shawl over her head and a rosary of beads in her hand. Through tears she looked at all this swarm. Then her frightened, wild eyes stared at the hospital below with its great white door. The rain fell like melted lead. Then she passed along the grey walls of the gaol.

There was a gust of fog in the street and the hard rain. The street looked wide and empty—the hard, black street. A hearse coming back from a funeral went by quickly at a trot. A thin cat coughed in the gutter. She was angry because she could not keep the tears from trickling down her face. Luckily it was raining—raining. ...

Then she saw a little crowd like a black lump at a corner. It was because of her tears that the crowd looked like a black lump, and when she got near she found it broke up into bits. They were all watching something on the ground. A policeman looked too. So did a lawyer she had seen in the court.

It was a mouse, and the were having a game with it. One had it under his foot; then he lifted his foot and let it run a bit till another put his foot on it—not hard—oh no—just enough to keep it a prisoner for a second and then let it run on again. Once a boy brought his foot down a little too hard and the mouse squeaked.

"Willie! Willie!" bawled a woman, "you'll kill it, and then you'll have no more fun."

She looked down among the boots and she saw the eyes of the little brown mouse. They looked like the other eyes—back there—not long ago. A fleck of blood was on his nose, and as he ran he left a thin smear of blood on the black slime of the road.

Ugh! … And it rained and the fog rolled pitiless and yellow. She felt herself hemmed in by people full of suspicion, who spied on her and wished her evil. Would she ever know peace again? She drew her shawl closer and counted the years since her marriage day. Then deliberately she pulled off her wedding-ring and dropped that and the rosary-beads in the gutter, and walked on with a rigid face.

Some time later she came back and sought for them, but they were gone.

~

The Speculation in Mrs. Catling

"Whether the object of your faith be real or false, you will nevertheless obtain the same effects."

PHILLIPUS AUREOLUS THEOPHRASTUS BOMBASTUS VON HOHENHEIM, *called* PARACELSUS

Chapter I

ALFRED NODD, THE YOUNG and sympathetic art-connoisseur, whose praises need no further singing, in one of his cruises through remote districts of the West of England in search of those treasures hid away in cottages and old manor-houses which may occasionally even yet be picked up for a trifle and sold again for extremely interesting sums, entered, rather brusquely, it must be confessed, Mrs. Catling's tiny dwelling. And there, after having scanned with a trained eye the meagre details of the room, and even the vestments of ancient Mrs. Catling herself—who might (one never knows) have been wearing some ornament of some long-dead ancestor—he hauled, with as little ceremony as a bailiff taking possession, down from the shelf, a large leather-bound Bible. A treasure—and what a treasure!

Old Mrs. Catling protested feebly, but Nodd with feverish hand was turning the leaves.

"Shall we say five pounds?" The meagreness of the offer, compared to the sum he hoped to realize, made his voice tremble.

Mrs. Catling began to cry. "You leave my Bible alone. What yer mean by comin' into people's places and pullin' their things about as if they was in the workhus! The very idea!"

Alfred Nodd turned upon her his celebrated searchlight smile which has so often brought a bargain to a favourable issue, when he is dealing with titled or wealthy clients.

"Fifteen?" he insinuated.

"No, nor a hundred-fifteen neither. I'll not sell my Bible—you leave my Bible alone!"—a response uttered with such vigour, and followed by such a blank of stubborn mutism, that Nodd, wonderfully skilful in such matters, decided that the battle was lost.

He rose with the intention of regaining his motor-car, left at the inn. But suddenly he had a very natural inspiration. Why not pick up the Bible and walk out of the cottage? Nobody was near, and the old woman's feeble cries would remain unheeded. Certainly, there is not anyone that knows him well who will do our friend Alfred Nodd the injustice to believe that he, a millionaire to-day by his unaided exertions, known and quoted upon the marts of Europe and America, was withheld from robbing an insignificant old cottage-woman by any ridiculous scruples of conscience. His clear brain had long ago perceived that all that kind of thing is twaddle.

But his hand already outstretched, trembling with eagerness, dropped, and his eye sought the window at the sound of a step outside. A man was at the little gate.

Thereupon Alfred Nodd adjusted his cap on his dark, fine-spun hair and took up his stick.

"Good-bye," he said blandly. "So very nice of you to let me see your beautiful book."

At the gate he stood aside to let the other man come in.

"*There's* a wealthy woman," said Nodd, jerking his head back at the cottage. He felt that if he could not get the book himself, he might as well boost up its value, for he was, like most of us, ready enough to do a good turn when it was not inconvenient.

"Wealthy? Poor old Mrs. Catling!" The doctor, who was attending her under the Insurance Act, laughed. "I wish she was. I come to see her often enough to make it profitable."

"Ah, the doctor!" Nodd became a little confidential and explained his importance. "Believe me, doctor, she has a Bible in there which is worth a huge sum. The Americans would give anything for it. The late Pierpont Morgan was searching for that very copy for years." ...

"Who do you think is nearly a millionaire?" said the doctor to his wife that evening. "Old Mrs. Catling."

"Say it again and say it slower," said the doctor's wife.

Chapter II

THE NEWS SPREAD. FROM the doctor's wife it reached the parson's wife, and from that opulent spring expatiated over the neighbourhood. Mrs. Catling, who had worked as a charwoman most of her days, had lived of late years extremely neglected, her soul strapped to her body mainly by the Old-Age Pension. Now she became an object of assiduous, if not affectionate care.

"My dear, did you ever? They say old Mrs. Catling's got money to leave."

Particularly interested were certain of her relatives who, having got on in the world, had hitherto ignored her existence, save that on very infrequent visits they were used to give powerful suggestions to her subjective mind as to the propriety of dying as soon as possible.

E.G.
{
1. "I do say, that when a body's come to the end of her workin' days and han't saved a bit, she's better dead."
2. "What's the use of talkin' of next winter, my dear? You won't be here to see it."
3. "What yer goin' to do with that eight-day clock? You haven't long to settle, y' know."
}

These relatives now rallied. Blood is thicker than water, and money thickens the blood. After all, who has the right to look after a body if it isn't her own relations? They came, often at great inconvenience, from the rather distant towns and villages where they lived, and covered her with attentions. Naturally, the hand which did the most would reap the most. Mrs. Bishop, who lived but half a mile from Mrs. Catling's door, had a strategical advantage of which she availed herself to the utmost; but, on the other hand, Uncle George Carney, the very prosperous draper, furniture dealer, and undertaker at Palebrook, had an unlimited command of horses and carriages. And as he was a very determined man, and had at his back a very determined family, he soon got control of the situation—became chairman, so to speak, of Mrs. Catling, Limited.

To do him justice, he took a generous view of his position. Mrs. Catling was moved to a much larger and pleasantly seated cottage, furnished with comfort, if not with taste. A fund was organized among the relatives to maintain her in a comfort which, if compared to her

earlier circumstances, might be called luxury. The relatives, even certain not very genuine ones, so-called distant cousins whom the closer
relatives objected to but could not very well keep out of the "deal," were
overlooking no chances that their calculating eyes descried.

The flaw was that the rapacity, the interested motive, was too pat-
ent. However, Mrs. Catling herself, it must be said, accepted all the
benefits regally, without any undue paroxysms of gratitude, and herein
shewed her wisdom. Her impassiveness, in fact, lent a note of dignity to
a situation which was truly in need of it.

In the new cottage, the BOOK, symbol of the movement, rested, por-
tentous, on the shelf in an apparent place. A cover had been made for it
by Uncle George Carney's daughter—purple flowers painted on pink,
certain to catch the eye. Dorothy was so clever! And at the frequent
tea-parties, when all, including Mrs. Catling herself, over-ate themselves with cakes and buttered toast and pastry, they would ever and
again turn their shiny faces reverently towards this immensely valuable
Object, the source of all their hopes. Uncle George had heard a man,
who knew a thing or two, say it might be worth £15,000; and Uncle
George's son, who was at Palebrook Grammar School, and was going
up to Cambridge on a scholarship, declared positively that it was worth
much more.

The reputation of the BOOK waxed and became considerable.

Lady Wednesbury, at Palebrook Court, who took an interest in
things artistic, invited some people staying in the house to accompany
her for a look at the treasure. She promised them some fun.

And she sailed into Mrs. Catling's parlour, very dainty, very well
dressed, very condescending.

"Oh, Mrs. Catling, I hear you have such a wonderful book! Do show
it us, will you?"

There were with her another lady who wore very thin embroidered
shoes and diamonds, and talked, either by nature or cultivation, with
the husky, not unpleasant voice and accent of the London coster-girl;
an old gentleman, who wore very tight clothes and was obviously doing
too much for his age; and another man who made jokes. The two ladies
clutched two chairs and sat down, and they and their men began talking very rapidly to each other.

"What a dear little room! What a perfectly weird picture!" *etc.*

Unfortunately, all went wrong from the start. They had walked into a gathering of the family—no such small beer either. It is true that in the looks of the elders there was at first, if not deference, at least something placating, deprecatory; and Mrs. Catling herself, a survival from those good times when "my lady" was a goddess who had power of life and death in her hands, stood up on her respectful old legs. But the young people were unfeignedly hostile. One son of Uncle George was on the way to Cambridge; another was training for the ministry. Above all, very clever Dorothy Carney was a promising student at a well-known Women's College, and a suffragist to boot. They all intensely resented this entrance among them without permission or apology. It was not because poor old Aunt Catling was a plain old peasant woman that there were not others to be considered! And what right had these strangers to come forcing their presence uninvited?

Dorothy began talking to her brothers loudly and flippantly in her pleasant voice, ignoring the visitors. She did it very well. Her brothers, and then her father, as soon as he recovered his poise, played up to her. Of course, Uncle George was too good a business man to act in this way if Lady Wednesbury had been a customer of his; but she was not and never likely to be. Indeed, certain undiplomatic remarks of her ladyship about "That abominable Radical Carney" had reached his ears. So he was not sorry to stretch his legs a bit and shew his independence and sense of equality, and he smiled encouragingly upon his self-possessed daughter.

Before long Lady Wednesbury noticed the atmosphere and rose. She was very cross, and still crosser because she knew that she ought not to let it be seen and she felt she was doing so.

"So you won't shew us your extraordinary book?" By instinct she singled out old Mrs. Catling as the only one there who would much mind her wrath. "Well, I think it is very uncivil of you."

"My lady——" stammered Mrs. Catling.

"The only thing we can shew you," interposed Uncle George, "is the door."

Dorothy began to laugh.

Uncle George pulled the door wide open. "*Good* afternoon," he said genially in his best manner.

Then he came back into the room. He was a little flustered. "If it was Lloyd George himself," he said, "who came and asked me like that, I wouldn't shew him the bl—bloomin' Book."

And Dorothy, although she disapproved of the expletive, could not but agree with the sentiment. From that day she conceived a real esteem for her father.

Chapter III

B UT THE VISIT TO Mrs. Catling of these lights of the social world, although in itself not a success, shed, even for those of the relatives who had thought it their duty to shew their indifference to such patronage, an increased lustre on the Book. For if people used to the estimation of things of no practical utility, who had also the guidance of experts at their call, desired to inspect the treasure, of what large and certain value it must be!

And the attentions to Mrs. Catling redoubled. Surely Uncle George and his family would come in first! How prettily Dorothy would tie the old dame's bonnet-strings! How assiduously the young Carneys adjusted the foot-stool! One day Mrs. Catling having remarked by caprice: "I wonder I h'an't got one of these 'ere motor-cars," Uncle George so worked upon the other relatives that they seriously thought of clubbing together to buy one.

The suspense became intolerable.

"Come now, Eliza," said Uncle George at last, resolutely, "we can't none of us live for ever. Why, I might be carried off myself any day. You're a woman of property. You can't go out as if you were on the parish, y' know. You must make your will."

Mrs. Catling began to whimper. "You want me to die, that's what it is. It's my book you're all after. I reckon you'd fair pison me to get my book."

"Tut, tut, Eliza," remonstrated Uncle George. Still, he was somewhat perturbed. He thought it safer to appeal to the other relatives for support. But all that their united efforts could bring about was that Mrs. Catling consented to see a solicitor in private. And try all they could, they could not arrive at a glimmering of the contents of the will.

The only thing was to keep on showering comforts on the old woman. They showered them on her more and more. It had the fascination of a gamble. Anyone might be the lucky one, and a failure of attention might mean that the will would be revised in favour of another.

And as every good action deserves a reward, there was some kind of justice in the fact that it was essentially the mass of attentions which brought about the consummation they all secretly wished for. Old Mrs. Catling was really killed by kindness. She drank too much tea; she ate a good deal too much; she had too many excitements. One day she was taken with a fit in her chair and died there.

The funeral arrangements were of the best kind. Uncle George did things on a lavish scale. It is something to have an undertaker in the family.

After the funeral the will was opened. Mrs. Catling had left the value of the Book to be divided among them all.

This was a blow. However, as Dorothy with her admirable common sense urged, there was only one thing to be done now, and that was to get an expert valuer down from London.

Chapter IV

On the appointed day the expert came, and the relatives assembled, for the last time all together, in Mrs. Catling's parlour. Most of them had not slept the night before, and even the youngest looked haggard. The Book, which had been distrustfully watched night and day since the death of the owner, was produced and solemnly laid on the table by Uncle George Carney's eldest son. The valuer gave a practised glance at the title-page, and a look of considerable astonishment came into his face.

"It is a very decent copy," he said, "but there are a good many like it. A bookseller might give you four or five pounds for it."

The relatives stared at one another aghast. Four or five pounds! Uncle George turned so pale and giddy that he had to clutch hold of a corner of the table.

"I say I've been swindled!" He tried to shout, but his voice was suffocated. He would feel this blow for the rest of his life.

The expert looked round at all these faces, flushed or livid, a little contemptuously. "Who was it," he asked, "that told you the book had any special value?"

Who was it? The relatives scanned each other with dull, furious eyes. Wouldn't they like to know, just! But nobody knew.

Alfred Nodd was become a myth.

Alone the doctor remembered, but he was a wise man and kept quiet. He reflected that if he began to explain, the relatives would probably hold him responsible for starting the rumour.

~

She Married the Vicar

Chapter I

A̲T THE JUNCTION, MACINTYRE found that he had nearly half an hour to wait before the train left for Palebrook. He sat down on a bench on the platform in the sun. The heat was great; a fine dust rose from the ballast on the line. Not far away men were working in the fields. They wore big white hats and their arms were the colour of rust. Poppies flared against the blue sky; larks soared and trilled. Nobody was about. He took from his pocket a small volume and began to read the great poetry again.

He knew a good deal of it by heart—all the love poetry certainly. Page after page of superb poetry—some of the greatest poetry, MacIntyre thought, ever written—addressed to Her. She lolled in the strophes—her lithe body, her heavy brown hair—how often MacIntyre had evoked Her! And now he was going to see Her. It was like seeing Beatrice, or Petrarch's Laura, or Helen of Troy.

MacIntyre somehow felt that he owned her. He had done so much for the fame of Raphael, the wonderful Jewish poet—the most wonderful since Heine—some would have it, since King David himself or the author of Solomon's Song—dead in his prime (he was only twenty-eight) some thirty years ago. If the world at large, the international public who care for poetry, have now come round to Raphael, it is chiefly due to MacIntyre. After all, Raphael was a poet who had only to be presented properly. Those lyrical cries of his, so poignant and even terrible at times by force of passion, were not mere splashes of rhetoric, verbal conflagration. There was no rhetoric about them. They were human: they rose like smoke from the smouldering heart of humanity, wording the passions, fears, yearnings, common to all in palace or factory or hut, in those hours when men and women repose, and dream the thoughts they have no words for. ...

A tramp, ragged, bruised, covered with the dust flung over him by hundreds of motor-wheels, came on the platform and sat down by MacIntyre. There was a vague look in him—in the crouch of the neck and shoulders; the sunken eyes; the suggestion of calcined lungs, of desolation and loneliness—of a pencil sketch made by Rysselberghe of the poet just before he died.

Looking at the tramp, MacIntyre thought of the poet's unhappy life. If there was ever a man who had a right to rebel against the tax often demanded from the lyrical or musical genius in return for his one gift, it was Raphael. Well might he exclaim, in one of the rare letters of his which survived (in his lifetime nobody thought it worth while to keep his letters), "I was never given the chance to be a *bourgeois*." Deplorable saying, lighting the very chasms of the tragedy! The only thing that relieved the tragedy is that it was not prolonged. His life was as other people had made it; he had never had very much chance to shape it himself. His cruel luck had cast him all his life among a kind of people who harassed and wounded him, did not understand him, tortured him, probably, to death. He had not even the consolation of any glimmer of success in his art. The newspapers sneered at him or ignored him. Even to other artists he was little more than a name. The Miss Nietzsches of the period called him a degenerate.

Of course there was Her. For a long time MacIntyre had hoped that he would come upon some letter or paper to shew just the part she played, to justify her immortality; for her name would last, he thought, as long as poetry lasted at all. But save her name and a few details, nothing of her relations with the poet came to the top—nothing. The world, from lack of material, had at length agreed that she had soothed him, broken his fall—that is, as far as she was able, for the texts seemed to indicate that she had been separated from him by the harshest fate.

One day the hazard of a report in the newspapers about a motor accident which she had witnessed revealed to MacIntyre that she was alive and living at Palebrook. It seemed she had married a clergyman in the neighbourhood, and upon his death had gone to live in the town. MacIntyre's delight was inexpressible. He told everybody. It was as if he had put his hand on the moon. Out of the long line of heroines stretching away to the beginning of the world, here was the one he wanted to see most. ...

"As for me," I said, "I should choose Bathsheba."

Others wondered why she had kept quiet about it. MacIntyre thought he understood that too.

Chapter II

THE PORTERS AT PALEBROOK Station knew her name quite well. The house, a fair-sized one, stood in a lane surrounded by other houses, but rising up before it was a good length of garden, ablaze with flowers basking in the sun of this hot day, with butterflies dancing above them.

The room where MacIntyre stood mopping his brows and feeling a little nervous was like thousands of other small drawing-rooms up and down England. There was some attempt at artistic effect, the main object being plainly to make the room cheerful. Flowers were about; light curtains swayed from the windows in the breeze, and the wall-paper was light. On the walls were the inevitable "Portrait of a Young Man, unknown," by Andrea del Sarto, a few reproductions of Watts' pictures, two etchings after Marcus Stone. Bronze frogs, in facetious postures, grinning cats and monkeys in porcelain, were on the mantel-piece and tables. Some photographs also—one or two men in uniform, one or two clergymen, an undergraduate, a barrister, a few women, and a nun. The room itself was old—seventeenth century probably—but what was possible had been done to make it look new. It revealed no emphatic personality in its owner, nothing which would stand her apart from other women who had drawing-rooms; but then there were so many strong personalities quite unable to express themselves by their surroundings, or indifferent to them. MacIntyre felt a little disap-pointed not to find any trace of Raphael; but, after all, a certain shyness, a certain delicacy, might account for that. ...

He was beginning to think he was being kept waiting, but ere he had time to think it definitely or to wonder about it, the door opened and a lady came in.

Just what kind of a person MacIntyre expected to see he could hardly have said. Although he was almost thirty, no longer young, he had the youth's difficulty in seizing the gradations of age. For him the young were those younger than himself, and those older were old. Now, Raphael had died more than thirty years ago: this span, for MacIntyre, had the imaginative value of a century. The woman the poet had loved would therefore look like——

Meanwhile, the woman the poet had loved was standing before him. She was a tall, handsome woman about fifty, with a very good figure, and perfectly white hair dressed high above her ruddy well-cut face. Under her straight eyebrows her clear blue eyes looked out frankly, a little imperatively. She was unmistakably Anglo-Saxon through and through; put her down in the most cosmopolitan city in the world and she would be spotted for English. MacIntyre, who had the journalist's gift of summarizing people quickly, took her to be a woman fond of sport, who lived much in the open air. Many a misty morning had those keen blue eyes watched between a horse's ears the hounds breaking cover. She was wearing a pair of buckskin shoes; doubtless she had a tennis match on for that afternoon. For the rest, she was dressed plainly but very well, with quite a contemporary cut to her skirt.

She held a tradesman's account-book in one of her firm capable-looking hands on which she wore a large wedding-ring and some other rings, and MacIntyre's card was pressed under her thumb on the cover of the book.

"You wanted to see me? I don't think I know your name, do I?"

She spoke in that quick, ungracious, domineering tone which many Englishwomen have, but her well-shaped mouth was smiling amiably enough, and MacIntyre could see her even teeth. There was not the slightest indication in her face or demeanour of a spiritual possibility.

"Raphael," he began; "the poet Raphael——"

And he continued his explanations to her who had survived. To tell the truth, he was rather muddled. The very modern, very capable lady before him looked so little like the mistress of a long-dead poet! Soon he got so confused that he stopped altogether. He felt he was a little superfluous. She was looking at him with her cool worldly eyes.

"Raphael," she mused. "Ah yes!" MacIntyre felt that she was ploughing back through the years, through all her wedded life with the defunct vicar … beyond. … "Ah yes. I think I remember the name."

"But he is celebrated! He will live for ages. He is like Heine—like——"

She bent forward a little. "Like whom did you say?"

"Heine."

"Ah yes," said Mrs. Brinton vaguely. "No doubt. Raphael was a clever young Jew."

MacIntyre felt indignant. "He has made you immortal, for one thing."

Mrs. Brinton looked a little alarmed.

"Oh, I hope he hasn't done anything so shocking." She laughed, but she was evidently much vexed. "Do you mean to say he has actually printed my name in his book?"

"I mean to say," replied MacIntyre sturdily, "that some of his greatest poems—in my opinion, some of the greatest poetry ever written—are addressed to you—not by name, of course, but it has been known for some time who was meant. Many women," he added, "perhaps most women, would think that worth living for."

"Would they?" said Mrs. Brinton. "Well, I don't. I think it was grossly improper of him. It only shows how careful you have to be about the kind of people you take up—well!" She paused a moment to control her annoyance. "I'll tell you, Mr.—er—"—she glanced down at the card—"MacIntyre, just what occurred with regard to young Raphael. He came to my father—my father, you may possibly know, was Squire of Rudstone, the next village here—and he was given some work in the library, to catalogue the books and pictures and so on. As I say, he was a clever young Jew, and my father took some notice of him—allowed him to dine with the family, and things of that kind. Then he began to prowl about after me, and make soft eyes, and one day my brother, the present Squire, who is a very observant man, said to me, 'Sophy, that Jew poetry fellow is falling in love with you.' I didn't like it, and I told my father. The upshot was that Raphael was put out by the scruff of the neck."

There was really nothing more to be said. But it was too miserable to leave the thing like this. MacIntyre made an effort and drew his book from his pocket.

"Will you let me read you one of the poems?" he asked.

Mrs. Brinton looked at him queerly, her head a little on one side, and MacIntyre knew that she was wondering whether he might not be a little mad.

"I'm so sorry," she said, "but I haven't a moment to spare. I'm frightfully rushed to-day."

Then, as he was going:

"If you are interested in poetry and art and that, you ought not to miss the church at Rudstone. My husband was vicar there for many years."

Chapter III

MACINTYRE REFRAINED FROM THE church. As he loitered at the station for the London train, he thought uncomfortably that he would never again be able to read of Beatrice, or Laura, or Sacharissa, or the others, with any confidence. Art could do too much. …

THE END

Also from Vincent O'Sullivan

Solis Press are proud to reprint this collection of seven short horror tales from Vincent O'Sullivan, the master of the decadent and macabre.

This edition includes the frontispiece from the first edition by Aubrey Beardsley. Each of the seven stories is illustrated with photographs commissioned for this new printing.

The Good Girl was first published in 1912 to a mixed reception. Some newspapers described it as "revolting", "unclean" and "ugly and depressing". Many authors of the time thought it distinctive and a work of genius.

The writer Robert Aickman wrote of O'Sullivan that: "The curious should try to find a copy of his novel, *The Good Girl*. The quest is difficult, but the product distinctive ... ."

Reviews for *The Good Girl*:

"It is not too much to say that *The Good Girl* is one of the top twenty best books by living American novelists"—*New York Evening Post*

"Its exceptional interest and quality are hereby commended to lovers of good fiction"—*Life*

Solis Press